One Step
At
A Time

Ian Yates

OTHER BOOKS BY IAN YATES

DCI Peter Carter Novels

One Piece At A Time
One Day At A Time
One Step At A Time

OTHER WORKS

Woolwich Shines
The Fighters
Pub Quizmaster Series of Books
Off The Beaten Track - (Walks in Western Crete)

For Helen & Patricia

May the road rise up to meet you
May the wind be always at your back
May the sun shine warm upon your face
The rains fall soft upon your fields and until we meet again

May God hold you in the palm of His hand.

Traditional Irish Blessing

IAN YATES

ACKNOWLEDGMENTS

First and foremost I have to thank everyone at Black Bay Publishing for their patience and editing skills. Without their help and at times, goading (especially Evelyn – a huge thank you for your persistence), this third book would have been left by the wayside as I left it to work on other projects.

I also have to thank my wife, Alison. Once again, it is only because of her understanding and quiet patience that I have managed to complete this third book in the DCI Carter series. I love you and always will xxx

I must also thank all those people that have allowed me to use their names in these books. It is so much easier when you can use a name that is 'real', rather than something invented...and once again I must reiterate that there are no similarities between the names of people and their characters in this, or any other book I have written. THANK YOU for allowing my manipulation of your characters as I see fit.

I cannot end without thanking you, the reader. You have made me continue writing with your support and encouragement and without *you*, this book would not have been possible – THANK YOU.

Crete, 2020

IAN YATES

'What saves a man is to take a step. Then another step. It is always the same step, but you have to take it.'
Antoine de Saint-Exupéry

"When the Fox hears the Rabbit scream he comes a-runnin', but not to help."
— Thomas Harris, The Silence of the Lambs

"Murder is not about lust and it's not about violence. It's about possession. When you feel the last breath of life coming out of the woman, you look into her eyes. At the point, it's being God."
— Ted Bundy

1

An airport's arrival hall is one of those few places where human emotions are raw and exposed. I don't know if it is the relief of surviving a trip in a thin metal tube that travels at hundreds of miles an hour and thousands of feet in the air, or the relief at having successfully negotiated a serious looking official who is scrutinising your documents without pulling you over for a cavity search. Either way it seems to bring out the best, and worst, in many people.

I look up as a young woman bumps into me in her attempt to rush out into the waiting crowd. She half turns with a huge grin on her face and bows her head in apology whilst mouthing, 'Sorry,' before she returns to her onward rush. Her bright orange rucksack bobs and weaves and occasionally sideswipes others who get the same treatment as I did. I follow her with my eyes and see her target. He is pushing his own way through the throng and his smile reflects hers. The joy and love on his face is something only seen after a long time apart or an eternity together. I smile as they meet and forget everyone else around them. True love. Raw emotion on show for everyone to see without a care in the world.

My smile drops as I realise it is very unlikely I will get the same treatment from the person waiting for me. How could I have been so stupid as to cheat on my fiancée?

I think of Julia and the last time I saw her. She was sitting in my sister, Helen's apartment with tears running down her cheeks. Tears which I had caused after my affair with a journalist which almost jeopardised my career as a Detective in the London Metropolitan Police force. It also looked like it was on the way to ruining my relationship with the only woman I have ever truly loved. To make matters worse, in the airport departure lounge whilst waiting for my flight I received a phone call. A phone call from that same journalist, Ann Clark, telling me that she was pregnant. For the last ten hours since I started my journey and even at the stopover in Athens airport whilst waiting for my connecting flight I have had my phone turned off. Partly because of the flight safety rules but mostly out of fear. Fear of hearing the awful news that I am to become a father with a woman I do not love.

As I am thinking through my problems I catch sight of Julia. She smiles lightly and my heart jumps, but then her face drops and she looks away. I know she is crying.

I recognise the tall, dark haired man standing next to her even though I met him only briefly almost nine months ago.

I walk up to them and he steps protectively in front of his niece, my fiancée.

I hold out my hand,

'Hello Babis. I hope you are well,' I say.

He grabs my hand and looks at me sternly,

'Yiasas Peter. Welcome to Crete. I wish it was under a better occasion that we meet again.'

His grip is as fearsome as his expression.

'So do I, Babis,' I say as I look past his shoulder to Julia, 'so do I.'

2

London Metropolitan Police Commissioner Patricia Wilks looks around her new office with barely disguised disdain. The move of the police headquarters of New Scotland Yard in Whitehall to the Curtis Green Building on Victoria Embankment is officially only a few months away but personnel have already started transferring across.

'This is half the size of the old office. How am I meant to conduct meetings when you can barely fit my desk and three people in here?' She asks the Minister for Redevelopment in front of her.

He clears his throat before speaking,

'Well, the desk you have at NSY is not making the move. That is being sold off at Sotheby's as part of the re-allocation of equipment and budgetary transfers. Due to the history of the item in question we expect it to raise a four-figure price which will help reduce your deficit during the transfer.'

Wilks look turns to anger, 'My budget deficit?' She explodes, 'This move was dreamt up by politicians as a way of saving money. You have cut the UK's police forces by over 16,000 and you are telling me about budget constraints. Do you realise what you are doing to the United Kingdom's policing capability? Do you?'

The minister sighs and looks out of the window to the iconic London skyline, 'Commissioner, we all need to be singing from the same hymn sheet for the press and the public. We cannot afford dissention from anybody within the ranks,' he turns to face Wilks, 'no matter how high up the chain of command they think they are. We all know that the new, smaller headquarters will help deliver a 21st Century police force to London and help Londoners to reconnect with the Met.'

'Yes, I've read the press statements from the Prime Minister also but you are running my forces down to unacceptable levels. Never has the thin blue line been a more apt phrase.'

'We all have our crosses to bear, Commissioner. I understand your reservations, but we have had thousands of man hours put into this study and the final result,' he waves his arm around the room, 'was the best option that provides security, stability and pound for pound best value policing for London and the United Kingdom as a whole. Now, why don't we pop downstairs and see the new computer security offices. I understand you have an outstanding record with cyber-crime and the like.'

Wilks takes another last glance around the empty room, shakes her head and gestures for the minister to exit the frosted glass door ahead of her.

'At least that is one department that you're leaving alone,' she mutters under breath as she closes the door behind her.

'Excuse me?'

Wilks gives her most charming smile to the Minister, 'I said that is one department where we can't moan.'

'Good. Tell me, how is it you can manage to attract such outstanding candidates.'

The Commissioner's smile widens, 'Oh I entrap them, bribe them and say they will go to prison if they don't work with us.'

The Minister laughs out loud, 'No really, where do you get them from.'

Wilks face changes instantly to one of hard seriousness,

'Really, that is what I tell them.'

The Minister looks at her, his laugh dying in his throat. The look between them seems to last an age before Wilks puts him out of his misery.

'Or I offer them a good wage, a decent pension and some of the most up to date equipment the government can afford.'

The relief on the man's face is comical, 'You nearly had me there, Commissioner, very good joke. Yes, very good.'

With that he turns and walks down the corridor without seeing if Wilks is following. She pauses a second watching his back before saying softly, 'And if they refuse, well then I throw them in prison for six months to a year.'

The strident ringing tone from her mobile phone causes the Minister to stop and look back towards her. She pulls the device from her uniform jacket pocket. On seeing the caller ID she starts to turn back to the office, 'I just have to take this. One moment please, Minister.'

She steps inside and closes the door gently. Swiping her finger across the screen, she answers the call, 'Wilks here, what have you got for me, JD?'

Detective Inspector Jonathon Dawkins sighs down the phone at his boss,

'It's the CPS. They've discontinued our proceedings against Helen Carter and say that whilst we have reasonable suspicion that she murdered Zoe Walker, there is no evidence to support a reasonable conviction in court. They've ordered me to release her as soon as possible.'

Wilks processes the information and comes to an immediate conclusion,

'It's the Crown Prosecution Service that calls the shots on this one, JD. If they say we have failed their threshold tests than there is nothing we can do. Apologise to Helen and let her know that she is still under investigation as a suspect in the murder of her partner, but we will be widening the enquiry to deal with other leads. Do not, I repeat, do not let the media get a foot in the door on this one. I don't need another media circus. Get Helen out of there quietly and take her back to her apartment. Offer her the standard guidance and support and inform her not to leave the Greater London area in case further questioning is required.'

'Yes, Ma'am. Umm, I was wondering, do you want me to inform her brother of the proceedings?'

Wilks pauses a little longer,

'No. I think it best if I contact DCI Carter myself and explain the findings. Thanks for letting me know JD.'

'All part of the package, Ma'am. I'll get on it straight away.'

'Yes, OK, thanks again.'

Wilks terminates the call and taps the phone absent-mindedly against the side of her cheek as she stares out across the grey skies and buildings of London.

3

After a moments uncomfortable silence where I stand waiting for Babis to say something more, I remove my hand from his grasp and lean slightly to my left,

'Julia?' I ask softly.

She turns to face me and I see her eyes glistening with tears. Her arm comes out and touches her uncle's back and then she is walking away. Walking away through the small crowd of smiling people, who are greeting and hugging each other, like I wish I was able to do with my fiancée. I make to take a step towards her but a strong arm blocks my way.

'Not here, Peter. Julia wanted to see you arrive but Stelios is waiting outside to drive her home. You are coming with me. We have our cousin's apartments ready for you. They are normally closed in the winter time but she has made an exception for us.'

'Babis, I just want to…'

He interrupts me with a gentle firmness,

'This is not about what you want, Peter. We are here for Julia and the family. I have spoken to Nektarios and we know his wishes and we also know your stupidity in doing what you did,' his strong grip digs into my shoulder, 'If it wasn't for her father I would be taking you somewhere quiet where we could speak in private about your problems. Do you understand?'

The pressure in my shoulder increases and I nod as I think back to the last time I spoke to this tall Cretan man in front of me.

He was in London to visit the critically injured Nektarios, Julia's father, after he had been beaten to within an inch of his life. He was intent on searching for the people who had hurt his brother-in-law and dishing out his own brand of justice. It was only the words of Nektarios' wife, Anna, who is Babis and Stelios' sister which stopped bloodshed on the streets of my city. I realise just what he means by having a private chat with me and I am grateful that Nektarios made the call.

'All I want to do is to try and make things right. I love Julia,' his grip lessens slightly and I feel the blood pumping back into my arm, 'believe me when I say that.'

He removes his hand and stares at me with his angry, dark eyes. I see them soften,

'We all do things we regret but it is only actions that prove our words mean something. Come, let me take you to Katarina's apartments. She is expecting us.'

He turns and walks away and I heft my small case in my hand and follow him outside.

As we exit the automatic doors of Chania airport the smell of wild herbs mixed with aircraft fuel fumes hits me like a soft, fragrant pillow to the face. I squint in the bright December sunlight and make out a tall mountain range that breaks the clear blue skyline ahead of us. Unlike the airports in London the road immediately outside the arrivals and departure hall is packed with cars. All have their hazard lights blinking and there are even some that are double parked.

I follow Babis as he weaves his way through the vehicles until he stops at a huge black, double cab, pick-up truck. It is blocking in a small white Nissan Micra where the driver is gesturing frantically at Babis as if his life depends on it. Babis rubs his thumb and forefinger together at the gesticulating man and gruffly shouts out,

'*Ena lepta, malaka.*'

This just forces a sharp beeping of the horn, but the driver stays in his car instead of confronting the tall man in dark clothes who is casually getting into the truck.

'Your bags go in there,' he says, pointing at the flat bed of the vehicle, 'it is not far.'

I throw the small case and my carry-on bag over the short metal wall into the wide load space and clamber in beside him.

As I shut the door I look out and up at the airport and try to mouth the words I see on the façade of the building,

'Iaann..uh..Iannis Das…'

'Ioannis Daskalogiannis, he was a great Cretan who was betrayed in 1771 by the Russians when leading a revolt against the Turks. He was skinned alive and executed, and it is said he never uttered a sound during his torture such was his bravery and strength. He was a true Sfakian.'

As we pull away the beeping of the small car fades along with a few words of Greek shouted out by the frustrated driver. Babis looks in the rear-view mirror briefly and mutters,

'If only all Cretans could be so quiet.'

4

The drive to the apartment building takes about thirty minutes and it is spent mostly in silence. The journey is punctuated only by a few words from Babis as we pass through certain areas.

'Souda Bay, the biggest natural harbour on the island. The Germans bombed it to hell and back but still we sailed our boats here to fight and fish.'

He says this as we wind our way down the side of a steep mountain and the view is spectacular to our left. The long expanse of water is flanked steeply on both sides by hills that tower above it and beyond these hills are even taller mountains capped with a blanket of snow. I notice military ships in the bay mixed with a spattering of smaller pleasure boats and fishing vessels, their windscreens glinting in the sunlight. A huge white ferry emblazoned with the words 'ANEK LINES' is just pulling away from its berth.

'The ferry to Athens,' Babis says helpfully before falling back into silence.

Nothing more is said and I watch the foreign landscape drift by in a blur. It is much greener than I expected. I imagined it to be more barren, yet along the sides of the roads are healthy green plants with vibrant orange, green and yellow flowers in bloom. We pull off the small road and enter onto what appears to be a main highway. Babis again resumes his sparse commentary,

'This is the new road.'

I look around and smile slightly. It looks like it was built in the 70's or 80's,

'New?' I ask.

'You should have seen the old road. This is the new road,' he repeats, 'it allows us to bypass Chania and save maybe an hour in the traffic.'

He accelerates and pulls out in front of a white delivery van which flashes its lights and beeps angrily. He just presses down on his own horn in reply and speeds away. I can see that driving with Babis is going to be a noisy past-time.

I stay quiet as he attempts to force the truck up to speeds a Formula 1 race driver would be proud of and try not to show any emotion as he pushes the vehicle through gaps of oncoming traffic that would make a motor-cyclist pause. I manage a sigh of relief as after ten frantic minutes we pull off onto a smaller road.

'It is not far now to Katarina's,' he says and looks over to me, 'Julia tells me you have family here. Why do you not stay with them?'

I stare out of the front windscreen whilst replying,

'I didn't want to bother Paul, my brother. I wanted this to be about Julia and me and not a family get together.'

'But it is family. Family are important too. You should make time for all and not sacrifice anyone. If not for family, who would you turn to?'

Luckily I do not have to reply as at that moment we turn into a small apartment complex.

'This is Katarina's.'

We skid to a halt in the gravelled car park and Babis is out of the truck as it still sways under its own momentum. He grabs my bags as I stiffly exit from the vehicle and I follow him towards a bar area which is enclosed by patio doors. He pulls them open, throws my bags inside and says,

'Wait here, she will be along shortly.'

He stops and looks at me, his face impassive,

'I will bring Julia to meet you later. Freshen up, have a sleep, you need it.'

With those words he leaves me at the cold, empty bar. I hear the engine roar into life and the gravel crunch under the wheels of his pick-up. I sigh and ease myself down into a traditional wicker thatched chair and wonder what I am going to say when I meet Julia.

5

JD is looking through the observation window of interview room one at Helen Carter. He glances down at the release form in his hands and digests the information on it with a shake of his head. He looks up again and sees that Helen has moved from the chair she was sitting on and has walked up to the one way glass. She stands there looking in, almost directly at him it seems, for a few seconds before raising her palms up in a 'what's happening' gesture. He turns to the woman standing next to him,

'Let's get this over with.' he says.

'You know I still think she's guilty?'

'Kate, I know you haven't been with us for too long, but when the CPS tells us we can't prosecute…'

Kate Jeffery, criminal psychologist and advisor to the Met, interrupts,

'I know, I know, but everything points to her as the guilty party.'

'Except any hard evidence,' JD replies, 'Come on. Let's not prolong this, I'll do the talking. I'll get her to sign the forms, and then I'll take her home. We'll have a uniform on detail outside her apartment as long as budgets will allow it.'

They both walk out of the darkened room into the corridor and JD opens the door to where Helen is waiting.

'JD, what is it this time?' Helen sounds tired, 'How many times can I tell you I had nothing to do with Zoe's murder?'

JD motions towards the table,

'Let's sit down, Helen. We're not here to ask any more questions, in fact, all I need you to do is sign a release form and you can go home.'

Helen folds her arms across her chest and looks suspiciously at the two of them,

'What? You're going to let me go, just like that?' She pauses and her voice rises in hope, 'Have you found the killer? That's it isn't it, you've found who killed Zoe.'

Her shoulders start to shake and she looks like she is about to fall down. Kate moves forward quickly and grabs her and gently guides her into the hard plastic seat as the tears start to fall. JD lets her cry for a few seconds before talking to her,

'Helen, we are no closer to finding Zoe's killer. I have to inform you that whilst you are still a suspect and a person of interest in this case, you're free to go home to your residence. I must also advise you not to leave the Greater London area until we can eliminate you completely from our enquiries.'

Helen looks up, tears still streaming down her shocked face.

'You still think I did this, don't you?' She looks between Kate and JD, 'You all still think I murdered her. What does my brother say about all this? Why hasn't he been in any of the interviews or been to see me?'

JD grabs one of Helen's petite, soft hands with his own two, large rough hands,

'It's not for us to apportion blame. We find the evidence and we use it make a case against the guilty party or parties. If you are innocent you have nothing to fear.'

Helen pulls away, 'What about Peter? Where is he?'

JD looks over to Kate with a troubled look,

'He's taken a leave of absence. In fact he was ordered to take some time off because he is personally involved with your case. The Commissioner thought...'

'So is he waiting to take me home?'

JD shakes his head, 'He's not here. He's gone to Crete to speak to Julia.'

Helen looks even more confused. JD pushes the forms over the table towards her with a pen,

'Why don't you sign this form saying you accept the terms of this release? I'll take you home and we can talk about it there,' he looks around the room, 'It'll be much better than this shit-hole, won't it?'

Kate looks disapprovingly at JD as Helen nods her head towards her brother's partner and friend. She slowly picks up the pen, scans the paperwork and signs her name at the bottom of the two sheets.

JD smiles at her and deliberately ignores Kate's look, 'Thank you Helen. Now how about I take you home?'

Looking in his rear view mirror, JD sees Helen with her eyes closed and her head resting against the side window. He understands how exhausting it must be for her to be accused and questioned over 72 hours about her lover's murder. He turns his attention back to the busy streets, his view distorted by the cold rain just starting to fall. Turning on the car's wipers he grimaces as it smudges the sparse water droplets across the glass making his vision worse.

'Just like this case,' he thinks, 'the truth is being blurred before we

can see it clearly.'
In his mind he runs through the main points from the case file,

1. It is almost certain the victim knew their killer.
2. The level of violence indicates a crime of passion.
3. The number of wounds, according to the psychologist, tends to be found in violence inflicted by women *on* women.
4. Helen knew the victim, was in a relationship with the victim and has a history of violence.

JD can see why Helen is the prime suspect but he cannot believe that she would be able to commit such an atrocity. He has known her and her brother for too long. He negotiates the tricky right hand turn across the oncoming traffic into Helen's apartment parking area and pulls the car into an empty slot. Helen stirs behind him and stifles a yawn with her hand.
'I never thought I could fall asleep so quickly,' she says.
'And just how much sleep have you had over the last few days?' he asks her.
She shrugs, 'I don't know; a couple of hours?'
'There you go. Your body needs it and it's been the first time you have been able to relax.'
Again he looks at her in the rear view mirror and tries to imagine her crouched over a body, methodically hacking it to pieces. Helen notices him looking at her and smiles back,
'Thanks for bringing me home, JD. Now please can you talk to me about Peter?'
'Yeah, but over a cup of tea. The stuff they give you back there, well, it's only just fit for human consumption.'
They get out of the car and hurry inside in an effort to keep out of the rain, which is falling more heavily now.

6

Stuart Masterson stands in the wide doorway. The slight breeze is

cooling his naked body as he looks out over the infinity pool to the azure blue sea of the Caribbean beyond. In the pool, a beautiful blonde woman is making slow strokes through the water. As she turns and heads back towards him she smiles,
'Are you coming in? The water is lovely.'
He smiles back but shakes his head,
'In a minute, Angie, I just have to make a phone call.'
He walks back into the shaded interior of the villa's dining room and picks up the telephone. He holds it in his hand for a second and thinks what he is about to do and how it will change his life. Then he punches in the numbers of a line in London that he memorised a long time ago and waits for the other end to pick up.
'Metro Construction, how may I help you today?'
Masterson pauses for a moment before speaking.
'Hello is there anybody there?' The woman's voice asks again.
'Yes, I'm here. Can you put me through to the renovation department please?'
'Certainly sir, do you have the name of a contact you wish to speak to?'
'Leahy, Andrew Leahy.'
Masterson is surprised to hear confusion from the woman at the other end of the phone. She is supposed to be trained to avoid such mistakes.
'Oh, um, yes sir. Straight away. Ummm....can I just confirm you said, Leahy?'
'That's correct,' and Masterson spells it out, 'his extension number is 66752.'
There is silence on the line and then a click as he is transferred.
'This is 66752, who am I speaking to?'
'My name is Stuart Masterson and I am the person who last saw Andrew Leahy alive.'
'We know who you are, Masterson, and we have you on surveillance cameras entering the apartment that day. Why are you contacting the office now?'
Masterson knows the call is being traced but he doesn't care,

'Leahy was a traitor to his country, our country and he needed to die. I want to come in for a full debrief and I want a promise from the Firm you will hear my side of events before you decide anything.'

'Leahy was high profile. His role at MI6 was important to us and his removal should have been discussed before you acted,' there is a pause as he attempts to find the correct word, '...independently.'

Masterson smiles, 'There wasn't time. It was a job that required instant action and the girl with him was on your renovations list too.'

'The girl was not your concern.'

'The girl was a known player in many countries who...'

'I do not care about the girl. We need to decide what to do with you after Leahy's unfortunate accident.'

Masterson's forehead wrinkles in confusion,

'Accident?' he asks.

'Yes, Mr Masterson. Andrew Leahy died tragically in a freak fall last week. He was alone at the time. Have you not seen any of the news over the last seven days?'

'I've been avoiding it.'

'We knew what Leahy was doing, Mr Masterson, we had plans in place for his retirement. It seems you just hastened them along. Unfortunately we now have to deal with you.'

'By now I must assume that you know where to find me?'

'I am looking at a satellite picture of your location as we speak.'

'I told Leahy I was quitting, I don't suppose you will accept that letter of resignation either?'

'Somebody will be in touch when we have reviewed the facts.'

'OK, but you will also need to speak to someone in the London Met. We were working together on the TSI thing when the shit hit the fan.'

'Masterson,' the voice growls, 'this is getting complicated.'

'I know but this man has all the facts and may help you to reach a, shall we say, a mutually beneficial decision based on the events leading up to the uh...accident.'

He hears a sigh,

'Who do we need to talk to?'

'His name is DCI Peter Carter. He is head of the Homicide and Serious Crimes Unit.'

'And this, DCI Carter, he knows all about the TSI situation?'

'He knows enough. Speak to him...it may stop you from killing me.'

'We shall see, but the odds don't look good from my position.'

'I understand. As I said, I'll be waiting.'

The line goes dead in Masterson's hand so he places it back in its charging dock.

He feels the cool breeze on his back and smiles.

'Well I might as well enjoy the time I have,' he says aloud to the empty room, 'they'll take at least a couple of days to get here.'

With the smile still on his face he walks out of the villa and dives in to the cool waters of the pool. In a few powerful strokes he is next to the woman. He grabs her and holds her in his arms, kissing her passionately on the lips.

'Now where were we before we were so rudely interrupted?' he says as he deftly slips her bikini top off.

7

Katarina arrives about ten minutes after Babis had left and opens a room for me. I cannot help but smile along with her and her bubbly personality.

'I am sorry about the mess, Mr Carter. We are not normally open for visitors in the winter-time.'

'If you think this is a mess you should see my apartment in London,' I reply, 'I really am very grateful you could put me up at such short notice.'

I watch as Katarina bustles around the room, tucking in the bed sheet and straightening the duvet. She flicks something off the cover and turns to me, her ever present smile beaming through her make-up.

'For family I will do anything. Now…is there anything you need? I am going shopping now so I will get you some water and supplies, but is there anything else you want?'

I shake my head,

'That is really very kind, but no, thank you. I think I have everything I need.'

She pulls out a notepad and jots down a number and her name,

'This is my mobile number, if you think of anything, just call. It is also the password for the wifi so you can use the internet if you wish.'

'Thank you,' I mutter.

With that she walks out through the open doorway in a whirl of perfume and I am left alone with my thoughts.

I look around. The room is a decent size for a one bedroom apartment, with a small kitchen complete with a two seater dining table in the living area. A comfortable looking sofa is placed against one wall with a coffee table in front of it facing a television set that is secured to the wall. On the dining table is a small tray of individually wrapped tea-bags and coffees and those small tin pots of horrible pasteurised milk that never seem to run out of date.

Walking to the kitchenette I fill the kettle with water and switch it on. As it boils I reach into my pocket and pull out my mobile phone. I cannot put it off any longer. I press the power button with my thumb and wait as it powers on. Once the messages welcoming me to Greece are disposed of the phone seems to rattle off for ever with a string of text and voice mail messages. I place it on the worktop as I ready myself a cup of coffee. Even though I hate the taste of the milk I have to put two of the small pots in the cup to stop it looking like gravy. Finally the musical melodies from the phone stop. I grab my hot cup of weak looking coffee, pick up the phone and slowly walk over to the sofa where I plonk myself down with a sigh.

'OK, this is it,' I say to the empty room as I open up the first of the text messages. Predictably it is from Ann Clarke,

Call me, we have lots to discuss

I open the next message,

Peter we need to talk. I love you

I keep scrolling, reading more of the same,

We can work this out this is not the time for anger. Please call me.

Scroll

This is not funny Peter - have you turned off your phone??????

Scroll

Why are you ignoring me!!!. I WILL NOT BE IGNORED

Scroll, scroll, scroll through increasingly angry messages, until finally.

Peter...I will come to you. I'm sorry you feel this way but I will show you what my love is for you. I will come to you.

I shake my head in a mixture of denial and anger. The anger is pointed at myself for getting into this position; the denial is because I want all this to just go away. I dial the code for my voicemail and brace myself for the angry torrent from my former lover.

It doesn't happen. Instead I hear Patricia Wilks talking to me,

'Peter, this is Commissioner Wilks. I have some news regarding your sister. I, uhm...I wish I could speak to you face to face but I know you are out of the country on personal matters. Peter, it's Helen. We will be releasing her from custody in the next few hours. It might be best if you can contact me when you get this message before trying to speak to her. Look, I know you have a lot on your plate at the moment but I wanted to keep you informed of any updates. So,' there is a pause, '...contact me when you get this message. Thank you.'

The phone goes silent. There are no other texts or voicemail messages so I place it on the table next to my now cold coffee. I think about checking my emails but realise it would probably only be more of the same. I place my head in my hands and lean forward, my elbows on my knees in a classic pose of complete and utter desperation and loss of hope. That is the pose Julia finds me in when she walks through the apartment doorway.

I jerk my head up in shock when I hear her soft voice,

'Peter, I couldn't wait until tonight. I thought it better if we talk straight away.'

I open my mouth as if to speak but nothing comes out.

She looks down at the cup on the table.

'I'll make us both a cuppa and we can talk. OK?'

I nod, still too dumbstruck and shocked by her sudden arrival. As she moves around the kitchen I grab my phone, press the power button to turn it off, and place it in my pocket. Now is not the time for any interruptions.

8

'Get me everything you can on a DCI Peter Carter of the Met. I want to know where he lives, who he sleeps with, his bank account details, any misdemeanours...anything and everything. If you can find it even his bloody inside leg measurements. Any scrap of information that is on file or in the public domain...get it, and get it fast.'

The young man he is talking to almost runs out of the office to get his boss the information.

The middle aged man at the desk pushes a red button on the intercom,

'Sue...get me Rowlinson. Tell him I need him in my office in ten minutes.'

'Yes Mr Groark,' is the reply from the discrete speaker, 'right away, sir.'

Jim Groark's thoughts return to the last conversation he had with his predecessor, Andrew Leahy. It was on the morning of Leahy's murder and involved what Groark could only consider as blackmail. If Leahy hadn't been killed in cold blood, Groark may well have had to instigate a drastic measure to protect himself and others higher up the pay chain. Now he was having to pick up the pieces of a very messy error...and it looked like it was getting messier by the minute.

He leans forward and types a few commands into his computer keyboard. His screen bursts into life showing a man and a woman at opposite sides of an expensive looking, leather topped, antique desk. There is movement at the bottom of the screen and he watches as a man comes in to view holding a silenced pistol in his hand. The extended, bulky, gun barrel comes up and the man behind the desk falls back in his chair with a violence that is unnatural, and then lies still.

The man with the pistol turns to leave then pauses. On screen he can see the lips moving and the woman turns around.

'Why didn't we install sound with the damn cameras?' he asks the screen as it develops into a torture scene.

The man shoots the woman twice, once in each shin. This seems to get the woman talking, but about what, he has no idea. The pistol is then raised one last time to press against the woman's forehead before the trigger is squeezed. He watches as her head snaps back to crash against the desk base, before she too lies still. The man with the pistol calmly walks out of shot. He has watched this scene many times and still he is amazed at the audacity of the assassin to walk into the private residence of Andrew Leahy, the head of MI6, and dispatch him so ruthlessly. He was even more amazed when the identity of the man was revealed as an operative of MI6. Formerly a Sergeant in the British Army's Parachute Regiment, he was also accepted for duties with the Special Air Service before he was poached by the government agency known as *The Firm*, to work in the clandestine world of Black Ops by the man he had just killed.

A salmon coloured UK Eyes – Top Secret file lies in front of him with the full details of the killer; Stuart Masterson, aka Neal Stephens, aka Robert Mansfield, aka Sergeant Tommy Wilson of the SAS.

He opens it and starts to read the contents once again,

'It would be a shame to lose someone of your talents Mr Masterson. A real shame.'

A voice crackles from his desk intercom,

'Sir, I have Mr Rowlinson here.'

He closes the file and reaches out to the intercom, pressing the transmit button,

'Send him in, Sue. Thank you.'

The door opens and a tall, muscular man walks in.

'Mr Groark, what can I do for you sir?' he asks as he walks across the room.

'David, we are all friends here, call me Jim. Please sit down.'

David Rowlinson pulls out a chair and settles his broad frame into the soft leather.

'OK, Jim. What's the job this time?'

Jim Groark, chief of Metro Construction's renovation department, aka The Firm, known to a select few as the government agency to go to when you need a person or persons to disappear, pushes the folder across the desk.

'Tell me everything you remember of your old friend Tommy Wilson,' he says and sits back in his own chair, interlocking his hands in front him as he does so... waiting.

Rowlinson looks down at the file but does not pick it up.

'Am I cleared for that?' he asks.

Groark nods his head once in reply.

'Tommy Wilson,' Rowlinson says with a smile, 'I've hardly seen him since, well it must be 2000 when we went into Sierra Leone together with 1 PARA.'

'Operation Barras?' Groark asks.

'That's right. He was a sniper deployed alongside us for support.'

'So he wasn't actually in 1 PARA with you?'

'Yes and no. I was in A company; the unit sent in to conduct the operation against the village of Magbeni, but we had a few new recruits with us. Instead of leaving these guys behind, the head shed,' Rowlinson notes the quizzical look on Groark's face, 'that's the officers, decided to supplement the teams with experience from other companies within 1 PARA. Tommy was in the sniper team of C company and we had both just passed selection for the SAS. It was good to see him out there with us, we became friends at Hereford and he was a hell of a soldier.'

'What happened after Sierra Leone?'

'We both got badged. I ended up in B Squadron's Air Troop, probably because of my Parachute Regiment background, but Tommy for some reason got deployed to D Squadron's Mobility

Troop. You would have thought with our similar backgrounds we would have both been Air. Anyway, Tommy excelled at it and by all accounts he loved it. We couldn't understand when he quit.'

'What caused him to quit?'

'No one knew. There were rumours flying around about a new unit opening up and they were stealing some of the best operatives, but those sorts of whispers were always flying around.'

'What type of unit? Tell me about the rumours.'

'There were always stories about a black unit doing even more deniable ops than we were involved in. When the shit really hit the fan, these guys were called in. You would sometimes see a familiar face in the strangest of places and then they would be gone. It was like a myth or a legend you know.'

Groark nods at the file,

'Read that, it might just answer some of the questions you have.'

Rowlinson picks up the file, looks at his boss over the top of it and then settles back in his chair as he opens the cover.

For the next few minutes, he is watched by Groark as he sometimes smiles, whistles and even once says, 'I don't fucking believe it…that wanker was there before us!' before apologising with an embarrassed look.

When he finally closes the cover he is smiling,

'I knew Tommy was good, but this…this is something else.'

'You seem a little impressed.'

'Well, what isn't there to be impressed about? Tommy, or should I say Masterson, if that's what he is calling himself now, has been there, seen it, done it and not only worn the T-shirt but set up a stall and sold the damn things on. What an operator.'

Groark leans over and turns the computer monitor so Rowlinson can see it.

'Take a look at this and tell me what you think afterwards.'

He replays the video of Masterson in Leahy's office.

'Shit…was that…?'

Groark nods.

'But he was supposed to have died in some kind of accident wasn't it?'

Groark says nothing but purses his lips and tilts his head to one side.

'Who sanctioned it?' Rowlinson asks.

'No-one.'

'Ah shit.'

'Exactly. If it comes down to it, could you retire Masterson?'

'What?'

Groark's face turns grim,

'I am asking, if it is required, do you have the necessary skills to remove Masterson from the picture?'

Rowlinson matches the other man's look,

'I can get close to him, that's for sure, he knows me. If it's required I can do it.'

Groark opens a drawer in his desk and pulls out a few pieces of paper, 'This is an open return ticket to the Caribbean. You fly out this evening at 2000 hours. Here are Masterson's location details. He is staying with a woman. If the decision is made, she is also expendable.'

'Do you want a message to be made or is it to look like an accident?'

Groark looks off to one side, considering the options before replying.

'The details will be sent to you when the decision has been made but, if it is ordered, then I think a clear message has to be sent to dissuade any other events of this kind. Get it all set up and await my orders.'

Rowlinson stands,

'No problem.' He turns to leave and pauses, 'Thank you for giving this job to me. With us being old friends I am sure it's what he would have wanted. It's what I would hope for if I was in his position.'

He walks towards the door to leave and hesitates only briefly as Groark speaks behind him,

'Be careful what you wish for, David. It sometimes has a habit of becoming true.'

9

JD reaches the door to the apartment building and pulls it open. Ignoring the rain slashing down, he holds it open for Helen to enter first. He cannot help but notice her long sleeved white shirt is plastered to her body revealing every contour. It is also unfortunate that the heavy rain has turned it almost transparent.

Following her into the building's hallway he removes his sodden jacket and places it over her shivering shoulders in an attempt to protect her modesty, and his discomfort. She turns her head towards him,

'Thanks,' she manages through chattering teeth, 'I didn't have time to grab a coat when...'

The rest of the sentence tapers off as she recalls the nightmare of being arrested for Zoe's murder.

JD runs a hand across his head and winces as his crew cut sprays droplets in every direction as he does so.

'Listen, Helen...'

'You don't have to say anything, JD. You were just doing your job. God knows I should know what that is all about having Peter for a brother,' her body shivers violently, 'Let's get upstairs and I can get into some dry clothes. I'm freezing, you look the same and there's that cuppa to warm us up.'

In front of them, the lift doors open with a soft ping and a well dressed young man steps out. He nods politely at Helen and ignores JD as he strides past, opens an umbrella and walks out into the teeming rain. JD gestures with his hand to the open door and follows Helen into the waiting lift.

During the short ride up he watches as Helen is shivering violently. He wants to hold her to keep her warm but knows how inappropriate that would be. He has to force himself to turn away to avoid staring at the glimpses of Helen's body as his jacket moves as she shivers. Helen notices and despite herself, cannot help but smile.

'JD?' she asks, 'Why is it that a perfect gentleman like you is still single?'

She watches as he takes a deep breath and sighs,

'Still looking for the perfect woman I guess,' he says looking at her, 'if that woman even exists at all.'

His gaze lasts a little longer than expected and Helen feels her face warming under it.

'I am sure there is someone out there just waiting for you to sweep her off her feet.'

As he turns away and nods at her words she blinks and shakes her head as if to clear it. What the hell is going on here, she thinks to herself as she struggles to regain her composure.

'Now, what about Peter?' she asks, trying to change the subject.

He doesn't even turn to face her, 'Thanks Helen, but he's just not my type.'

She punches him playfully on the shoulder, 'Idiot,' she says with a smile as the awkward moment between them passes, 'you know what I mean,' her tone turns serious, 'What does he think about my arrest? Does he think I'm guilty?'

'I don't know what he thinks,' he turns back towards her. 'Truly, I don't. The case against you was compelling and we had to bring you in. If we hadn't done that and the press found out or the story leaked somehow, well that would open up a whole new can of worms.'

Helen feels her face warming again, but this time in anger, 'But did Peter think I was guilty?'

There is a pause as JD considers his answer before softly replying, 'He was the one who signed off on the arrest order.'

'So he does that but can't even be bothered to come to arrest me himself, and now he's fucked off to Crete to be with Julia?' her voice is angry now, 'Wanker!'

'It's not like that, Helen. He had no choice, he...'

'There's always a choice,' she shouts, 'he could have at least... he could have...'

Helen's shoulders shake as the tears flow as freely as the rain outside. JD moves to her and holds her in a bear hug. His huge arms wrap around her small shoulders, attempting to soothe her frustration, anger and fear away. Her own slender arms encircle him in an attempt to cling on to her own sanity as the events of the last few days come crashing down upon her. The lift judders to a halt and the doors open automatically to let them escape the claustrophobic box.

They un-wrap themselves from each other's embrace and say nothing as Helen leads the way to her apartment. She stops outside her door and stares at it.

'I don't even have a key,' she sobs softly before rapping gently against its surface with her knuckles, 'I just hope Ewelina is in.'

In answer to her statement, the door is opened a few seconds later by her flatmate.

'Helen, oh my God...look at you.'

Helen allows herself to be dragged inside and hugged. JD's jacket is pulled off and thrown to one side where it lands in a damp heap. Ewelina looks at JD, 'What have you done to her?' she asks, her Polish accent more apparent with her anger.

'It's OK, Ewelina. JD brought me home. They have finally released me.' Helen replies for him.

The Polish woman shoots a venomous look at JD,

'It should have been sooner. Everyone knows she would not do such a thing.' She turns her attention back to the shivering woman before her, 'And you, my poor baby. I missed you...I missed you so much,' she smothers Helen with kisses before holding her chin and staring into her eyes, 'and me, did you miss me?'

Helen smiles back, 'Of course, babe. You know how much you mean to me.'

Ewelina drops her head down so their foreheads touch, 'That is all I wanted to hear,' she whispers before pulling her head back and saying brightly, 'now let's get you into some warm clothes.'

The two women walk away leaving JD on the apartment's threshold, 'A towel would be nice,' he says as he walks in and kicks the door closed behind him with a satisfying slam.

10

It's a rare day in London when there are no victims of unexplained deaths, but today, so far at least, it is one of those days. The Chief Medical Examiner, Graham Young, is sitting behind his desk and reviewing notes from yesterday's autopsies. There were three carried out by him and his team and again, in a rare turn of events, none were attributed to violence or unexplained circumstances. Two were simple cases of the vulnerable, homeless people that London is never short of, who simply succumbed to the effects of hypothermia, possibly due to excess alcohol consumption and the failure to wrap up sufficiently. At this time of year, he thinks, there will be many more before the month is out. The third is a tragic case of a small boy who was struck by a taxi whilst out playing with friends. The CCTV footage from the taxi showed there was nothing the driver could do. The young lad simply stepped out from between two parked cars and that was it. Graham shakes his head as he thinks of a young boy's future taken abruptly by a twist of fate and the failure of a family to teach basic road safety.

He closes the folder, hiding the graphic pictures from view and places it to one side. His fingers drum on another file for a second before he pulls it slowly towards him. He reads aloud the name written in thick black ink from the front of it,

'Zoe Walker.'

He opens the flimsy front page and is startled as Kate Jeffrey's voice rings out from the doorway,

'I hope I am not disturbing anything.'

He closes the cover and smiles up to his lover as she walks across the room,

'Hey there…not disturbing a thing. Thankfully it is a quiet day so I was just…'

Kate looks across the desk,

'Hmm, I see. Zoe Walker. Do you want to discuss it?'

As a criminal psychologist attached to the Metropolitan Police,

Kate is fully aware of the Zoe Walker case. In fact it was her recommendations that were used to get Helen Carter arrested on suspicion of the murder. She sits down on the soft chair opposite Graham and leans forward on his desk.

'You know I still feel we were on the right track with Helen.'

Graham nods, commenting,

'Yes I do too, but I wonder if we were a little too aggressive with the findings. Perhaps we should have waited before taking our conclusions to Peter.'

'And let a possible, violent and psychotic killer remain loose? I think we did the right thing.'

Graham stares at the file on the table and once again drums his fingers on the cover. Kate waits for him to voice whatever is troubling him. She knows that silence is often the best way to get somebody to talk. His fingers stop their movement.

'What if...?' he starts and pauses.

Kate cocks her head to the side and waits.

'What if someone knew our procedures and how we analyse the victim and suspect?'

'In what way,' she prompts.

'Let's suppose that the killer knew about suspect profiling and how we use it.'

'It's not an exact science, Graham, but it does have results. All of us in the profession ensure that those making the decisions to arrest and charge suspects are always aware of that. We offer recommendations and advice only.'

'Except in this case it was presented as evidence and...'

'Are you accusing me of professional incompetence or negligence in my duties?' The words fly quickly from Kate's mouth.

Graham sits back in his chair in mild astonishment,

'What? Where did that come from? I am merely saying that *we* presented supposition as fact. We should not have done that.' He watches as Kate slowly calms down, 'What I was saying was what if the real killer knew our techniques. It is not hard to find that information on the internet. Everyone uses Google nowadays.'

'If all offenders used the internet to make their crimes untraceable,' Kate smiles thinly, 'well that would make our job so much easier. Ninety-nine per cent of the information available is absolute rubbish.'

'But what of the one per cent?'

'Graham, listen, violent crimes broadly occur because of three circumstances; you have a motivated offender,' she holds up an outstretched finger, 'a vulnerable and suitable victim,' another finger flicks up, 'and the lack of a suitable protector or guardian for the victim,' her third finger rises quickly and then she places her hand back in her lap. 'In most cases these crimes are just extensions of the suspect's normal life as they occur in the areas they live or work and they occur against people they are acquainted with. We can also infer some behavioural aspects from the crime scene.' She taps the folder in front of Graham,

'This case has all the hallmarks of a killer who was intimate with the victim. A killer who was methodical and precise apart from the initial frenzy of the act itself.'

Kate flips open the file and removes a few photographs. She sorts through them and places them down as she describes each one,

'This shows the loss of control associated with a crime of passion. See the large number of entry wounds to the torso?' Another photo placed down, 'Here we see how the killer has arranged the body parts into a neat pile. A neat pile,' she repeats, 'why would someone do that after the damage that was inflicted upon the body? It shows they must have everything in order, that they are naturally a neat and tidy person with no place for chaos in their life.' Another photo, 'The words here, *MISS ME?* They show a longing to be recognised. It reveals a person who is a loner and yet wants, no, craves human interaction.'

Before she can place another gruesome picture down, Graham grabs her hand to stop her.

'The characteristics of which do not belong to Helen Carter.'

Kate gently pulls her wrist free and sits back down,

'What do you mean?'

'I was so caught up in the moment...so caught up with you that it clouded my judgement.'

'Graham?' Her voice is questioning now, 'What are you saying?'

'I am saying that with all the devastation caused by the TSI incident and the whirlwind of meeting you, my mind was elsewhere. I should have said something earlier but I went along with you. You were compelling, full of life and so...so...just so...you. I hadn't realised how long it had been since I was around someone like you.'

'You're worrying me now, Graham. Please, stop.'

'I can't. I don't think Helen is the killer, in fact, if I think back I don't think I ever did.'

Kate opens her mouth but Graham holds up his hand to stop her.

'I cannot allow my judgement to be affected in this way. I should be impartial and let the physical evidence speak for itself and in this case I was wrong to let my emotions get the better of me. I have known Helen for as long as I have been friends with Peter and she is nothing like your profile description. She has never been a loner. She does not crave human interaction as it is always around her,' he pauses and smiles slightly, 'and as for a tidy person, my God, you could not be further from the truth.'

'But the photos of their apartment...'

'Three women lived together in that place Kate, and Helen was the most untidy of the lot of them. I remember Peter telling me that Ewelina was constantly...'

He stops mid sentence as his eyes widen in realisation,

'Ewelina,' he says staring at Kate even as his hand reaches out for the telephone on his desk.

11

JD is standing in the kitchen and attempting to dry his face and scalp with a sodden piece of paper towel.

'Jesus,' he says out loud as the fragile material crumbles and breaks up as he rubs it over his stubbly head. He looks around and spies a cloth tea towel hanging from a hook on a cupboard

door,
'That'll do.'
The rough material dries him quicker and easier than the paper towel. He looks up, surprised, as Helen walks in and laughs.
'What have you got all over you?' she asks as she laughs softly.
His eyes look quizzically at her as she steps forward.
'Here, let me help you.'
Her hands move swiftly over his face and head, deftly removing small, balled up pieces of paper that have been rubbed into his short hair and the folds of his skin. She holds them out to him and he obediently stretches his hand out for her to drop the detritus in.
'The bin's under the sink...unless you want to keep them as a memento?' she says with a smirk.
'Ha ha, very droll.'
Helen looks him up and down, 'At least your jacket kept the worst of the rain off but your trousers are soaked. Come on, get them off and I will freshen them up in the tumble dryer.'
JD's cheeks turn a bright pink making Helen laugh again.
'What, JD? Are you embarrassed about undressing in front of a woman?'
'No...it's just that...I...uh, I...'
'What is it? Do you wear women's underwear or something?' Helen chuckles.
His cheeks turn an even brighter shade of crimson and Helen's face drops,
'You're not seriously telling me...'
JD stops her before she can continue, blurting out,
'I'm wearing tights. Woman's tights.'
He watches as Helen's eyes widen and she starts to laugh.
'Oh God I thought it was something kinky for a moment. It's about the warmth thing isn't it? Peter, when he first started on the force used to get me to buy him tights as he was too embarrassed to get them himself. He told me that when you are standing outside all day in the cold that the tights help to keep you warm.'
It is JD's turn to widen his eyes in astonishment.

'Listen, as long as they're not fishnet stockings, it's nothing I've not seen before. Come on, get them off.'

JD shakes his head as he reluctantly and slowly starts to unbuckle his belt,

'I don't believe this,' he says without looking at her.

'Don't believe what?' Ewelina asks as she enters the small kitchen and sees JD with his trousers pulled down just below his waist, 'What are you doing?' she asks with alarm as she looks between Helen and the red faced JD who hurriedly pulls his clothing back up.

'Nothing…it's nothing. I'll live with the wet trousers,' he says hurriedly, 'but thank you anyway for trying, Helen.'

As he tucks his shirt back in to his waist band and re-buckles his belt he does not notice Helen's laughter or the look that Ewelina gives them both.

'Helen,' Ewelina says stiffly, her Polish accent making her words sound harsh, 'I must go for some milk. Will you be OK for a few minutes?'

Helen, still laughing can only nod.

'I will not be long.'

She turns, almost angrily, and strides out of the kitchen. They hear the door slam and JD cannot help it as he starts laughing out loud along with Helen.

'Now that was awkward,' he says when he regains a bit of composure.

'Thank you JD, again.'

His smile grows wider,

'What for? What have I done this time?'

'For making me laugh, giving me a sense of perspective, for…I don't know, just being here.'

Helen leans forward and kisses him quickly on the cheek, She pulls back quickly and puts her fingers to her mouth, pulling a small white blob of damp paper from her lips,

'Urrgh, but not thanks for that.'

JD turns away to hide his reddening face and busies himself with filling the kettle with water,

'Let's make sure we've got everything ready for when she gets back with the milk,' he says, as he feels the warmth of her lips fade rapidly from the side of his face, 'Where do you keep your coffee?'

'I'll get it, it's in the fridge. The cafetiere is in the cupboard above the kettle.'

As Helen turns her back to him he glances over his shoulder and watches her as she bends down to the under-counter fridge. He closes his eyes and shakes his head before turning back to the kitchen counter.

Stop it JD, just stop it right now, he tells himself as he grabs the large glass and steel coffee filter and places it down in front of him with a bump. *Not only is she a suspect in a murder investigation, she is your best friend's sister, and don't forget he's also your boss. To top it all off she likes women. You are definitely barking up the wrong tree here.* He chuckles to himself as he places some of the hot water from the kettle into the cafetiere to warm it.

'What's so funny?' Helen asks as she places an oblong pack of Dowe Egbert's filter coffee and a carton of milk down on the kitchen counter.

'Oh, just thinking that this day is not going how I expected it to,' he replies.

Helen nods her head slowly, sadly, 'Tell me about it, my whole week has been like that.'

JD points to the green carton,

'I thought Ewelina said she was going for milk?'

Helen picks it up and shakes it from side,

'It's about half full, hmm, maybe she just wanted to stock up.'

JD suddenly turns rigid and lets out a small cry before dropping to the floor, banging his chin off the kitchen counter for good measure.

Helen jumps back, dropping the carton and seeing, for the first time, Ewelina standing behind her holding a small black and yellow device that she had just pressed against JD's neck. She focuses on Ewelina's hands and what she holds between them.

'I don't want to have to taser you too, Helen. But we must talk. I really need you to tell me how much you missed me and I can show you how much I love you too.'

Helen is too shocked to speak.

'Zoe was not good for you, I know you understand that, and him,' she shoots a contemptuous glance at the still form on the floor, 'I saw how he was looking at you and how you were with him. Tell me it's not true.'

Helen can only just shake her head, her mouth moving but no words are formed as she looks at the woman before her in shock.

Ewelina steps forward menacingly,

'Tell me it's not true, Helen.'

12

Julia walks towards me with a steaming mug in each hand. She places them both down on the table, pulls a chair back and sits down.

'Just one question, Peter, just one,' she leans forward embracing the mug in her delicate hands and stares into the depths of the liquid. She says it quietly, 'Why?'

I want to reach out and hold her hand. I want to pick her up and embrace this beautiful woman in front of me, to show my feelings for her. But I know that it is too soon. If I do that she will turn away and I will lose her.

I watch as she brings her face up to look at me,

'Why?' she asks again as the tears start to form. A droplet appears at the corner of her eye, and mesmerised, I follow it as it rolls down her cheek, past the crease of her lips and hangs heavily on her chin. Another follows and the combined weight forces it to break loose and drop into the coffee with an imperceptible splash. Only the ripples on the surface of the cup show it even existed.

'Julia, I don't know. I was lost with so much going on around me, I have no excuses, I was so wrong to…'

'You were lost? What does that even mean? Lost? Jesus, Peter. You have to do better than that.'

Her face turns away in disgust and anger.

'Julia, I can only say I am sorry, truly sorry for my actions. I wasn't thinking, I deliberately wasn't thinking of anything.'

'Do you love her?' she asks, facing me once more.

'No, of course not.' I blurt out.

'And me,' a pause as she looks at me with a fierce intensity, 'do you love me?'

'Oh sweetheart, I love you more than I can put into words. I wish we weren't in this place right now, I wish I could turn back the clock and things would be so different.'

'But you can't, Peter. You can't just wish this away and pretend it never happened,' she bangs the table with her fist causing both cups to spill part of their contents onto the wooden surface, 'How could you be so fucking stupid?'

At the sound of her fist hitting the table, a shadow casts itself at the door,

'Julia, are you alright?' It is Stelios, the younger of her two uncles, standing in the open doorway, 'I heard a noise.'

Julia wipes her eyes with one hand as she stands up, '*Ine endaxi*, Stelio, everything is OK.'

I want to grab her again as I see her eyes, normally so soft and loving, turn to a hardness I do not recognise. It is a steeliness within her that I have caused.

'I shouldn't have come, this is a mistake.'

'No, Julia, no. Please stay. We need to talk about this.'

She shakes her head as she walks towards her uncle,

'It's too soon, Peter. I need time.'

'If you go without us talking it will fester like an open wound, because that is what this is. We need to deal with it and if you get angry then so be it, but we must talk to each other. I love you, Julia. I don't want to lose you and I'll do anything to try and get back what we had.'

She stops in her tracks,

'How do you give me back the trust I have lost for you?' She faces me again, 'Can you do that, Peter? Make me trust you again?'

I want her to feel the sincerity of my words as I lock her eyes with my own,

'With time I hope so. I will do anything to make that happen.'

The seconds tick by slowly as we just stare at each other, not even Stelios moves as he watches us.

It's Julia who finally breaks the silence and I let out a long breath I didn't realise I was holding in,

'Stelio, would you be able to come back in one hour to pick me up?'

'Are you sure?' he asks, ignoring me.

'Yes I'm sure. We need to talk, just like Peter says,' she smiles, but it is not for my benefit as she looks at the man in the doorway, 'It'll be OK, thank you.'

Stelios alternates his gaze between the two of us and nods his head.

'One hour and I will be here to get you. If you want to leave earlier I will be in the kafenion just across the road,' he walks in and kisses her on both cheeks then whispers something in her ear. She nods at him, her smile widening at his words. He walks out of the apartment whilst casting a warning glance towards me.

As Julia once again sits down opposite me her smile disappears,

'So, Peter, you've got an hour. Where do you want to begin?'

I take a deep breath and begin talking.

13

'It truly is an impressive setup you have here, Commissioner.'

Wilks smiles politely at the minister and glances at her watch, 'Thank you but I hope you don't mind, I do have other engagements to deal with today and...' she leaves the sentence hanging.

'No problem at all,' he offers, 'why don't you go and work on your other issues and I will get this young chap to see me out,' he clasps him on the shoulder as he speaks, 'It's Luke, isn't it?'

The young man sitting in front of the double monitors turns to Wilks with wide eyes, 'Ma'am?' he almost pleads.

She smiles at him, 'That would be a great idea, thank you for being so understanding. And Luke, please ensure you show the minister the stats for DDoS attacks against our offices and how we combat them.'

'DDoS? What on earth is that?' the minister asks.

She watches as Luke's shoulders slump as he realises he is dealing with a person who knows as much about IT as a dead parrot.

'Dedicated Denial of Service. We regularly receive hacking attempts into our servers and most of them are just kids trying out their skills. But what really hurts us, and many other large companies, are DDoS attacks by sophisticated hackers. The simplest way to describe it would be as a swarm of requests hitting our servers at the same time, increasing in frequency until the processors cannot handle any more requests,' he glares at Wilks. 'Legitimate information requests are lost in the swarm and if we miss the attack we can lose vital connections for our real police work.'

She shakes the minister's hand as Luke continues his explanations and walks out of the new IT Crime Laboratory with a wry smile on her face. She is heading for the underground car park on the same level. She has driven herself here today as budget cuts have forced the removal of a driver for her except on the most official of occasions. Fumbling in her small bag for her keys, she is startled when the woman's voice appears as if from nowhere.

'Commissioner, is it true that the only suspect you have in the Walker case has been released?'

The damn press, Wilks thinks as she turns to face the questioner, 'One; I cannot comment on individual cases without a press conference, and two, how did you get in here? Oh, Miss Clark,' she says, recognising the Metro reporter and the cause of Peter Carter's troubles, 'I really shouldn't be speaking to you.'

Ann drops the hand holding the small digital voice recorder down to her side,

'I need to get back to work, I need to do something.' Tears start to glisten in her eyes and Wilks can see that she is hurting.

'Peter won't answer my calls, my boss is trying to force me to take a leave of absence and get my head together after the assault in my apartment...'

Wilks looks away with a shamed look on her face,

'We are doing what we can about that incident, but we don't have much to work on,' she says hearing the defeat in her own voice.

Ann had been badly beaten in her own apartment a few weeks back.

She had been left for dead and it was only pure luck that Carter had found her when he did.

'I'm not here about that. I need to speak to Peter. I want to know what he wants to do about the baby.'

Wilks whips her head round quickly at Ann's words,

'A baby? Your baby?'

Ann nods at her questions.

'I left a voicemail with him this morning,' Wilks is almost talking to herself, 'he must have his phone turned off in Crete.'

'Peter's in Crete? Is he with his brother?'

Wilks realises her mistake too late. She looks at the woman in front her and sees how she is confused and vulnerable. She nods her head,

Ann's eyes lose focus as she goes through something in her head,

'Is Helen with him? Is that why you let her go?'

Wilks waves one hand in a dismissive gesture. She has been caught off guard but will say no more,

'That's enough of this conversation it is stopping right here. If you need any more information regarding ongoing cases then you must contact the Public Relations officer dealing with the case.' She starts to walk away to her car, but pauses,

'I'm sorry about what is happening, Miss Clark...Ann... but please let Peter sort his own life out before he has to deal with the issues back here.'

Ann casts a venomous look at the Commissioner as she climbs into her car and drives up to the exit barrier where she stops. There is a brief conversation with the uniformed man at the small kiosk who looks back to where Ann is standing, and then the car drives out into the grey light.

With a resigned sigh, Ann begins walking towards the private security guard who is making his own way towards her with a less than friendly look on his own face.

14

Graham's hand is resting on the phone as he pauses,

'Hold on,' he says, looking at Kate, 'I want to be sure about things this time. We may have already caused an innocent woman to be arrested because we didn't think about the evidence properly.'

He picks up the receiver, 'I'll get JD down here with the case files and we'll talk this through together.'

His fingers start punching in numbers but after a few buttons have been pressed, he stops and replaces the phone.

'What's wrong?' Kate asks.

'I tell you what, why don't we take a trip to see him. It will do me good to get out of this office for an hour or two, and we are quiet today,' one hand reaches out and taps twice on his desk, 'and I hope it stays that way, touch wood.'

He pushes himself up from his chair, but Kate stays sitting.

'What about us, Graham? It sounded like you wanted to turn this unfortunate event into something that could affect our relationship.'

Graham places his hands on the desk and leans forward slightly,

'I am just worried that I missed something, hell, I am still worried, and that's why I won't go off half-cocked with this theory. If it is going to affect our relationship then we need to talk about it after this has been reviewed between us and JD. I don't want to discuss this here, or now.'

He stays in that position, waiting for a response. Kate finally nods her head slowly,

'OK, let's go upstairs and talk to JD. As you say there are more important things we need to resolve before we even think about what is happening between us.'

She stands up and gives Graham a cold look,

'After all, why should it matter what the living feel, when there is dead body to talk about.'

Not giving him a chance to reply, Kate turns and walks briskly out of his office pausing only at the door to ask,

'Are you coming or what?' before disappearing from view.

Graham shakes his head and says softly before following,

'I will never understand women.'

The journey through the labyrinth of corridors and elevators, like a life size version of snakes and ladders, is taken in silence. An occasional nod of the head and a smile to a recognised colleague is all the interaction that occurs.

Stepping into the offices of the Homicide and Serious Crimes Unit is like entering a new world. They walk past the open plan desks and the detectives burrowed into their workstations or making phone calls, and wend their way to the rear of the area to where the glass-walled office of DCI Carter resides. With Peter on forced leave, it is now the domain of his deputy, Detective Inspector Dawkins, JD. Finding the office empty, Graham turns to the nearest detective,

'Do you know where the DI is please?'

The woman shakes her head and picks up her phone to dismiss the two interlopers into her territory. She places the handset in the crook of her neck and rummages on her desk for her notepad.

'Do you know when he will be back?' Graham asks again getting a disinterested look for his query.

The woman takes the handset from its resting place and holds it in both hands in front of her like an offering,

'Can't you see I'm busy here?' she asks, her voice dripping with venom.

'And we are trying to find DI Dawkins so we can attempt to find the murderer of Zoe Walker, remember her? She was a young, pretty girl, violently murdered just a few nights ago…or are you too busy to try and help us?'

She looks between the two of them slowly before responding,

'The last I heard he was releasing the bosses sister from custody. I overheard him speaking to the Commissioner on the phone earlier today. What he was doing after that I have no idea,' she gestures with the phone, 'now can I make my phone call. It's following up a lead of the shooting of two men outside a nightclub two nights ago...or are *you* too busy to let me do my job?'

Kate grabs Graham's arm to lead him away,

'Thank you for your help,' she says sweetly as they walk away and whispers to Graham, 'Let's find the Commissioner.'

15

I cannot believe it when after what seems like just five minutes, Stelios re-appears at the door. Both Julia and I have tears streaming down our faces with the things said between us but we both know we needed to have this conversation.

Stelios stands silently and waits.

Julia stands up and I match her movements. She takes a hesitant step towards me, leans forward and kisses me on the cheek.

'This is just the beginning, Peter,' she says as she takes a step backward, 'We have a long way to go yet.'

I nod as I feel the impression of her lips on my cheek fade away and with those words, she is gone. I am still standing there as I hear a truck's engines roar into life and tyres crunch through the loose gravel of the car park. My hand is shaking as I bring it up to my face to wipe away my tears and I take a long, shuddering breath in an attempt to calm myself. A small grin appears on my face as I think of her parting words,

'*...we have a long way to go yet.*'

That means there is hope. I have not lost her.

Taking the half full cups of cold coffee to the tiny kitchen I rinse them out and wonder what is going on back in London and why I have heard nothing.

'My bloody phone's switched off.' I say out loud to the empty room.

I fish the phone out of my pocket and turn it on, waiting for it to run through its power up sequence and the annoying musical interlude as it does so. With dread I hear the tones announce voice mail and text messages are waiting for me and I think that most of them will be from Ann. As I scroll through, my fears are confirmed but two voicemails stand out. Both are from Commissioner Wilks. I punch in the code to retrieve them and hold the phone up to my ear.

'Peter, it's Wilks. I wish I didn't have to contact you like this, but you are not answering your phone for some reason. I have some news regarding your sister, Helen. We have released her today with no charge. The CPS has no case against her but we will be continuing our enquiries with her as a major suspect. Again I am so very sorry for letting you know like this, but please, once you get this message I will be waiting for your call to give you more details. Peter...' the line is quiet for a second, 'Peter, I cannot imagine what you are going through at the moment, but rest assured we are all behind you, I am behind you. When you are ready to come back to work just let me know. I await your call.'

The phone beeps at me and gives me instructions on whether I want to delete, replay or hear the next message; I press the number for next message. This time Wilks sounds a lot less sympathetic and much more direct,

'Peter, its Wilks. I have just been accosted by Ann Clarke. She knows you're in Crete and she knows about Helen. I don't know what her plans are but she sounded desperate and she also told me about the pregnancy.

I know her editor at The Metro, and I will talk to him to see about delaying any story she may be coming up with. But I can't promise anything. Be prepared for some kind of media backlash about this whole thing. I just thought you should know and try and prepare yourself.'

Once again I hear the options from the phone in my ear but I just disconnect the call and place it back in my pocket as my mind races.

Closing my eyes, I rub my temples as I think of the damage it could do to the progress made between Julia and me just moments before.

'Fuck it,' I say as I walk over to my small rucksack and pull out the bottle of Laphroaig I picked up in Duty Free. Taking it to the small table I rip off the foil protecting the cork stopper and pull it out with a satisfying pop. The wonderful peaty aroma instantly fills my nostrils and I breathe it in.

'I hope you're not planning on drinking all of that on your own.'

I look around in surprise to see my brother, Paul, standing in the open doorway.

'You could have told me you were coming over little brother. I have a spare room you know,' He walks in and gives me a big hug whilst grinning broadly, 'now how about we get a couple of glasses and sort this out like the old days?'

Smiling myself, I look between him and the open door,

'I really wish people would learn how to close the fucking doors around here.'

I get a fist shown at me for my cheek,

'Don't think I'm not afraid to use this, Pete. You may be a copper but you're in my manor now.'

'Paul, you read too many cheap crime novels. No-one talks like that. Jesus, *my manor*, who are you, Reggie Kray?'

Paul lets out a small laugh but his face stays serious, 'Seriously mate, you should have called. You know we're always here for you and Helen. How is she by the way? I haven't spoken to her for a few days.'

Instead of replying I walk to the kitchen cupboards and pull out a couple of glasses which I place next to the Scotch on the table.

'Let's talk about it over a drink, eh?' I ask, 'But first, how the hell did you know I was here?'

Paul starts pouring the amber fluid into the glasses with a smile,

'It's a small community here, Peter. I knew you were coming while you still in the air.' He hands me a glass, and clinks his against it, 'Stin yiamas, to your health.'

We both take a healthy pull on the fragrant whisky and saviour the peaty taste explosion for a moment. Paul drags a chair from under the table and sits himself down upon it with a satisfied groan. He gestures with his glass for me to do the same in the chair opposite his. As I do his bidding he places his glass down, 'Now talk, and don't leave anything out.' Paul says

Taking another, longer sip of the whisky. I pause as I wonder where to start and realising that there is only one way to do this. I start at the beginning.

16

JD's head crashes back and his eyes fly open in panic. He snaps them shut again as he winces at the pain in his jaw and he tastes blood in his mouth. Running his tongue gently around his teeth, he feels the jagged edge of at least one broken tooth and the ripped flesh where it has punctured the skin on the inside of his lip.

He tries to raise his hand to his mouth and discovers he is restricted in some way. Gingerly opening his eyes again he looks groggily down at his body. As his head clears he realises he has been placed in a chair. His eyes focus on the duct tape that is attaching his own arms to that of an office chair.

'Wha..?' his voice is muffled due to his swollen tongue.

Flexing his arms he tries to rip them away, but the tape is too strong for him. He feels his legs are also restricted and he bends forward to see them attached to the sturdy metal legs. An attempt to stand just forces the chair forward a half inch on the thick carpet and he stops as he feels himself begin to topple over.

He looks around and breathes heavily through his damaged mouth, not with the exertion, but with fear that is close to turning to panic. The curtains are drawn but a chink of light pierces the gloom and provides just enough illumination for JD to see he is in someone's bedroom. But that is all he can make out in the semi darkness. He tries to think back to what happened, but all he can remember is talking to Helen about coffee, then…nothing.

He stops his movement suddenly,

'Helen,' he thinks as his eyes dart side to side as he runs through scenarios in his mind before he comes to a single conclusion that makes any sense, 'Zoe's killer was in the house.'

At that moment the door is pushed open and a figure is silhouetted in the bright doorway. He cannot make out who it is, but all he is really focussed on is the long blade, glistening in the hand.

'I thought I heard movement.'

His eyes widen in shock as he recognises Ewelina's voice and he is too stunned to speak as she steps into the room and advances towards him.

She stops in front of him and holds the knife out, gently pushing the point into his cheek. His head is pushed back as far as he can move and he freezes, afraid to move in case the blade slips towards his eyes.

'I see how you look at her,' as she says this she moves forward and straddles him, 'I see you want her. Do you think that a pig like you could ever be anything to her?'

JD feels blood begin to drip down his cheek like a warm, red tear. She removes the knife from his cheek and places it near his left eye. He can see his own blood on the tip as it catches the faint light from outside the room.

'Maybe I should take your eyes to stop what you see. What do you think to that, pig?'

'Ewelina…Ewelina, stop it now.'

JD wants to turn towards the sound of Helen's harsh voice but the knife is so close to his eye that he dare not move. As time seems to stands still he watches as the blade moves slowly away from his face.

'Why, Helen? Why not just kill him now and be done with him?'

'If we do that we will never know how much they know about you. We need to find out what the police know before we escape.'

JD turns his head slowly to look at Helen, his face questioning and incredulous. He catches a glimpse of her shaking her head rapidly and silently mouthing 'no' before a punch from the hand holding the knife rocks his head back. The sharp blade catches his ear as the punch is thrown, slicing it open cleanly.

'You don't fucking look at her,' Ewelina screams at him, 'and after all, it doesn't matter how much you know with the protection I have.' She moves backward quickly to avoid the blood pouring from his wound, 'Ha, look at how he bleeds…like a pig. It will be even better when it is his throat.'

'Let's leave him be a moment,' Helen says from the doorway, 'He's not going anywhere.'

JD sees Ewelina's knuckles turn white as she grips the knife handle tightly in frustration.

'Come on Ewelina, we have time. Let's go back to bed.'

Ewelina looks between the two of them and a sly smile crosses her face, 'Yes, let's go to bed,' she leans across and flicks a switch, bathing the room in light, 'but here. We do it here where he can see how he will never have you.'

There is a metallic clunk as the knife is placed on a surface out of JD's sight,

'But if he gets an erection I will cut if off and feed it to him.'

JD takes a deep breath, thinking if that were to happen under the present circumstances it would take a lot of doing.

As Helen steps into the room, she is pulled into an embrace with Ewelina. Watching as they start to kiss and slowly remove each other's clothes JD's body reacts automatically and he realises he may well be in serious trouble.

17

My head is thumping. I can feel the warmth of sunlight on my face but I cannot bear to open my eyes at the moment as I move my tongue around the inside of mouth. It feels like I have been licking sandpaper laced with whiskey.

I bravely open one eye and have to shut it rapidly as my brain screams out in horror at the sudden bright light. Still with my eyes closed I push myself up to a sitting position and place my feet on the floor. My eyes fly open in shock at just how cold the tiles are under my bare feet and as I breathe out I see little plumes of breath coming from my mouth.

'Bloody hell, I thought this was meant to be a hot country,' I say as I roll my head to loosen the knots in my neck.

'Morning sleepy head. It's a bit chilly at the moment but as soon as the sun comes up properly it'll soon warm up.'

Paul's voice surprises me.

'What are you doing here?' I ask as he hands me a steaming cup of hot aromatic coffee.

'After putting you to bed last night there was no way I was driving home. So I rang the missus and told her I would be staying here to look after you. She had sort of expected it. Do you remember that time when I was based in Lincolnshire? She still hassles me about it now,' he says with a grin, 'How I managed to get to work that morning is still a mystery to me.'

I place the coffee down on the floor next to the bed, groaning as I bend down and my head threatens to split in two.

'Got any ibuprofen and water? I'm not sure I can face this coffee.'

'Peter, that is the finest Cretan hangover cure of traditional Greek coffee. Bring it through to the kitchen and I'll get you a brufen.'

I watch silently as he walks away, humming a small tune as he does so. I am always amazed at Paul's capacity for alcohol. So why do I always try and keep up with him, I ask myself.

Pushing myself up from the bed with considerable effort, I follow him out.

'Jesus, where did all that come from?' I ask as I gesture to the row of empty bottles lined up on the kitchen counter. I see two empty Laphroaig bottles, a bottle of Metaxa and two one litre, plastic water bottles.

'At least we were drinking water with it.' I add.

Paul shakes his head, 'Nope, that's raki. The local firewater out here. You took quite a shine to it after the brandy and it was lucky that Katarina had a few bottles behind the bar.'

He pours the dregs of one of the plastic bottles into a couple of shot glasses and hands me one with a small white pill.

'Take these together. It'll sort you out.'

I place the tablet in my mouth and swig back on the offered glass. In my impaired mental state I had expected water and the taste of the raki as it hits my throat makes me gag. I throw myself out of the chair and rush towards the kitchen sink where I violently throw up. It seems to go on forever.

Paul's voice is full of laughter,

'Yep, that's you sorted but remember to swallow when you see a small brown circle come up...that's you chucking your ring up. The water is in the fridge for when you need it. Oh and that was a tic-tac I gave you, I don't have any pills.'

He grabs his jacket and goes to leave,

'Don't forget you're coming to ours for dinner tonight. If you can get Julia to come that would be great, but I understand the situation, so...' he leaves the question hanging.

I wave at him with one hand as my body attempts to remove the alcohol from my system.

'There's a *pharmakeio,* a pharmacy, just around the corner in the village. I'm sure a walk in the fresh air will do you a world of good so pop in there for some tablets. They speak good English and they always stock hangover cures for the tourists.'

With a shake of his head he walks out of the door,

'I'll pick you up at eight 'o' clock tonight. See you later little brother.'

If I didn't have my head in the sink I would punch him. Instead all I can do is groan and expel softly,

'Bastard!'

18

Stuart Masterson leans over the table and digs a fork into a sausage on the plate opposite him.

'Hey, I wanted that.' Angela exclaims playfully.

'I am helping you watch your figure. I would hate to see that perfect body laid waste by a...' he takes a bite from the sausage and saviours it for a second, '...oh wow, such a fantastic meaty treat.'

Angela looks down at her body and arches her shoulders back to push her chest out,

'I suppose you're right. I also suppose that I should keep your greasy paws off this perfect body in case your flaws rub off on it.'

Her grin flashes a glimpse of white teeth and he smiles back, 'How about after we finish here, we go back and see what happens when I rub my flaws against you?'

Her head cocks to one side and her playful grin turns to wide smile, 'I have a good idea what will happen then, Mr Masterson, and I like it.'

She watches his face as it changes from one of happiness to one of concern as he looks over her shoulder. She turns her head to see what he is looking at but only sees other tourists as they go about their breakfast.

'What is it? What's up?' she asks as her own smile melts away.

'Oh, it's nothing. I find it hard to believe but I think I just saw an old friend,' he places his fork with the half eaten sausage down on his plate and stands up, 'Do you mind? I just want to say hello, I won't be long.'

She watches him as he walks calmly through the restaurant towards a man sitting on his own at a table facing the sea. Shrugging her shoulders, she reaches over and grabs the remnants of her sausage from his fork.

'Well this isn't going to go to waste,' she says as she starts nibbling on it.

Masterson walks across the restaurant until he is standing behind the man and waits.

'Hi Tommy. How's tricks?' The question is asked even though the man sitting in front of him has not turned around.

Masterson walks into view.

'Please, sit down. It's been a while.'

Pulling out the chair, he sits down, still saying nothing.

'I'm sorry I forget you're not Tommy anymore,' he places his fork down and holds out his hand, 'Good to see you again, *Stuart*. It's been far too long.'

Ignoring the proffered hand from Rowlinson, Masterson speaks calmly,

'There's only one reason you're here, so tell me. Why have you shown yourself?'

'Look, I'm not going to hide the fact I've been sent here by the firm after your little stunt. But all they want me to do is to keep an eye on you. They knew that sooner or later Leahy would have to go, and all you did was bring that timescale forward slightly. Unfortunately he had a lot of influential friends and they might not be quite as understanding as our bosses.'

'Your bosses, not mine. I quit remember. So, why you?'

Rowlinson sighs, 'They thought it would be good if you saw a friendly face, you know... someone you could trust.'

Masterson stands up,

'Then they don't know me. I trust no-one.'

The men stare at each other for an uncomfortable moment.

'Look mate if I was here to kill you we wouldn't be having this conversation. You would be dead already,' he gestures over his shoulder, 'along with your little blonde bombshell over there. So do me a favour, give me some credit and take what I say at face value.' He points to the jagged, white scar on Masterson's chest, 'I remember how that bled like a bastard. I thought I was going to lose you but we managed to get you on that chopper and out of that shit hole before it was too late.'

Masterson's hand comes up involuntarily and traces the raised ridge of scar tissue.

'I'll be watching you, Dave. If I even suspect the tiniest thing I ...'

'Yeah, yeah, yeah, I know. You will disembowel me with a spoon and feed my remains to the sharks.' He holds out his hand again, 'Trust me; I'm only here to observe you and keep an eye out for any attempts on your life by interested third parties.'

There is another pause before Masterson finally accepts the handshake,

'So you're here as my unofficial body guard?' he asks.

A shake of the head from the man opposite and the handshake is released,

'No, that's not what I said. I am here to observe and keep an eye out. They haven't told me to get involved one way or the other, so...'

'OK, yeah. I understand.' Masterson looks back to Angela who has turned to see what he is up to, 'Look, thanks for being up front with me. This is as strange a situation for you as it is for me. I think I... well... I don't know what I think.'

'Why don't we meet up later and catch up. I read a bit about you, but most of the file was classified and there are a few things I would give my right arm to hear about. I would also love to hear how you met up with her. She's amazing.' He nods his head towards Angela.

Masterson smiles, 'Stay away, big man. I remember your conquests after jungle training.' They both smile and their minds wander back to more forgiving, but not innocent times. 'OK, let's meet up after dinner. She knows what I did for a living so I will introduce you as an old Para colleague.'

'Just what we are, mate. I look forward to it.'

As Masterson walks away, Rowlinson's left hand moves up from beneath the table and places the steak knife held within it back onto the fresh white table-cloth. Picking up his napkin he wipes the sweat off his palm and nonchalantly goes back to eating his breakfast.

19

Ewelina is nuzzling her lips into Helen's neck as her hands move slowly up and down her naked body. She stops for a moment and looks up at JD,

'This is what you want isn't it? You want to watch her fuck, yes?' She spits out these words towards him like verbal bullets.

JD takes yet another deep breath through his broken mouth and just stares at her. He tries desperately not to take in the erotic sight before him, but fails. Thinking of only one thing he can do, he closes his eyes.

'Open your fucking eyes or I will cut off your eyelids!' Ewelina's Polish accent makes it sound like something from an old war movie.

Reluctantly he opens his eyes and looks straight at Helen. Their eyes lock and he sees confusion and anger in Helens dark eyes, then her head bows as if in shame. JD is almost as surprised as Ewelina when Helen's head whips back with force and smashes into the exposed face behind her. From where he is sitting JD can clearly hear the crunching of cartilage and bone as the nose is broken.

Ewelina flies backwards, screaming and clutching at her bloody face as Helen quickly turns her body around and starts beating her with her fists. Ewelina lashes out with a foot, catching Helen off balance and throwing her off the bed. Her head crunches against the wall near JD and she lies silent and unmoving. Pushing herself groggily off the bed, Ewelina stumbles out of the room.

Knowing he hasn't got much time JD again starts pulling on his restraints. Using the arm of the chair as a lever, JD starts to pull up on the tape, panic giving him renewed strength. It stretches slightly and gives him hope. Pulling again he feels a muscle tear in his shoulder. He screams through the pain as the tape stretches even further and suddenly with a rip his arm is free.

Before he can reach over to release his other arm, Ewelina appears in the doorway holding something in her outstretched hand. It is only when he sees the flash does he comprehend it is a pistol.

The bullet hits him high in the right side of his chest and pushes him backward in the chair. He teeters on the edge of gravity for what seems an eternity before crashing painfully over onto the ground.

He loses consciousness for a second and when he comes around he is only inches away from Helen's face. As his vision starts to go once more he looks into her wide, staring eyes and cannot tell if she is alive or dead. His world fades to grey, then black.

Ewelina stands there, the pistol still outstretched in her hand for how long she can't tell. She hears shouting from outside the apartment and it brings her back to the moment. As people react to the sound of gunfire she knows it is only a matter of time before the police arrive. Her mind moves quickly and she comes to a decision.

Throwing the pistol onto the bed she hurries around the room to gather up her clothes, which she shrugs on. She grabs a small backpack from the wardrobe and stuffs a few items inside it before taking one last look at the two people on the floor of her bedroom. She smiles cruelly as she looks at the blood pooling around JD's smashed shoulder but this disappears when she turns to Helen's prone body.

'I am sorry, *moja miłość*...my love. We could have been good, but now it is *dobranoc.*'

She picks up the gun from the bed and places it in her jacket pocket, sighs deeply, and walks out of the room. She can already hear sirens in the distance as she closes the front door of the apartment behind her.

She does not wait for the elevator but uses the stairs and exits the building from the back door just as a police car screeches to a halt in front of her. The young policeman in the passenger seat jumps out of the car leaving the door open behind him. He stops as he sees her,

'Bloody hell Miss, what happened to you?' He is staring at her bloody face.

Ewelina moves to him as the driver, an older, larger man, pulls himself up and out of the car.

'In there...a man, he hit me,' she holds her hand to her face and cries out as she touches her battered nose, 'I think he had a gun, he was going upstairs...I just ran.'

The two policemen look at each other, unspoken words pass between them by their facial expressions. The driver moves quickly to the rear of the car and opens the boot to reveal the metal gun safe within. He punches in the combination and brings out an MP5 sub-machine gun and a Sig Sauer 9mm pistol in its black plastic holster. He hands the MP5 to the younger man who is talking into his radio and asking for more armed response vehicles to get to their location. The driver turns to Ewelina, 'This man, what did he look like and what floor was he on?' She shakes her head and plays on her Polish accent, 'He was big, he punch me. I don't know what floor, I ran. I scared of him.' 'OK, love…OK. Look, sit down in the back of the car and wait for the paramedics. They will be here any time now,' he looks over to his colleague, 'We're going in yeah?' He gets a nod in reply, 'Shit, and I was hoping for a quiet day.' He opens the back door of the car, 'Wait here. You'll be safe.' As they both head towards the building they are too focussed on the apparent threat inside to see the bruised and bloodied woman quickly hurry away and disappear around the corner.

20

Angela watches Stuart as he walks back to their table. She notices his eyes darting around the room, scanning faces as he passes people and turning quickly towards each movement in his peripheral vision. By the time he returns and sits down she is as nervous as he looks. 'Stu, what the fuck is going on here?' she asks. Masterson just grins, grabs her left hand in both of his and brings it to his lips to kiss it gently, 'Hey babe, it's nothing to worry about. I just got spooked by seeing an old army friend in a place I never thought I would recognise anyone.' Angela pulls her hand away and stares at the man's face before her, 'I may not have known you for very long Stuart Masterson, but I know when a man is lying to me.' She pauses and slowly looks around the room as if scrutinising every diner, 'Are we in danger here?' she questions as she looks back into Stuart's eyes.

The half second Masterson takes to rub his hand across his chin, the soft bristles making a sound loud in his head yet unheard by anyone else is enough for Angela.

'Shit! It's bad isn't it?'

Stuart just stares across the table at the beautiful blonde woman in front of him and nods his head. He watches as she takes a deep breath, their eyes never moving away from each other.

'How bad?'

He responds softly, 'Life or death,' and is surprised to see her eyes harden and narrow slightly before her soft lips turn upwards in a small grin.

'Well at least now I know where we stand.'

She leans forward and kisses him passionately on the lips for a brief second before moving her head back a few inches to stare intently into his eyes and asking, 'So what do I have to do?'

Grinning back at her he shakes his head slowly and incredulously, 'Bloody hell woman, you keep surprising me at every turn.'

He turns his head slightly to look at Rowlinson, still eating his breakfast, 'This one we have to play by ear,' he pauses as he turns back, his grin now gone, 'we play it by ear and when it blows we make sure we are ready for it.'

He watches her face as she nods her head with a grim determination set on her features.

'How about we hit the beach, I have a feeling we might have to leave pretty soon and I really want a tan to piss off the folks back in London.'

'London?' Angie asks, 'Why are we going back to London?'

'We need to find Carter and let him know just how serious this is becoming. For a copper he seems alright and...well, he reminds me a lot of my dad at his age. Full of ambition, solid... you know reliable. I admire that in a bloke and I don't want to see him become collateral damage in my mess. I should never have said anything about him and I think he deserves better.'

'Won't London be dangerous for you, for us?'

'Babe, that man sitting over there shows that London can find us whenever it wants. We face the same dangers there as anywhere else now.' He looks down at the table top and shakes his head again, 'I shouldn't have involved you in this. I should have realised they would come after me like this.' He stands up, 'I have to go back and face the consequences, but right now I am going to drag you down to the beach, strip you naked in the warm sea and have my wicked way with you.'

He holds out his hand which Angie takes with a smile,

'Why Mr. Masterson, you really know how to treat a lady don't you?'

'Live every day like it's your last, that's my motto.'

He watches as her smile falters, 'Not today, don't say that today please,' she says with a small shake of her head, 'not with him sitting over there.'

'Don't worry about him. If he had been given his orders we would be in a very different situation here, but they made a mistake. They've sent someone I know to send their message and it's plain to see what that message is going to be.' He looks down at his watch, 'They are five hours behind us at the moment so I think we have until at least lunch time before we have to worry about anything. Come on, get up I have a promise to keep for a lady.'

21

Wilks is sitting at her desk trying to decipher the figures from the latest budget cuts in front of her when there is a sharp knock on her door. Looking up she finds Graham and Kate standing in the open doorway. She closes the file and lets out a sigh of relief,

'You have just saved me from jumping out of this window in frustration.' She notices the look on Graham's face and her tone turns serious, 'What is it?'

'I think we may have a problem,' Graham says with a worried inflection in his voice, 'do you have a few minutes?'

Wilks gestures them to enter and sit down as she stands up and walks across the office to close the door behind them. She pauses with her back to them both,

'Is this to do with the Zoe Walker case?' she asks softly.

'Our case was based against Helen, but we think it may be prudent to have a closer look at her flatmate, Ewelina.'

Wilks digests this information as she walks back to her own side of the desk. She had actually been expecting the news that the story had broken in the newspapers from Ann Clarke, and to hear this is almost a relief. She sits down and leans forward, resting her elbows on her desk and clasping her hands in front of her,

'Tell me more and explain why I should do this, especially after the wild goose chase you two have sent us on over the last few days.'

Kate stands up angrily, 'We gave you the correct advice at the time given the facts and evidence given to us...to me,' her voice raises, 'I will not be accused by anyone, even you, of sending anyone on a *wild goose chase*, as you call it...'

'Kate,' Graham tries to calm her down, 'Kate, sit down and let's stick to the facts we have before us now. This is not the time for getting angry.'

Kate looks at him with a hard look of betrayal on her face, but sits down and stays quiet.

Wilks nods her head, 'I understand this is an emotional time for everyone. I apologise if I belittled the contribution your work has done, Kate, but I will not be rushed into making another mistake. If we have a prime suspect I want a water-tight case brought against them before I even think about getting an arrest warrant.'

Graham nods his head, 'I understand your concerns, but I believe that there may be a danger to Helen.'

'Why do you think that?' Wilks asks, tilting her head to one side in a questioning manner.

Graham and Kate look at each other. Kate nods her head towards him, 'Tell her.'

Graham turns back to Wilks, 'Our assumptions that Zoe Walker knew her killer we think are still correct. The violence of her murder and the way in which she was killed make it a personal issue for the killer. We assumed it was Helen because of her recent history and because it could have been a crime of passion.'

'Graham, sorry to interrupt you but we have been through all of this and the CPS say that the evidence is weak. Actually to say it is weak is doing it a favour. There is no case against Helen Carter that we can prove.'

'I know, and that was our mistake. We were rushed into the decision by the high profile of the case and we should have taken a step back and confirmed the assumptions that were made. But we don't think that Helen is the killer. We have reason to believe that Zoe and Helen's flatmate, Ewelina, should be considered our primary person of interest.'

Kate starts speaking before Wilks can respond,

'Ma'am, the profile fits the flatmate, Ewelina. We were on the right track from the beginning but we just may have accused the wrong woman. With Helen's history of violence it was a logical choice to think of her as the prime suspect, especially with such a limited amount of background data on her flatmate.'

Wilks pulls out a small wireless keyboard from the side of the monitor and places it on the folder before her which now bears the soft imprints of her elbows upon it, and starts typing. After hitting the 'Enter' button she starts reading,

'Ewelina Jankowska, Polish origin. Moved to England in 2010 to seek work aged 25. No living family members and no relatives in the UK according to her paperwork.' She looks back to Kate, 'Is this all we have on her?'

Kate nods as she replies in a calmer tone to Wilks,

'As soon as Poland became part of the EU we stopped requiring immigration services to do any background checks. We only have that information because of the recent investigation into Zoe Walker's case.'

'And you're telling me she's now our main suspect?'

Both Graham and Kate nod in unison.

'Kate, Graham...can you see how this looks to me? I have a team of highly talented police officers and detectives working this case who at the moment have not come up with a shred of useable evidence, and you come in here, the second time in a week I must add, with your theory about the killer.'

Wilks leans back in her chair and looks intently at the two people in front of her. There is a moments silence as they all stare at each other across the wide desk waiting for someone to speak. Graham opens his mouth to say something and is interrupted by the harsh ringing of a phone with a red sticker on the handset that is sitting on the desks surface in front of them.

'I have to get this,' Wilks says, 'would you mind waiting outside one moment.'

Graham and Kate stand up and leave the room, looking like naughty schoolchildren dismissed from the headmaster's office. As Graham closes the door behind him he hears Wilks pick up the phone and answer with her name before her words are muffled by the closed door.

'Well this isn't going as planned,' Kate says angrily with her arms folded across her chest.

Graham looks at her and shakes his head,

'Why do you think that everything is a slight against you or your character? You're meant to be a psychologist, yet you don't seem to notice when you're the one being irrational.'

His words are like a slap in the face to Kate as she stares at him with an open mouth. Her expression is incredulous and Graham finds himself stifling a small laugh.

'Jesus, Kate. You need to calm down, you have to...'

He doesn't get to finish his sentence as Wilks come flying out of her office, her mobile phone held up to her mouth as she is barking instructions into it,

'You two with me,' she commands, 'there's been a shooting.'

'What? Why..., why do you need us at a shooting?' Graham asks as he blindly follows her instructions and struggles to keep up.

Stopping in the corridor, Wilks takes the phone away from her mouth for a second to reply to him,

'Because it occurred at Helen Carter's apartment and there are two critically injured people there. It seems your theory may have been correct.'

22

My head is throbbing as I make my way down to the small village. The bright December sunlight seems to have the sole intention of making my eyes hurt more than my head. The pharmacy is easily found by the neon green electronic sign that flickers between a green rotating cross and a numerical display of the temperature. All around me the local people are dressed in heavy winter coats, woolly hats and wrapped up as if to take on an arctic challenge. Glancing up again at the sign I see the temperature indicate 22 degrees Centigrade. I take off my jacket in what would be a fine summer's day for London and wonder how the people around me are not dropping with heat exhaustion.

With my jacket draped over one arm and one hand held up against the glare of the sun, I enter the dimly lit pharmacy. My eyes take a second to adjust from the bright sunshine outside.

A young woman in a white coat smiles to show her brilliant white teeth, emerges from behind the counter,

'Ah, Mr. Carter. It is Paul's brother, yes?'

'Um, yes it is. I'm afraid you have me at a disadvantage.'

She laughs lightly,

'You look so alike it almost as if you are twins. He just has a little more meat on his bones, no?'

It is my turn to laugh, which only causes a shooting pain to lance up the back of my head. She sees me wince,

'I see you are in some pain. Let me guess; raki?'

I nod and smile grimly, almost apologetically.

'Don't worry, we have many people who enjoy our tsikoudia a little too much on their first night.'

She turns around and scans quickly along the well stocked shelves before grasping a small packet of tablets.

'Try these. They will take away your pain without making you drowsy. They are best taken with some food and some liquids so it may be best to have something to eat first.'

I grab my wallet from my back pocket and only then realise I do not have any Euros on me.

'Oh God,' I look at her quickly, 'is there a cash point or a bank near here?' I feel I must explain more, 'I didn't have time to exchange any money before travelling, I am so sorry.'

Again a flash of brilliant white teeth,

'No problem, come back when you have managed to get some money and pay me then,' she pauses and her look turns pensive, ' but you need to eat.'

She walks around the counter and thrusts the box of tablets in my hand.

'Follow me, *pame.*'

I follow her obediently out into the sunlight as she marches straight across the road without looking. There is a small squeal of rubber on tarmac and a beep of a horn but she just waves at the driver and reaches the other side of the road without harm. I check both ways and cross with a little more caution to where she is waiting amongst some café tables.

'Sit here,' she commands, and again I do as I am told. My head is in no mood for conflict this morning.

'Giorgo, *ena proino parakalo. Tha pliroso, nai, eine o adelfos tou Paul.*'

She faces me again with a beautiful smile,

'Now when he comes with your food don't worry about money. It is all arranged. Take two of the pills with a coffee and maybe drink a little less tonight.'

Then like a white coated whirlwind she hustles across the road back to her pharmacy, leaving me bewildered about what has just occurred.

'Thank you,' I say lamely as she disappears inside.

A shadow is cast over me as a large Greek man stands at my shoulder also looking across to the pharmacy,

'She is a real beauty, no? That is Aristea, my cousin's daughter. She studied in Manchester to learn the chemicals for the pharmakeio. It is good she comes back and works in her family business,' he grasps my hand and pumps it vigorously three times, 'welcome my friend. I am Giorgo and this is my taverna.'

'Peter,' I respond, 'pleased to meet you.'

'Your brother he is a good man. He comes here many times.'

'How does everyone know my brother, and how does everyone seem to know who I am?' I ask with an incredulous tone.

'It is a small village and it is wintertime. No tourists, so to have a stranger arrive is big news for us. I would say that everyone knew who you were by the time your bags were unpacked.'

Giorgo lets out a huge belly laugh and continues, 'And I bet that some of the yia yia's even knew what was in your suitcase!'

A young boy appears beside him carrying a small cup of coffee and a glass of water which he places almost shyly in front of me.

'My son, Apostolos, one day he will grow up to be the best waiter in all of Crete. Say hello, Apostole.'

The boy moves slowly behind his father's leg and peeks out at me with that innocent wide eyed look of children the world over. I nod my head to him and smile, to which I receive a smile back.

'Now I will leave you to your coffee and make you breakfast like the English; eggs, bacon, toast and sausage, but not your fake English sausages, real Cretan ones with flavour. You will love them.'

With those words, Giorgo claps me on the shoulder and turns away to the depths of his dark taverna and somewhere hidden in the gloom, his kitchen.

With his words ringing in my ears I wash down two of the tablets with the ice cold water and take a pensive sip of the thick, yet delicious, coffee.

I suddenly remember the message left by Commissioner Wilks on my voicemail. I glance at my watch and do the mental arithmetic to adjust to UK time. It's early but she is normally in her office by now. I pull out my phone and place the call only to hear it ring out and ask me to leave a message.

'Good morning ma'am, just checking in after receiving your messages. Thank you for letting me know about Helen and also the heads-up about Ann Clarke. There's not much I can do from here about either of them but I'll be back in five days. Boss, I'm sorry that Ann Clark dragged you into this, I know it's a personal matter and it shouldn't interfere with the job.' I pause, looking for the right words, what I come up with sounds lame, even to me, 'It won't happen again, boss, I promise. Thank you again.'

I hang up and look at the phone, wondering if I should call Helen and explain why I am not there to be with her. I can imagine her hurt and frustration not only with me but with the whole police department. I shake my head and think to myself,

'No conflict today. Give her a chance to calm down, besides I need to concentrate on Julia.'

Thinking her name makes me dial her number, I want her to know that I am here for her, here to try and mend our fractured relationship, but the call goes straight into a recorded message about the number being unavailable. I know she hates using voicemail, saying that if someone wants to talk to her and she is busy, 'then they can bloody well ring back' and that forces a smile out of me. I start constructing a text message.

Hi Julia, just wanted to say how good it was to talk yesterday. I love you and I am going to keep telling you that over and over. Would you like to get together this evening, Paul has asked if the two of us would join them for dinner. He knows the situation and I thought it might be good for us to be somewhere 'normal'. No pressure, I love you x

I hit send just as Giorgo reappears with a plate full of food that looks like it would feed a family of four.

'*Kali orexi*, enjoy your meal my friend and if you need any more you only need to ask.'

The rumbling in my stomach makes me realise I have not eaten anything since the flight over, and an in-flight meal does not supply the amount of the calories I need compared to the amount of alcohol consumed last night. I tuck in with relish as my phone signals that I have received a new message. Placing down my fork I pick up the phone with a smile as I hope that Julia's reply is a positive one. Instead my heart goes cold when I read the four simple words from Ann Clarke.

I am in Crete

23

EMAIL HEADER:
To: **Rowlinson@123construction.com**
From: **Financialservices@commerce.co.uk**
SUBJECT: Successful bid on project Ref 113/A/4

Mr Rowlinson,

Your bid on project ref 113/A/4 has been approved. Please action ASAP and send final detail to the admin office by 1700z today.

Greek office has been advised of the decision and we are also awaiting their response.

L. Wallis
FSC HR Consultant

Rowlinson breathes slowly and deeply as he re-reads the vaguely coded e-mail. The message explains succinctly that the hit is to go ahead on Masterson.

He walks over to the large built-in wardrobe and removes his suitcase, placing it on the bed. Opening the case he takes out his neatly folded clothes, putting them on the bed spread next to his case. He pulls a small Velcro tab in the top right hand corner of the false base to reveal an impressive set of weapons arrayed neatly in the cut-out foam that lines the real floor of the suitcase. Reaching in he pulls out a nasty looking black bladed, serrated knife and a small automatic pistol with a silencer attached. Turning the pistol over in his hand he narrows his eyes and shakes his head before placing it back in the small cut-out in the foam saying, 'Sorry mate, it has to be bloody.'

The knife disappears into a cleverly disguised sheath in his cargo shorts. With the Velcro pocket closed it is almost impossible to see, yet can be pulled out for a swift attack in an instant. In another pocket he places a compact digital camera. This is to be used to take photographs of the bodies which he will then via encrypted e-mail to Groark back in London.

Moving towards the door he catches sight of himself in the full length mirror and pauses to adjust the knife pocket slightly until he is satisfied with his appearance. He exits his room, closing the door softly behind him.

*

Covered only with a thin sheet, Angie Wilson is lying naked on her bed and listening to the sound of the shower as it splashes noisily from the adjoining bathroom. Her body is aching with that exquisite pleasure that only comes after energetic and passionate love-making. She closes her eyes and stretches her body out with a silkiness that resembles a big cat lazing in the sun on the Serengeti. Hearing a door latch click gently into place her smile spreads even further,

'If you're back for more then I hope you are feeling suitably refreshed after your shower.'

She says this without even opening her eyes, waiting with mounting anticipation for her lover to join her on the bed. Still hearing the splashing from the shower she frowns ever so slightly. As the hand clamps down across her mouth her eyes fly open to stare into the face of the man she saw Stuart talking to at the breakfast table.

'Sorry love, nothing personal,' he says as his fist smashes into the delicate skin just above her left eye. Angie's body goes limp as the force of the blow on her temple stuns her.

Rowlinson gets off the bed and pulls the sheet back to reveal her lightly tanned and naked body. He glances over his shoulder at the bathroom door with a smile on his face before turning his attention back to the still form on the bed.

'I'll be back in a minute love,' he whispers into her ear, 'no point in not having some fun while I'm here is there?'

He leaves the unconscious Angie on the bed and walks stealthily to the bathroom door.

'Let's do this,' he says softly as he slowly turns the door handle.

Masterson, in the shower, sees the light change in the room and smiles in anticipation as he imagines Angie entering the bathroom.

'Come to join me have you beautiful? I have to say that I think I need a little more time if you are looking for an encore. You've really…'

His words are cut off abruptly as the opaque shower door flies open and a heavy body hurls itself in towards him. He senses rather than sees a fist coming towards his head and instinctively raised a hand to block the coming punch. Warm blood mixes with the shower water as his left arm is sliced open. It is only his lightning reaction that stopped it from being his throat that was slit. With his good hand, Masterson reaches and grabs out, pulling the attacker forward in an attempt to throw him off balance. They both tumble backwards in the shower cubicle and Masterson's head is smashed into the tiled wall behind him. He fights the blackness that threatens to engulf him but feels his knees begin to buckle. He struggles to remain upright but his head is spinning and he collapses to the floor.

Rowlinson reaches out to turn off the water that is spraying down on them both. As the water stops he feels his neck gingerly where he was grabbed in the talon like grip of his old friend.

Masterson groggily opens his eyes and raises a bloodied arm in an attempt to push Rowlinson away. Rowlinson just smiles grimly as he raises the knife in front of him,

'Sorry mate, orders are to make you suffer. I was hoping it could be quick for you, what with you being a mate an all, but you had to fight back. I'll make it quick with the girl though, there's no need for her to pay for your mistakes.' He pauses a second. 'Of course I'll have a little fun with her first. No point in letting a fine body like that go to waste is there?'

Masterson grabs weakly at Rowlinson's trouser leg but it is pushed away with ease.

'Fighting to the end as always,' Rowlinson places the knife against the inside of Masterson's thigh as he talks, 'because I liked you I'm going to just nick your femoral artery. You'll bleed out in a few minutes but unfortunately for you they are going to be painful minutes as I have to make an example of you.'

Masterson pushes the arm holding the knife away from his leg. There is slightly more power in his muscles this time and it forces Rowlinson to smash his head one final time against the wall. Masterson's body goes limp and his eyelids flutter as even now he struggles to remain conscious.

Rowlinson makes a loud sigh, 'It would be easier for you if you were out of it, but if you want to fight it and stay awake, it's your funeral.'

He places the knife blade once more against Masterson's upper thigh.

A scream of anger causes his head to turn sharply just in time to see the heavy lamp from the bedroom swinging towards him. What would have been a heavy blow to the back of his skull turns into a glancing one off the side of his face. The knife is pulled away from Masterson and is lashed out at his assailant as the lamp comes back for a second time. This time it lands square and Rowlinson sees nothing more as he blacks out.

Angie stands above the two men, panting heavily as she stares down at their inert bodies. She raises the makeshift club in her arms in an attempt to deliver another blow, but finds it suddenly too heavy for her to lift even above waist height. She looks down at the lamp in her hand as if to will it to do her bidding and notices a strange black object protruding from her chest. She drops the lamp and in confusion touches the rubber gripped handle that appears to be growing from her body. As her fingertips brush it a wave of pain courses through her as the knife's blade is minutely moved across a rib. She collapses to the floor as blood starts to spread from her wound out onto the floor where it drips slowly into a small stainless steel grill that covers a drainage hole.

The bathroom is silent save for the laboured breathing of the injured, and the relentless soft sound of dripping and splashing blood that echoes up from the vent.

24

The scene around Helen and Ewelina's apartment is one of chaos. Dozens of police officers are trying to keep bystanders and worried apartment dwellers at bay behind the blue and white barrier tape, and struggling. The officers look alert and angry, a dangerous combination, and Wilks can understand why; word has got out that one of their own has been critically injured. Mixed amongst the anger of the younger officers is a sense of disbelief about the situation. For many of them this is their first experience of a colleague being seriously injured, and Wilks knows it will not be the last time if they make a career of the force. Cutting a swathe through the uniformed officers and followed closely by Graham and Kate, she decisively makes her way to the SOCO, or Scenes of Crime Officer, at the small white, pop-up tent that is kept for such purposes. The SOCO will have the most up-to-date information about the situation. Looking at the perimeter barrier she notices that luckily, for now, the media presence is limited at the moment. She knows it will build to a crescendo of shouted questions and flashing lights before too long and she wants to be prepared for this media circus when it is time to give the press conference.

Entering the tent she hones in on a burly looking inspector who is looking stressed as he speaks to two officers from the Armed Response Unit.

'Bill, what have we got here?' she asks.

'Ma'am,' he sounds shocked, 'we weren't expecting to see you here.'

'Bill, when I'm told this is one of our own we all chip in. What's the situation?'

Inspector William Michaels indicates to the two officers by his side, 'This is Sergeant Morecambe and Constable Waters of the ARU. They cleared the building and found the injured parties. They were also the first officers to arrive at the scene.'

Wilks nods her head to the two men, 'Sergeant, Constable, what did you find?'

PC Waters looks instinctively to his Sergeant, who answers.

'Ma'am, upon entering the building we took up a tactical posture to cover the two exits and awaited backup which arrived less than five minutes after our request. Our information stated there was a lone gunman in the building but it was not a definite situation. On the arrival of the ARU team we moved forward in an attempt to identify and apprehend the gunman before he could leave the building.'

'How did you come by the information about the armed intruder?' Wilks asks.

The Sergeant glances at his young partner with an angry look on his face, 'A young woman in obvious distress exited the building as we arrived. She informed us she had been assaulted by a man with a gun as she was leaving her apartment. Her injuries were consistent with her story.'

Wilks looks around, seeing no young woman.

'Where is this woman now, Sergeant?'

'She, uh…we left her in the back of our vehicle as we took up our tactical posture. She was informed to wait for the paramedics as I felt that her injuries were not serious enough to warrant one of us remaining with her. Especially with the reports of an armed person and that gunshots had been fired.'

'So she is still in your car or is she around here somewhere?'

'Well ma'am, she appears to have left whilst we were clearing the building. I would say that she perhaps felt apprehensive about being in the vicinity of a firearms incident.'

Wilks folds her arms across her chest in a vain attempt to contain her anger,

'So you let a witness, possibly the only person who could identify the assailant, just walk away?'

She turns to the SOCO, dismissing the two ARU officers from the conversation with her glare.

'Do we have a description of this woman so we can possibly attempt to find her?'

'Yes ma'am. She's in her late-20's or early 30's, slim build, dark hair and of Eastern European origin. Possibly Polish or Russian according to her accent,' he looks apologetically at Wilks, 'I know that could account for a few thousand women in London but Sergeant Morecambe will be working as long as it takes to ensure there is a detailed composite to be handed out to the officers on the ground, that is if she does not come forward. He has even offered to forgo his overtime to do it.'

The look on Morecambe's face is almost comical before he regains his composure and nods his head in compliance, but Wilks misses this as she has turned to face Graham and Kate standing behind her. Her voice is angry as she talks to the SOCO whilst staring at the two.

'The witness sounds like it could be a person of interest in a separate homicide we are investigating, and I have reason to believe she may also be the person involved in today's incident,' her voice turns softer as she turns back to face the inspector, 'The two involved, do we have any information on their condition?'

Sergeant Morecambe nods his head and starts speaking before his Inspector can answer.

'The male who was shot is DI Dawkins, ma'am. I recognised him from when I was working the Chinery murder last month. We also ran a check of the apartment and the owner is Helen Carter. We have good reason to believe that she is the injured woman at the scene.'

The Constable pipes up with the fervour of youth,

'It's definitely her ma'am, I saw her on that TV show when she was talking about the kidnapping and her escape from that psycho...'

The look he is given from the combined higher ranks of his Sergeant, Inspector and Commissioner, shuts him up.

'Bill, do we have a positive ID rather than hearsay?' Wilks asks.

Reaching across a trestle table, Inspector Michaels pulls an open topped box towards them and pulls out a small, clear plastic bag containing a wallet.

'This belongs to the male gunshot victim. It contains the warrant card of DI Dawkins,' he fishes out another small bag, 'and this is the driving licence of the injured female. I'm sorry ma'am but we can confirm it is Helen Carter and DI Dawkins who were involved. They are both in a critical condition. DI Dawkins was shot once in the chest and Miss Carter has a head and spinal injury. I don't know any more as they are en-route to the hospital,' he checks his watch, 'actually they will be there by now.'

As if on cue his radio crackles into life but the first part of the message is lost in the general background noise of sirens over the air,

'…unfortunately has been pronounced dead on arrival.'

25

I am still staring at those four words from Ann Clarke on my phone's screen when another message comes through. With dread I scroll through the menu to open it and let out a breath I didn't know I was holding when I see it is from Julia.

Peter, I can't do this today and in company. We need to sort things out between us first. This is too soon. Can you meet me tomorrow evening in Kolymbari? Stelios will pick you up.

My mind is racing. Tomorrow evening might work out better for me. I wonder if I would be able to sort out the Ann situation without Julia finding out.

'My friend,' Giorgo's voice booms out to me. I had not even seen him walk up to the table, so engrossed was I in the text messages.

'My friend,' he repeats when he sees he has my attention, 'you look troubled. Is the breakfast not good?'

I hastily place the phone face-down on the table, 'No, no. The food is delicious, I was just, ah…' I struggle to find the words as Giorgo nods his head knowingly.

'Woman trouble I guess, yes? We all have these my friend.'

His heavy hand clasps me once again on the shoulder and he

leans in, almost conspiratorially,

'Things have a way of working out. Try not to force things, eh?'

I nod my head, not just at his words, but also as I realise that everybody truly does know each other's personal business here. It makes me wonder how I can prevent Julia finding out that Ann is here.

'Hey,' he continues, 'your brother is coming. I will bring you both a fresh coffee.'

He disappears back inside once again with a swiftness that defies his bulk. I smile half-heartedly at Paul as he climbs out of a battered and faded, red Renault Twingo and walks towards me, calling out greetings and gesturing to the locals who all seem to know him.

'Hey little brother, how's the head?' he asks as he sits down opposite me and takes off his sunglasses, placing them on the table.

'Jesus, Paul. Don't ever let me touch a drop of that raki stuff again. I feel like crap.'

He laughs out loud. A true and pure sound of humour at another's expense,

'You'll get used to it,' he says as he reaches out and grabs half a sausage from my plate. He takes a bite from it as I speak.

'I seem to have another headache as well this morning,' I pause and he sees the look on my face.

'What is it? Is it Julia? Has she…?'

'No it's not Julia, well not entirely.'

I turn over the mobile phone and seek out Ann's message before sliding it across the table towards him. The last bite of the sausage pauses midway to his mouth.

'Oh shit,' he states simply.

'Exactly, and I need to stop Julia from finding out that she's here. If she does she'll think this has been my plan all along in case we didn't work out.'

'Hold on mate, you're not thinking straight about this. I reckon you need to let her know, and as soon as possible, in my opinion.'

He pops the remains of the meaty morsel into his mouth and

chews slowly, waiting for my answer.

I shake my head, 'I can't tell her, I just can't. I know how she would react.'

'OK, what are you going to do about this shit-storm you seem to have found yourself in?'

I make a decision quickly, 'I need to see Ann and get her on a flight back home.'

Giorgo breaks the conversation by placing a tray bearing two tiny coffee cups, a decanter containing something clear, and three shot glasses.

'Coffee and a little something to make the day seem brighter,' he says, opening the small glass bottle and filling each of the small glasses in turn.

'Is that...?' I ask.

Yep, that's raki,' Paul says nodding with a grin on his face, 'and it's impolite not to drink it when you receive it as a gift.' As he says this he raises his glass in a salute to Giorgo.

'Yiamas my friends,' the big man says as he raises his own glass. They both look at me, waiting.

With reluctance I pick up my own shot glass and raise it alongside theirs until they touch with a resounding 'clink'.

'Yiamas,' I say, before we all knock back the innocuous looking drink and slam the glasses down on the table. I am the only who grimaces and close my eyes as the harsh liquid burns its way down my throat and into my stomach. It is all I can do not to let it come straight back up alongside the food I have just eaten. Only when I open my eyes do I see that the glasses have been refilled.

'Oh shit,' I mutter as my two companions grin at me.

'Giorgo?' Paul asks, 'How do you stop a woman from finding out your private business here in Crete?'

Giorgo strokes his moustache as if in thought,

'Easy my friend. You marry her and make sure she stays at home to cook for you and look after your children. Of course that means your mistress will know all of your secrets, ahh...*ti na kanoume*, what can you do? Women, you can't live them, you can't shoot them.'

He downs his glass for the second time, 'I must go. I am making stifado for tonight's customers.'

He shakes both of our hands and gestures across the table, 'This is from me, *kanena problema fili mou*, no problem my friends.'

With that he leaves us, taking his empty glass with him. Back to his kitchen and his stifado.

Paul waits a second before looking at me soberly,

'I'll meet with Ann and talk to her. I think I should be able to make her see sense and why she should leave you alone.'

I shake my head, 'No Paul, you can't. I won't let you do that. It has to be me.'

'Think about it for a second mate,' he responds as he leans forward in his chair to place an elbow on the table, 'you meet a strange woman out here and get seen by someone and it will be back to Julia and her family before you even get to say hello. If I go and meet the same woman then it is just me meeting up with a friend for a coffee and a chat.'

I mull it over, seeing the logic of his words and he senses my thoughts.

'Come on. Send her a text message now and tell her you'll meet her this afternoon in the Monastiri Taverna at the Old Harbour in Chania. It's a public place, and at this time of year it will be quiet.'

'But you don't even know what she looks like,' I try to protest.

'Trust me, she'll probably be the only one there at this time of year, plus you'll be watching from a nearby café and directing me towards her by phone. That way you can point her out to me without being seen.'

'It sounds like you've done this before,' I say.

'Ask no questions, I tell no lies.'

He raises his shot glass towards me,

'Is it a plan?'

I stare out into the village street at the hustle and bustle of daily life in this foreign country, and can see no other option. I still have to ask one further question,

'Are you sure you can persuade her to leave?'

I turn back to him as he answers.

'Trust me. I can be very persuasive when I need to be.'
I raise my own glass and we once more bring them together in a toast,
'Then I guess it's a plan.'
This time as I gulp down the raki my face stays impassive.
Paul watches on silently as I pull the phone back towards me and compose a short message. I hit send and sit there waiting like an expectant father for a response. It is less than 30 seconds in coming,
See you there
'It's on,' I say.

26

Masterson's eyes open groggily, his arm is stinging and his head is a mass of pain and confusion, He takes a second as he struggles to comprehend why he is slumped in a shower cubicle. He focuses on the prone figure laying at his feet and even through the mask of blood covering his former colleague's face, recognises it as Rowlinson. Pushing himself out of the wet cubicle with a groan, he crawls forward and sees another body come in to view. Angela, his perfect Angela, her naked body lying motionless in a pool of blood.
Forgetting his own pain and ignoring his would-be assassin, he moves as swiftly as his body will allow to reach his lover's side. He sees the black rubberised grip protruding with an alien ugliness from her perfect skin. He reaches out as if to touch it, to prove to himself it is real and not some imagined horror, but before his fingers can brush against the knife's handle, Angela's eyes flutter open to rest upon his own. Her mouth moves silently as he brushes back the hair across her face with a gentleness that belies the anger he feels welling up from his core. An anger that threatens to explode with a destructive force. It takes all of his will-power to sound calm,
'Don't try to speak, don't move, babe. I'll get help, I'll…'

He loses his ability to speak himself and Angela produces a pained smile and almost imperceptibly shakes her head,

'Too late,' she whispers.

Masterson closes his eyes and shakes his head. The hand that grasps his feels weak and he opens his eyes to look at the dying woman he loves.

Angela feels as if she has used every remaining ounce of strength to reach up and hold his hand in hers, but she somehow manages to squeeze his hand and pull it towards her lips.

'No, we can…I can go and get help,' Masterson is pleading with her now, but inside he knows the truth. He can see the truth in the blood that has escaped from her body. The dark, red blood that is now slowing in its race from the jagged wound in her chest.

'It's ok,' she says softly, 'it doesn't hurt anymore.'

Her eyes drop and her gaze loses focus for an instant. Quickly she locks it back onto his. Masterson's vision blurs with tears he thought he would never shed again as the hand holding his begins to shake.

'I love you,' he says, his face just inches away from hers, 'you know that, don't you?'

He watches as her smile widens and she nods her head slowly,

'I know,' she manages to whisper.

Masterson smiles back and grips her hand tightly.

Then she is gone.

He sees her eyes drift to a point above his shoulder and focus on something only she can see. The spark of life disappears and he is left staring into a set of two lifeless orbs.

He kisses her gently on the lips and slowly lowers her body down to the tiled floor. He whispers, 'I love you,' one last time as he closes her eyes with one hand and lets out a silent roar of anguish.

The groan from behind him makes his expression change from one of grief to a murderous snarl. He swivels around, still crouched down on the balls of his feet to face the man who has taken away the only person that he has truly ever loved.

Standing up slowly, his pain, both physical and mental, for the moment ignored, he steps forward to tower over Rowlinson who is starting to stir from his forced slumber. Masterson scans the bathroom, he knows what he is looking for and spies it where it has dropped into the wash basin. A cruel smile spreads across his face.

With his bare feet he delivers a swift and brutal kick into Rowlinson's abdomen to ensure his continued incapacitation. Masterson walks across the bathroom taking care not to step in Angela's blood. He avoids looking at her body, his eyes fixed on the implement in the bowl that he needs. His hand grabs the old-fashioned bone handle of his straight razor from where it has fallen during the struggles. With one hand he deftly flicks the long, flat blade open which glints with a passive viciousness in the light.

The grim smile still on his face, Masterson once again steps over the dead body of his lover and makes his way back to the groaning Rowlinson.

27

JD can hear the wail of the ambulance siren but it sounds muffled, like it is being smothered with something. He is sitting in the back of the ambulance opposite the paramedic who is working with her patient on the other wheeled trolley.

His memory is vague. JD knows he was shot. He remembers seeing the flash and then being knocked over from the force of the bullet hitting him, but what happened after that is gone. Also the fact that his shattered shoulder is strapped up and his right arm is in a sling sort of brings the reality home to him. He attempts to force his groggy mind to recall the events but just cannot remember anything. He puts it down to the painkillers that must have been pumped into him for he also cannot feel any pain.

Opposite, the paramedic is oblivious to him as she is she is focussed on her task, and JD realises that it must be a serious, if not life threatening situation for her patient.

'Come on,' she says out loud, leaning over the body as she squeezes a clear plastic diaphragm that is attached by a short length of tubing to a mask that covers her patient's face. 'Don't give up on me. Don't give up on me now.'

JD watches as she reaches up and flicks a switch on the green and beige coloured box that is attached to the wall by thick rubber straps which hold it in place. A high pitched beeping fills the cabin and a second or two later it changes into a steady whine. Taking the two paddles that are stored on either side of the box she places them onto the still form and shouts out, 'Clear,' more from protocol or habit than because it is needed to warn medical staff to take their hands from the body. She presses the rubberised buttons in the handles and JD watches as the body jerks on the gurney. It is not the same action you see in the films or on TV he notices, but more of the action made when someone coughs, a flexing of the chest that stops as quickly as it started. The lights dim and JD looks up before realising that the system must be connected to the ambulances power circuitry. The high pitched beeping returns before changing once again into the electronic whine to show the machine is ready for use once more.

The paramedic is leaning over her patient, checking vital signs and hoping to see a reaction to her life saving work. She stands up and places her hands back on the paddles, 'Clear' she says again and the ritual of the jerking body and the dimming lights is repeated.

'Shit,' she says quickly and punches the handles back into their assigned slots, causing their cable flex to start swinging violently. They slow to rhythmic motion that matches the swaying of the vehicle. Pulling open a drawer to her side she moves with a sense of increased urgency. She reaches in and grabs a pre-filled syringe, double checks the printed label, then removes the small blue protective cap that covers the needle. With no time to lose she drops the cap on the floor where it rolls around with the other detritus of her work; bandage wrappers, blood-stained material and even a pair of scissors that she dropped earlier.

JD winces as he sees the long thin needle exposed and lets out a sigh of relief that he is not its intended recipient. The paramedic pauses and places her head down so that her ear is close to her patients head. She stands back up, shaking her head, which causes her pony-tail to whip back and forth.

'Come on, come back to me,' she mutters as she feels along the chest in front of her with two thinly gloved fingers. When she is satisfied she has the correct spot she presses the point of the needle into the skin, careful to avoid her own flesh.

JD cannot believe just how much of the needle is inserted before the plunger is slowly pushed down and the life-saving drugs are administered. As he watches he starts to feel a dull ache in his shoulder that rapidly becomes very painful. He considers asking for more pain-killers but knows that there are far more serious things that the paramedic is working on than to give him a shot for pain. He leans back and eases himself down so that his head is resting on the thinly covered pillow and waits, hoping that the pain will not increase in its intensity whilst the paramedic is busy. He closes his eyes in an attempt to stave off the growing pain and cannot help himself as he lets out a small groan. He opens his eyes and is shocked to see the young looking face of the paramedic staring down at him.

'Shh, shh. It's ok,' she says to him soothingly, 'you're going to be alright.'

A racking pain courses through his body and he slams his eyes shut in reflex against the pain. He feels a cool liquid pour through his body and the pain is eased away. JD lets himself go with the feeling of liquidity as he succumbs to whatever drugs are being pumped into his body. He wants to thank the paramedic and opens his eyes to be able to see her and show his gratitude, only to find himself looking up at the fluorescent lighting on the ceiling of the ambulance. He turns his head to one side in an attempt to see what drama must be unfolding on the opposite side and stares straight into the eyes of the person on the trolley. Realisation hits him with a feeling that is uplifting, terrifying and exhilarating all at the same time. JD stares at the face he knows so well. He stares into his own eyes with a sense of calmness he never knew when he was alive. For JD there is a flash of light that blocks out all of his senses, then nothing more.

The paramedic suddenly stops her movements and her head drops in defeat. With her chin resting wearily on her chest and with tears of frustration in her eyes, she turns to the front of the ambulance. One hand is resting on the still form of JD as she raises her head, 'Mick, you can turn off the blues and twos. I've lost him.'

The driver sighs, knowing how badly this will affect his partner. He clamps his teeth together, sharing in the same frustration and eases his foot off the accelerator. Reaching out with his left hand he flicks a bank of switches that rests in the centre console and the sirens fall silent. He detaches the microphone handset from its cradle and presses the button on the side of the mouthpiece,

'Base, this is Alpha 034. Inform the ER that our patient has expired en-route. Repeat, patient has expired en-route. Out.'

The now silent and slow moving ambulance continues its journey through the London streets.

28

'We've got a few hours to kill, Pete. How do you fancy a little sight-seeing tour?' Paul asks me after we have both contorted ourselves to get into the cramped confines of his car.

'As long as we don't have to spend too long in this shoebox I'm up for it,' I reply, attempting to shuffle sideways so my left leg is not resting against the gearstick.

'I was thinking we could pop in to a local winery and pick up a couple of bottles to have with dinner tonight. The owner is a really friendly guy and it will stop us waiting around like lemons until 3 o'clock. What do you say?'

I let out a small groan before replying.

'More bloody alcohol? I don't think I can face anymore after raki for breakfast.'

Paul chuckles good-naturedly, 'That was just to get the day started, besides we can't eat without wine. That would be just wrong.'

'Well,' I say, resigning myself to the fact, 'it doesn't look like I am going to have much choice in the matter does it?'

'That's the spirit. Let's crack on then.'

With these words Paul starts the car which to my great surprise starts first time. He casts a quick glance over his shoulder and pulls away from the curb with a squeal of rubber on tarmac. Apparently everyone drives like a Formula One driver over here.

'Go, go, go,' I say in my best Murray Walker impression.

'You need to work on that one mate. I mean, seriously, that was crap,' Paul says with a smile on his face.

'Piss off,' I respond, also smiling but it quickly turns to a look of alarm as he completes a U-turn across the street in front of an oncoming taxi. The large silver Mercedes weaves around us as if it was an everyday occurrence, which I realise it probably is. To take my mind off the driving I reach out and turn on the radio, immediately wishing I hadn't as a cacophony of what sounds like a group of droning monks assaults my senses.

'What the hell is that?' I ask as I attempt to retune the radio to something resembling music I recognise.

'That little brother is known as Cretan *mantinades* and is music for the soul. If you're looking for Radio 1, well you're going to have to wait until you get back to London for that.'

I am surprised when I hear a voice blare from the crackly speakers in an American accent.

'...AFN – The Eagle, serving America's best,' before launching into some rap music.

'Turn that crap off,' Paul says, 'it's the US Navy's radio station at Souda Bay. I try not to listen to it even though it's the only English speaking station in the area. It's either country, hard rock or this shite that they play all day and they intersperse it with infomercials about how to pass fitness tests and how not to piss off the locals.'

He reaches his hand out and rotates the dial until the readout displays 93.2 and we are suddenly listening to 'Stuck In The Middle With You' by Stealers Wheel.

'Very apt,' I mutter as we listen to how there are clowns to the left and jokers to the right, 'another US station?' I enquire.

'No, this is Easy FM. They mostly play stuff from the '70s through to the '90s. Pretty good it is too, but they do repeat the songs a lot.'

'This is more like it.'

Paul nods, 'Yeah but this song just makes me think of some poor guy getting tortured and having his ear cut off.'

'Reservoir Dogs, Tarantino's finest film.'

'It was good, but I watched it for the first time in a tent in the middle of the Kuwaiti desert. Sort of spoiled it a bit for me.'

I stay quiet as I think back to the days when the whole family was worried about Paul and what was happening during and just after the first Gulf War.

'Do you miss it?' I ask, breaking the silence between us.

'What, the army? Yeah, I miss the blokes you know, but the job...the job had changed over time. I mean, it was getting so I was never at home, and when I did get back I always had a bag packed in the spare room so I was ready to move out.' He shakes his head, 'That's great when you're single, but when you have to leave your family behind and not really know when you are coming home, that's a lot tougher.'

I look out of the window and see we are passing what looks like an old military base comprising a small airfield, some barracks and a few very dusty, obviously unused planes and anti-aircraft guns. I am just about to ask what it is when Paul starts talking.

'This is Maleme airfield. It was the main invasion point in 1941 for the Germans during the Battle of Crete. Brit, Aussies, Kiwi and Greek soldiers were based here and in the surrounding areas and they should have managed to hold the airfield. But in the confusion of the attack there was a cock-up in communication and the Germans managed to take it. I remember we looked at the order of battle at Sandhurst and we had to plan our own methods of defending the airfield. Nine times out of ten we managed it successfully with the troops that were on hand and beat off the invasion, but there was always that small chance of a SNAFU that gave the momentum to the attackers.'

'SNAFU?' I ask.

'Situation Normal, All Fucked Up,' Paul explains, 'military speak for if it can go wrong, it will.'

We take a sweeping left hand bend, then a right hand one to cross a bridge and Paul slows the car.

'If you look at the old bridge on your right you can still see the scars and damage on the concrete and bricks that were made during the fighting. That is the original bridge that crossed the river.'

I am amazed that I can see the pockmarks in the coarse, heavy bricks that make up the stanchions, from fighting that occurred so many years ago. Paul continues his running commentary,

'Some German gliders managed to crash land in the river bed. To start with it was a slaughter and so many of their paratroopers died before they could even fire a shot. Apparently the locals were even in on the act, coming out with pitchforks and knives to hack at the troops as they landed, but the numbers were too great and enough survived to mount attack after attack on the hill behind the base, Hill 107. Once they had taken that it was easier for them to control the runway, bring in reinforcements and it was curtains for us.' Paul lets out a half laugh as he accelerates away from the bridges, 'The thing is, Hitler never used paras or glider troops in such an assault again. The loss of so many of his elite fighting men in just one operation stopped him from using them apart from as normal ground troops. It also meant a delay in his planned invasion of Russia which meant he had to invade in the winter-time. And we know what a disaster that was for him. So, you could say that this was a major turning point in the Second World War. If it wasn't for Crete and what happened here, then we may well have been speaking German today.'

I try and take in the enormity of the invasion, an invasion I know nothing about, 'How long did the battle last?' I ask, wondering if it was months or years to inflict such casualties.

'Eleven days,' Paul answers, 'eleven days of fighting and retreating across the island to try and escape by boat to Egypt. The Cretan's continued the fight for the rest of the war with disastrous consequences for many of the villages.'

'What do you mean?' I ask, my interest piqued.

'There's a village called Kandanos, it's about 20 kilometres inland that was completely destroyed, I mean just razed to the ground after a German patrol went missing in the area. Just up the road from here in a place called Kontomari, they rounded up all the males and took them to the edge of the village. They even handed out cigarettes and took pictures for Christ's sake, then they calmly shot them all. Massacred because a few German troops were killed by Crete resistance fighters.'

'Bloody hell.' I am shocked by the level of violence against a civilian population.

'And that's just the half of it,' he continues, 'it was a terrible time for the locals, but they put up a hell of a fight. It's in their character.'

We drive through the small village of Tavronitis. It is just a few shops with baskets of fruit and vegetables displayed outside on the pavement, and a few bars that appear to be doing a roaring trade if the number of old men sitting at the tables in the morning sun is anything to go by and then we through and past it. We drive on for another kilometre or so before taking a left turn and heading up into olive groves that stretch out to the flanks of the snow capped mountains rising up in the distance.

We drive up to an impressive looking building with an old style, but modern built wall and arch that fronts it.

'Welcome to Karavitakis Winery' the sign proudly exclaims at the entrance as Paul brings the Twingo to a sharp stop.

'The brakes work then,' I say out of the side of my mouth as a young man exits the building and walks towards us with a friendly smile on his face. I extract myself from the car that was not built for anyone over 5 foot 8, yet alone my 6 foot plus frame.

'*Yia sou Paul, ti kanis?*' the man says.

'*Yia sou Adoni, ola kala. Esis?*' Paul replies as I stand there with a bewildered look on my face.

'Adonis,' Paul continues in English, 'this is my brother, Paul. He's over from England for a few days and I thought he would like to see your wines here, maybe take some back with him.' Paul looks over Adonis shoulder, 'Niko not here today?' he questions.

'No, he flew out to Berlin this morning, we are getting another reward for our wines.' The smile on his face is one of ecstatic enthusiasm, 'Great news, no?' After shaking Paul's hand he grasps mine, 'Yia sou Peter, hero poli…uh, pleased to meet you.'

His smile is infectious and I can't help but smile back as I respond.

'You too, a great place you own here.'

He laughs, 'Oh I wish I owned it. I only work here, Nikos Karavitakis is the owner and he gets the awful job of having to leave Kriti to accept the rewards. I mean, who would want to leave this beautiful island?' he says, letting go of my hand and gesturing to the scenery that surrounds us.

I look across the wide vista of rolling, tree covered hills, rugged mountains, long coastline and a deep blue sea and reply,

'I can certainly see why people would want to stay.'

Adonis holds his palms up in a questioning manner,

'So Paul, you want your usual order?'

'How about a tour first? Show Peter your setup here and then a little tasting to help him decide on which wines to buy.'

'For sure, no problem, just follow me guys.'

I turn to Paul with a raised eyebrow, 'Oh, I'm buying the wine am I?' I ask.

'Hey,' Paul says in mock indignation, 'I'm a retired old soldier, you need to look after us veterans, and besides, when was the last time you bought a drink for your big brother, eh?'

'I seem to recall your stag-night in Soho cost me a fortune in champagne.'

'Yeah, but you had just been promoted,' he pauses, 'besides as my best man I remember you insisted on doing it, just like I remember what, or should I say, *who*, you insisted on doing as well that night.'

I have no reply to that and the next 45 minutes is spent listening to the incredibly knowledgeable and enthusiastic Adonis as he walks around the machinery, vats and cellars of the winery before finishing off in a small courtyard where he brings out bottle after bottle of wine for us to taste. I am enjoying the experience so much that I almost forget why I am here on Crete in the first place...almost.

As Paul and I sip the last remnants of the final wine we were given, a sweet dessert wine that is delicious, Adonis darts into a side room for a few moments.

'I think perhaps I should talk to Ann this afternoon,' I say.

Paul shakes his head, 'No way. If you start talking to her she will be all over you like a rash. Stay out of sight and stick to the plan. Trust me, Peter, it's a safer option for you and Julia that way.'

Adonis reappears holding a small box under one arm and carrying a paper bag emblazoned with the winery logo in his other hand.

'These are yours,' he says, handing the box to Paul, 'and these are for you,' he hands the bag to me.

I glimpse inside and see two bottles, one red and one white. The two I had expressed a preference for during the tasting.

'How much for everything?' I ask him.

'Paul has an account and your bottles are from me, a gift.' Then in an exaggerated whisper, 'Besides, your brother buys enough wine here to keep us in profits all year,' and he winks at me.

'Don't I bloody know it,' Paul says, 'but by God they're worth it.'

Adonis walks us back to Paul's car and opens the boot so we can place the wine into the small space.

'Adonis, thank you very much, uhhh *efcharisto poli*,' I stumble over the unfamiliar Greek words, but it brings a grin to his face.

'Peter, you speak Greek. Bravo!' and he grabs me in a bear hug that almost knocks the breath from my lungs, 'before long you will be speaking like a local.'

Paul glances at his watch as he shuts the hatchback door with an empty thud.

'Adonis, give Niko my regards when you see him next and

congratulations on the new award. You guys deserve it,' he looks at me and his expression has turned serious, 'but I am afraid we have to rush off to a prior appointment. I hope you understand.'

'Not even time for a tsikoudia?' Adonis asks, a hurt puppy look on his face.

Paul grasps his hand in his own, 'Next time, Adonis. I promise, but we really have to go.'

I miss the friendly Greek man's reply as my phone starts ringing in my pocket. I pull it out with a feeling of trepidation as I wonder who is calling and see Graham's name on the screen. I breathe out a sigh of relief as I answer his call.

29

Wilks is impatient and cannot wait for the message to be repeated.

'Who is it? I need a name,' she snaps at the inspector.

The tented area seems to close in around her as he transmits her request. The officers and civilians alike have all fallen silent as they realise they are now all at the scene of a murder investigation. The voice over the radio seems to take an age before it crackles back into life from the tinny speaker.

'Identity of the deceased is unconfirmed but it is a white male, approximately 30-35 years of age with what appears to be a gunshot wound to the chest...'

The transmission continues but Wilks has blocked it out. She does not move or say a word as the reality sinks in. Graham exhales two words in an automatic reflex,

'Oh God.'

His words seem to galvanise Wilks into action.

'Get this scene locked down. Nobody else in or out of the cordon apart from forensics,' she addresses Graham. 'How soon can you get a team here and set up?'

Graham responds immediately,

'I can get a full team on-site within an hour,' he says confidently;

glad to have something to do that will take his mind off the death of his friend and colleague.

'You've got thirty minutes,' Wilks says and turns her attention back to Inspector Michaels as Graham pulls out his mobile phone. She continues her orders, 'I want statements from every person in the apartment block and I want uniforms knocking on the doors of every home and office within 500 metres of this place. If anyone has seen something I want to know about it.' She points to the two officers of the Armed Response Unit, 'You two! Written statements and a full report to me within the hour. I'll get a photograph of the woman I believe you let slip away while you are working on that to confirm it is Ewelina Jankowska, then I want you out on the streets searching for her. You'll be out all night if needs be.' She sees the expression on the face of the younger man of the two and takes a menacing step towards him, her voice low and angry, 'If it wasn't for you rushing in to play hero, ignoring protocols and orders, we would at least have a suspect in custody. A suspect who may have now completed a double, even triple homicide.'

She realises her fists are clenched by her sides, her knuckles painfully tight and white. She forces herself to take a step backwards from the shocked young officer.

'Ma'am, is there anything I can do?' Kate asks in an attempt to defuse the situation by removing Wilks' focus from the man in front of her. Unfortunately it was the wrong thing to ask a fuming Wilks.

'Anything you can do?' bursts from Wilks with a quiet venom, 'What you can do is get the hell out of my crime scene and out of my way. Your incompetence has directly resulted in the death of one of my officers and a critical injury to a woman you described as our prime suspect.'

Kate's eyes widen as the accusation hangs in the air of the now deathly silent tent. Graham moves protectively in front of Kate, pausing his phone conversation to do so.

'Patricia,' he says quietly, 'Patricia,' even softer as he seeks to calm her down, to break the spell of the anger coursing through her veins, 'that was uncalled for but I understand why you feel so angry, so frustrated. He was my friend too.'

Surprisingly it is Kate who answers his calm voice,

'No, she's right. It was my fault we went after Helen, I sent us all on a wild goose chase after the wrong person. It is my fault that I didn't see the signs as I should.'

'If we are laying fault at people's feet then I must also be to blame,' Graham says, 'I was the one who went forward with the information you provided without giving you the chance to think things through. If anyone is to blame, it is me.'

Grahams shoulders slump with the burden of his confession.

Wilks, having been given a few seconds to regain her composure while Kate and Graham were talking puts up a hand to stop them both.

'Kate, Graham is right, not about who is at fault, but that my words were uncalled for and I apologise. As for who is to blame we should be concentrating on finding the real culprit, Miss Ewelina Jankowska, and ensuring that this time we make no mistakes in our judgement or in our actions,' she looks carefully at each person before her, 'and I include myself in that statement. Now,' she claps her hands together to bring everyone's attention firmly to her, 'shall we get to work?'

The small group breaks up but Kate stays. Graham raises his eyebrows but receives a shake of the head from Kate and he retreats to his phone calls, contacting the forensic team and issuing them orders.

Wilks pauses a second before speaking, going through options in her mind.

'Kate, what do you know about Ewelina?'

Kate blinks; once, twice, as if she is computing information in her head.

'Polish origin,' she starts, 'no real information on her background before coming to the UK, in fact no real information on her since she arrived here either.'

Kate pauses and looks hard at Wilks,

'In fact all I can offer is professional advice and assumptions on her state of mind based on similar cases.'

'What do you think she would be doing now? Where would she go and who would she turn to for help?'

'I need to know more about her but I think it is safe to say that she will go somewhere she knows, somewhere she feels safe. A friend unknown to Helen perhaps, or another family member here in London. The problem we have is that she may have lived elsewhere before moving here, another city maybe. If that is the case then she would likely try and get back to that area and lay low until getting off the mainland and travelling back to Poland. There are just too many variables to say for sure.'

Wilks has an idea forming,

'Would access to computer records help?'

'Definitely, but we would need her to have left a trail with bills, mobile phone records, that sort of thing. Access to that information requires a court order.'

'Or someone who is willing to bend the rules,' Wilks says with a far off voice as she runs through the ramifications of her idea. If what she is about to suggest comes to light and, God forbid, the press gets hold of it, then her career would be ruined for circumnavigating correct procedures.

'I can't order you to do this Kate, you are a civilian under contract to my department, but it might help us track down Ewelina. And,' she pauses as she wants to ensure she gets the wording right, 'as a civilian you would not require to wait for the lengthy process of obtaining the correct paperwork. You could be doing it as background research for your profiling.'

'But I would still require permission before sharing any information I find with the police, with you. Until I get that then it is illegal for me to give it you.'

'I understand Kate, but this woman killed JD and she has mutilated an innocent girl who somehow crossed her.'

'I know that, but I can't. I'm bound by my own rules and convictions, I...'

'Listen, if you don't do this then she will disappear within the next 24 hours and we will never find her. There will never be justice for JD's murder and it will be your fault. Your fault because of your incompetence in putting forward Helen Carter as a suspect.' Wilks waits for a reply but gets nothing back. 'Do you think that any force in the country will ever take you on after I dismiss you?'

'Are you threatening me?'

'No, I am offering you an option. Do this. Work with me and help me find some answers. It would help your own work too, but all I ask is that a copy of your research is left on your desk, or perhaps in the canteen, when you find something. It only has to be forgotten to be filed away, somebody finds it and hands it to me. You get your research, I get a chance to find my suspect and,' her voice becomes hard, 'you get to keep your job and redeem yourself in my eyes.'

Kate knows when she is beaten and Wilks sees it in her expression.

'But I don't know how to access the information you want. I mean I know what I am looking for, but how to find it is beyond me.'

Wilks has her phone out and is scrolling through the contacts. She finds the name she wants and hits CALL. As the phone rings she says,

'I think I know just the person to help you with that.'

After three rings it is answered,

'Afternoon commissioner, what can I do for you today?'

'Luke,' she replies, 'I'm sending someone down to work with you. Whatever she wants, you give it to her. Anything. Do you understand?'

'Sure boss, no problem. Uhm, can I ask what this is about so I can prep, or does it need to stay underground?'

He hears a long drawn out sigh from Wilks before she responds.

'It's about JD, Luke. He's dead.'

'Oh shit...how is DCI Carter taking it? I know they were close.'

Wilks hasn't even thought of telling Peter and feels embarrassed to answer. Instead she ignores the question,

'She's on her way down now, Luke. Work fast on this one,' she hangs up before he can say any more.

'Kate, go to the new building and make your way down to the computer labs. He will be expecting you.'

As Kate walks away, Wilks looks around the room until her eyes rest on Graham. He is just finishing his phone call and she beckons him over.

'My team will be on site with all the necessary equipment within 20 minutes, maybe a little longer according to traffic at this time of day,' he says, thinking she is after an update.

'Graham, we need to tell Peter what has happened, I know you are close and I think it would be best coming from you.'

'If that's what you feel would be correct, Patricia,' Graham answers carefully.

'Yes,' she says with more conviction, 'I have a lot to be getting on with here and it would be of a great help if you could update him about the situation.'

Graham holds up his mobile phone,

'I'll do it straight away.'

'Thank you,' Wilks says, turning quickly away so that Graham cannot see the tears forming in her eyes, 'thank you very much.'

Graham takes a deep breath, dials the number and walks away to a quiet area of the tent in order to break the sad news to his closest friend.

30

Masterson, now wearing a pair of shorts, grabs his wash-bag and a towel from where they are hanging on a hook on the back of the bathroom door, and studiously ignores looking at the scene of carnage. He closes the door behind him to block off the view from the bedroom and sits down at the long, mirrored dressing table. Opening the small black bag he pulls out a packet of antiseptic wet-wipes and a small yellow tube of super-glue which he places on the surface in front of him, next to the open bladed razor. He folds the towel in two and lays it flat upon the light coloured wood. The wash-bag is tossed next to a roll of duct-tape on the bed behind him, narrowly missing Rowlinson who is gagged and tied to a chair.

He opens the narrow drawers of the dressing table in turn until he finds the complimentary sewing kit he was searching for,. He places it next to the other articles. Pausing for a moment, his eyes darting around the items in front of him as he runs through his requirements in his mind, he nods to himself. Pushing himself up from the chair he walks out of the bedroom. Rowlinson is watching his every move silently. Even with his old friend out of the room, Rowlinson does not struggle, or try to break free. He knows his only hope now will be for a swift, merciful death.

Masterson returns with a bottle of Koskenkorva 013 Vodka, places it on the table and sits down to start his work.

He rests his left arm on the towel and surveys the damage done by Rowlinson's heavy knife. The edges of the wound are clean, the sharp blade slicing cleanly through the layers of skin and muscle, luckily not cutting a tendon or a major blood vessel on the way. He opens the vodka bottle with his right hand, the cork loosened by his thumb until it falls away. He places the same thumb over the top of the bottle and sprinkles the 60% alcohol liquid across the bloody wound. He grits his teeth against the pain of the fluid as it washes through the gash in his arm. Putting down the bottle he pulls one of the antiseptic wipes from the flat, oblong package. Carefully wiping away the watery looking blood and alcohol reveals the depth of the cut. The red piece of cloth is dropped to the floor as he reaches out for the small yellow tube. He uses his teeth to unscrew the black cap and places, into the wound, the exposed white, hollow tip which he moves along the full length of the cut, squeezing the thin metallic case to force the superglue out as he does so. The pain is sharper this time as the tacky liquid starts to attack the open and raw nerve endings of the cut. The tube is placed back on the desk, he will need that later.

Using his thumb and first two fingers of his right hand he squeezes the edges of the wound together. The glue inside is compressed and spreads itself over the full surfaces of the sliced flesh. The chemical reaction of the glue is it bonds creates heat and the burning sensation causes a hiss of breath to escape from Masterson as he holds the wound edges together. After twenty or thirty seconds he tentatively releases his grip on his flesh, watching for any signs of the wound edges pulling apart. If that happens he will have to resort to the sewing kit to crudely stitch himself together. Ten seconds pass and the burning in his arm intensifies, but the skin stays glued together. He leans back, smiling to himself in the mirror, then his eyes flick to the man in the chair behind him, and it fades from his face.

*

He takes his time working on Rowlinson, not because he doesn't believe the answers being given, but because he wants revenge. He wants to see pain on the face of this man before him. If it was the other way around and Masterson was tied to the chair then it would have been just business as the cuts slice through wielding flesh. With Masterson wielding the knife it is personal and painful. The gag stuffed in Rowlinson's mouth suppresses most of the volume but the tortured screams still pierce the air. Unfortunately for the victim, Masterson has turned up the volume on the small, yet powerful, Bluetooth speaker and the muffled screams are drowned out by the music of Iron Maiden,
'You take my life but I'll take yours too,
You use your musket but I'll run you through...'
The music continues as the screams and breathing of Rowlinson both subside. He heaves his chest, his body straining for oxygen but the amount of blood he has lost cannot carry enough of it to his vital organs. Bright red frothy foam forms at the corner of his mouth to mix with the darker blood that has dried upon what is left of his face and he falls still.
Picking up Rowlinson's phone, Masterson turns it on and takes a photograph of the mutilated and unrecognisable figure strapped to the chair. Even though Rowlinson had told him everything, his thoughts of vengeance and the knowledge of the damage that would have been inflicted on his own body spurred him on to inflict these acts of depravity before him. He surveys his

handiwork and feels nothing; no remorse, no satisfaction, no pain, nothing. Just a sense of numbness.

He picks the name from the contact list that was given to him during the interrogation and composes a short message.

Task completed. Is this the sort of message you wanted to convey to others?

He adds the bloody photo and sends it on to the recipient.

Not wanting to re-enter the bathroom where Angela's body lays, he washes the blood and sweat from his body at the kitchen sink. As the dark red fluid is sluiced away, Rowlinson's phone signals an incoming message. Drying off his damp hands, arms and body to leave pink stains on the white towel, he picks up the phone to read the reply.

Confirm with picture ID before returning to this location for debrief. Good job.

Picking up his own passport, Masterson opens it to the back page to display his photo and address details. Creasing the pages back so they stay open he places it in the gore on the dead man's chest and takes another picture with the phone. This he duly sends off, adding,

ID confirmation as Masterson, S. No longer active.

The cool air from the air-conditioning unit that is humming quietly away on the wall causes goose-bumps to raise on his exposed flesh. He rubs his arms to wipe the small nodules away and looks around for the remote control to the unit. Finding it next to the bed he lowers the temperature even further and sets it to the minimum temperature setting of 15 degrees centigrade. He hopes this coolness will give him at least 24 hours before the smell from the bodies will become apparent to tourists as they walk the grounds past the small villa. As an extra measure he ensures the 'Do Not Disturb' notice on the handle of the front door is still firmly affixed. Walking back inside he grabs his small, black day-sack from the open wardrobe near the front door and pulls out his mobile phone. He taps his finger on the screen in thought as he composes the words for the conversation he is about to have in his head. Satisfied, he dials Carter's number with a view to warn him about the attempt on his life that is likely to happen soon. Masterson hopes his call will be in time to stop the likeable policeman from getting a bullet in the head.

As the phone runs through the connection sequence, Masterson walks around the room and gathers a few things together which he places into the day-sack. Masterson takes one last glance around the room. He knows it won't stand up to a scrutinised forensic examination, he has left too much evidence and DNA around the room for that, but at least it will buy him some time. Leaving his passport with Rowlinson's body he leaves. He has ways and means of travelling through borders that will not require the documents required by legal travellers, and besides, he wants to disappear for a while as he plots the revenge he has burning inside him. He pauses as the call is connected and he hears the ringing in the earpiece. It is answered simply,

'This is Carter.'

'Carter…Peter. It's Masterson. I've got some bad news and you need to hear me out.'

There is a sigh heard down the line that is not diminished even by the thousands of miles journey through cables, fibre-optics and satellite signals.

'Great, I could do with more bad news right now.'

The voice is strained and Masterson can almost feel the pressure that Carter must be under.

'Peter, I have reason to believe there is going to be an attempt on your life. Can you get to a secure area and…'

The shouts and screams from the other end of the phone stops Masterson mid-sentence.

31

Paul's driving does not get any better as we enter the crowded streets of Chania, but at least I can see that he is attempting to avoid the other cars, mopeds and pedestrians, unlike the rest of the motorists it seems.

'Jesus, it's like the bloody bumper cars at the fair,' I say as I breathe in to try and make the car smaller and fit between the gap of a moped and parked car.

'You should see it in August when the tourists are in full flow,' Paul beeps his horn at a freezer truck that is attempting to pull out into the flow of traffic. The fact that the van is running a red light is lost on the driver who waves his arm out of the window.

Paul expertly swerves the small car around the front bumper, causing horns to blare behind us and continues on without even acknowledging the cacophony he has caused,

'Today is pretty quiet really,' he adds.

I look at him and see the smallest of smiles spreading on his face before he bursts out laughing.

'To be honest mate the traffic here is horrendous. I try and avoid coming into town unless I can avoid it.' He slams on his brakes as a woman dressed in a black dress steps out from between two parked cars and proceeds to cross the road as if it were empty instead of teeming with all manner of speeding vehicles. The horns increase in volume behind us as w, and the car next to us waits for the elderly lady to cross. She stops and gives us a toothless grin and a nod of her head as she climbs back up on the pavement.

I let out a sigh of relief.

'This makes London at rush hour look like a walk in the park. At least back home we have lanes and people obey traffic lights.'

We turn off the main route and enter a narrow road with cars parked on either side making it narrower still. Just when I think we are going to just stop in the middle of the road or drive into the sea, Paul turns into a narrow gap and I am surprised to see we are in the middle of an almost empty pay-and-display car park.

'You're kidding me, ' I say, 'this place is empty and the streets are packed.'

'Out of season they don't seem to give out too many parking tickets so the locals take their chances on getting a fine. Half the time they won't pay it anyway, or more correctly, can't pay it. If you can't afford three Euros to park up how are you expected to find 60 if you are fined? So it means that this time of year we always find plenty of places to park.'

He pulls into one of the empty parking slots and jumps out of the car to get the ticket. As he strolls back he shields his eyes against the glare of the bright December sun as I extract myself from the cramped confines and place my coat on the back seat.

'Are you using that jacket?' he asks me as I pull myself out of the car.

'In this heat? I don't think so.'

He shivers slightly as he places the ticket in the front window, leans over the passenger seat to grab my coat and pulls it on. He stretches his arms out, moving his body around as he does so,

'A little short in the arms and a little big around the waist, but it'll do. I'm freezing.'

'You try wearing a fitted jacket over a Kevlar vest and see how long that lasts you.' I defend my slightly larger size with a plain-clothes detective's standard response.

'The last time I wore body armour you couldn't put a jacket over it,' he replies with a grin, 'come on. Let's get you set up where you can see everything.'

We avoid the harbour front and take the narrow back streets between three and four-story tall houses that leave the quaint lanes and alleyways in shadow. I begin to feel a little of the chill now we are out of the sun and wish I had not given up my coat, no matter how thin the material is. We come out into a wide square that has a fountain energetically flowing with water. I notice a Starbucks Coffee-House looking out of place opposite and Paul follows my gaze.

'Progress,' he says shaking his head.

Even so, there are not many empty tables inside the coffee chain's store.

We skirt the harbour with its impressive looking lighthouse tower on the opposite side and I follow Paul up a dark flight of steep steps. The café at the top is a surprise of modern furniture and glass fronted balcony. He walks with purpose to the wall of glass and chooses a table that is set on the left near the wall and looks around.

'You are in shade here with the sun behind you. Anyone looking up will be dazzled by the glare and you can't be seen from anywhere along the harbour.' He points off to his right, past a pink domed building that stands alone on the harbour, to a row of small restaurants, 'I'll be meeting Ann at the Monastiri, it's the one with the blinds up and the flames coming out of those glass heaters, do you se it?'

I follow his outstretched hand and see the establishment he is pointing at. I nod my head.

'Good. There's a white bench in front the mosque,' his hand moves slightly to point at the domed building, 'where I'll be waiting for your call when you see her.' He drops his hand and ushers me down into a seat at the table he is standing next to.

'I've just thought, do you have a picture of her on your phone so I can identify her.'

I shake my head, saying 'No.'

He doesn't believe me, 'Pete, I'm not judging you here. This is to help you out. Now do you have a picture?'

I reluctantly pull out my phone and go to the picture gallery. I find a picture of Ann, one that is the least revealing and hold it out to him. Paul lets out a low whistle as he looks at the image of Ann on all fours facing the camera. She is naked. He goes to take the camera from my hand and I snatch it back,

'No way. You see this one only.'

He takes a moment to study the picture and when he has memorised her face he shakes his head,

'I think it would be best if you deleted all of those, don't you?'

I feel foolish, like a child caught with his hand in the biscuit barrel as I realise he is right.

'I don't know why I've kept them,' I say.

'You're a bloke. It's what we do. Now get rid of them and give me a call if you see her before I do.'

He turns and walks away as a waitress in black trousers, white blouse and a red waist bib comes over to take my order. She glimpses the photograph on my phone and smiles slightly, an eyebrow raised.

'What can I get you?' she asks, and I am not sure of who is the more embarrassed, her or me.

'A coffee please,' I mumble, 'white, no sugar, thanks.'

'No problem.'

She turns away, no doubt to go and tell the other staff about the pervert who is sitting outside flashing naked pictures around on his phone. I stroke my forehead and hide my face as I start deleting the pictures from my phone. It takes me longer than I expected and just as I finish removing all the files my coffee is placed down in front of me along with a glass of water, a small plate of biscuits and a receipt rolled up in a shot glass. The waitress turns and walks away without saying a word. She doesn't need to, the smile says it all. I let out a groan and look out over the harbour, looking for Ann Clarke. I see Paul sitting on the bench as he is looking up towards where I am seated but I can see my exact position is hidden from his view. I take a sip of my coffee and scan the people milling about and even in December the promenade is busy with tourists. It is easy to see why.

The harbour is built out of old, yellowed stone that is easily three or four hundred years old. The lighthouse at the entrance to the open sea dominates the area and catches your eye wherever you look. The row of restaurants where Monastiri sits is ideally located to get the best of the views of the lighthouse, the imposing fortified building behind it and beyond, across the bay to the island that looks like a large turtle emerging from the sea.

I easily spot Ann as she walks around the corner heading directly towards me. I sit back in my seat trying to hide myself even more amongst the shadows, and watch as she pauses to look around. Her eyes rest briefly on Paul and I see her hand come up, almost in a wave, before she realises it is not me. She looks embarrassed and takes a deep breath before entering the restaurant. I am about to call Paul when I see him stand, give me the thumbs up and make his way towards Ann. With my hand paused on the CALL button I jump when the phone rings and even more surprised when I see that Graham is calling me. Knowing that I can do no more to help Paul, yet keeping one eye on the unfolding situation, I answer Graham's call,

'Hello Graham, this is an unexpected pleasure.'

'I'm afraid that's not so Peter. This is not an easy phone call to make.'

I can tell from the tone of his voice, not just his words, that I am not going to like what comes next and I think of what may have happened with Helen.

'Has she been arrested again?' I ask quickly, watching as Paul enters the restaurant, 'Has there been new evidence found?'

'No, no. Nothing like that, although Helen has been involved in an incident. There was a shooting...'

'What?' I exclaim, not giving him a chance to continue.

Graham's voice remains calm as he carries on,

'Helen's OK, she was not shot although she does have some serious injuries the doctors are saying she will be OK.'

'What the hell happened? Is it related to the Zoe Walker case?' Although I am watching Paul introduce himself to Ann, my mind is back in detective mode.

'It's believed so. Look I can't say anything more about the case over the phone and I am sure Commissioner Wilks will want to talk to you in detail about it,' he pauses and his next few words are chosen carefully, 'I have to let you know that JD was involved in the incident and received a gunshot wound to the chest.'

'How's he doing?' my thoughts are reeling with the details of the case and how this new incident will affect it. I hear the next words but they don't make any sense to me, I have to ask Graham to repeat them.

'I'm afraid he didn't make it Peter. He died on the way to the hospital from what looks like massive blood loss. I am doing the autopsy to determine the cause of death tomorrow.'

Everything slows down around me and I feel faint. JD is dead, I can't believe it, I won't believe it.

'Peter...Peter,' Graham's voice on the phone slowly drags me back into reality.

'But Helen,' I try and focus on something else, 'Helen is going to be alright?'

'Yes she is. Listen, Wilks will contact you within the hour with full details. She asked me to let you know the situation so you could decide upon your course of action. She thought you may want to return home.'

'Yes, that's exactly what I need to do. I'll start arranging things and I'll wait for her call.' I look out over the calm water, the sunlight glinting of the small ripples that bob and dip in the currents. 'Graham, thank you for letting me know.'

I hear 'You're welc…' and I hang up, cutting him off.

I don't know how long I am sitting there just staring at the sea but it can't have been more than a minute or so, when my phone starts ringing again. I shake my head to clear it and look back towards Paul. He is standing up with his phone to his ear and I realise it must be him trying to contact me. Without looking at the display I answer the phone automatically,

'This is Carter.'

At first I don't recognise the voice.

'Carter?' His tone softens, 'Peter, it's Masterson. I've got some bad news and you need to hear me out.'

I let out a deep sigh as I stand up. The waitress, seeing my reaction walks towards me anticipating me paying the bill, 'Great, I could do with more bad news right now,' I say.

I am staring at Paul as Masterson continues, trying to work out how I am going to explain the situation about Helen and also how I will justify my leaving Crete to Julia.

'Peter, I have reason to believe there is going to be an attempt on your life. Can you get to a secure area and…'

I hear nothing more as my whole world is shattered.

32

Tim Burke holds up his camera and scans the harbour front. Unlike most tourists he swiftly moves past the picturesque domed mosque and he doesn't even glance at the mountains in the distance with their covering of snow that stands out starkly against the blue sky. Instead he moves with a determined speed as he searches for something, someone, in particular. As he looks at the small screen he watches as his target walk into view and into a small taverna. He moves fast.

The walking pole resting against his holdall is picked up and he clamps the camera to a special attachment that sits just below the pole's handle. He removes a large metallic water bottle from the bag and clips it onto the pole with a small, high pitched hiss. Pulling back on the T-shaped, rubberised handle, Tim extends the length by another few inches and with an audible 'click' a small curved spur pops out from a hidden slot. Reaching into his trouser pocket he pulls out two AA batteries. Pushing the curved metal spur forward reveals a gap in the side of the pole big enough to fit your little finger into. Tim deftly screws off the top of on of the batteries to reveal a pointed slug within. He drops the two halves of the fake battery into the open bag and places the slug into the hole. With his forefinger he pulls the spur backward to seal the slug within the chamber. When he is satisfied that everything is as it should be he presses the record button on the camera and the sophisticated device automatically places a call. It is linked to a tiny Bluetooth earpiece in Tim's ear and it buzzes once before his call is connected. He doesn't wait to hear a voice and starts talking in a low voice.

'Requesting authorisation. Target is on screen and you should be receiving a picture any second.'

'Stand by, stand by,' is the reply.

Pressing the record button on the camera also links the small GPS chip in the device to the military grade communications satellite in a geo-synchronous orbit that covers the eastern Mediterranean and parts of the Middle East. The signal includes a live stream from the camera and apart from a few seconds delay the man in his office in London will be able to see exactly what Tim sees.

Jim Groark, sitting at his desk receives a phone call. He picks up the receiver and after a second he reaches out and presses a button on his keyboard that is sitting beneath the twenty-two

inch Samsung monitor on his desk. He watches the images for a few moments and recognises the man on screen as Carter. Even with his back to the camera he can clearly identify the police detective from surveillance photographs taken over the last few days. He watches as Carter takes a phone from his pocket and place it to his ear. As he watches, Carter shakes his head and he can see the jaw moving as he talks. Groark wonders who he is talking to and whether his last words will be memorable. Groark says just one word into his own telephone,
'Authorised.'

Back in Crete and waiting for a response, Tim has placed the T-shaped handle of his simple yet technologically advanced weapon into his shoulder. His left hand is placed under the metallic water bottle, which is in fact a compressed air storage tank, and his right hand moves forward and removes the rubber cap from the bottom of the walking pole to reveal a rifled barrel. Looking back at the screen he sees a red arrow pointing just left of the head and shoulders of the man in focus and Tim adjusts the barrel slightly until the arrow is resting on the man's neckline.

The camera is an advanced optical system that compensates for wind-speed and atmospheric conditions and instantly provides feedback to the shooter.

'It's a great tool,' he thinks to himself, 'but it doesn't half take the fun out of it.' He makes a shucking sound from one side of his mouth, 'Any monkey can take a shot with this bit of kit,' he mutters.

The word, 'Authorised' is relayed to him through the Bluetooth headset and he rests his finger lightly on the trigger.

'Affirmative, stand by, stand by,' he says and changes his focus to the skill of taking a long range shot.

Even with the advanced technology at his disposal he reverts back to the basic marksmanship principles which have held him in good stead over his career. His mind talks him through the stages;

Relax, steady your breathing, gently take up the tension on the trigger,   breathe   in...and   out,   breathe in...stop...squeeze...CRACK...follow through...watch target.

The rifle does not produce a small explosion as a conventional weapon would do. The projectile, which in this case is a 0.45 inch calibre slug, is forced from the barrel using only air pressure forced from the cylinder. There is enough compressed air in the fake water bottle for two full power shots, which is one more than is normally necessary for Tim. The crack that is produced is made by the slug as it passes through the sound barrier on leaving the barrel. The pneumatic action of the rifle also produces no significant recoil and that means a lighter and smaller weapon can be produced for covert activities such as this.

The 350 grain slug leaves the barrel at 1650 feet per second and produces more stopping power than Clint Eastwood's famous Dirty Harry character's .357 Magnum, with over 2,000 foot pound (ft/lb) of energy.

On their respective screens, Tim and Groark both watch as the slug smashes into the nape of the man's neck. He drops instantly amid a haze of red mist.

'Shit,' Tim says as he sees a woman who was blocked from view appear in the screen as the body drops. Groark just watches impassively as she brings a hand up to her chest to try and cover the blood splattered white blouse she is wearing. The woman wavers slightly as she takes her hand away in confusion and looks at the gore slowly dripping from it. The blossoming spread of red across her shirt shows that the heavy slug was hardly stopped by the main target and has continued its journey into her body. She coughs once, a dark red explosion of blood and then she too collapses to the floor and lies still. Groark smiles,

'Task completed, exit and follow extraction plans. See you tomorrow,' he waits for his commands to be relayed before hanging up.

Tim rips the camera off the walking pole and places it back around his neck on the wide black webbing strap. He twists the air tank off and places it in the holdall. Pressing a small button he compresses the pole back to its normal length and replaces the rubberised foot on to the end of the barrel. He checks quickly around the area he has been standing in and seeing no evidence, walks away from the ancient battlements and towards the entrance of the maritime museum. At the main foyer he smiles good-naturedly in to the guard who is tied up in his chair. He makes sure the frightened man gets a good look at his face as he walks towards him and deposits two fifty euro notes on the desk, 'Thanks for that,' he says in a rich Texan accent, 'a very interesting day. Sorry about shutting the place up but I really don't like to be disturbed when I work.' He points to the money, 'That's for your trouble, son.'

He opens the tall, heavy doors, turning the small sign from KLEISTO/CLOSED to ANIKTO/OPEN as he walks away. Glancing around and seeing no-one watching he darts up a small side street and is quickly out of view. He rips a Velcro panel from the base of the holdall to reveal two webbing straps that turn the bag into a medium sized backpack. Unzipping a compartment at the base, he pulls over a waterproof cover that changes the colour from black to light blue. Reaching up to his face he removes the light brown wig, goatee beard and moustache which get stuffed into the bag and he pulls out a baseball cap and a pair of gun-metal gray spectacles which he puts on. To finish of his disguise he turns his black lightweight jacket inside out to reveal a trekking style shirt. To complete the effect he rolls up the sleeves and unzips and removes the legs of his trousers over his sandalled feet. Transformed now into a geeky looking tourist, Tim strolls out of the alleyway and into a narrow shopping street. He takes pictures of the buildings and wares on display, just like any other visitor to this beautiful city. As he walks away from the harbour and the growing noise of sirens and shouting, he smiles lightly at the thought of another job well done and another nice little bonus. Smiling apologetically at a shop owner who is trying to entice him in, Tim walks over to the waiting car and bends down to peer in the passenger side window.

'Any chance of a lift, love?' he asks the blonde, female driver, his accent now has a light Suffolk twang to it.

She looks at him and laughs,

'Get in you moron, we have to get back to the ship before it leaves.'

Tim throws his bag on the back seat and clambers in. He leans over and kisses the driver on the cheek,

'Come on then Jude, I could murder a cuppa.'

Jude reaches over and pops the glove-box open to reveal a small flask.

'There's tea in there,' she shakes her head as she drives away; 'sometimes you are so predictable.'

As Tim takes a sip of the hot, sweet tea he lets out a long satisfied sigh,

'This is why I married you, great in the kitchen and you know just what I want.'

The drive back to the Royal Navy frigate that is berthed at Souda Bay is completed with the chatter of a typical husband and wife on holiday. The perfect cover for a paid for pair of assassins.

33

Kate has to wait in the lobby of the new offices of the headquarters of the Metropolitan Police as she is not yet registered on the security system of the building. Even with her New Scotland Yard pass and her identification that shows her working for the Met, the security officers will only allow her access with an escort. She understands their concerns but is a little exasperated with their diligence and wonders how many other colleagues have had the same problem.

She is carefully reading the signs on the walls in an attempt to stave off her boredom, but there are only so many times you can read the same anti-terrorist procedures without letting your mind wander.

As her thoughts drift to Graham and where their relationship is heading, a young man, a boy almost, she thinks, opens one of the doors opposite and walks towards her with a smile on his face.

'Miss Jeffery, Kate Jeffery?' he asks.

Kate stands up and nods her head,

'Yes that's me. Are you here to sort my security pass?'

He smiles, 'No, sorry that's in the hands of the private firm they brought in,' he furtively glances over his shoulder at the uniformed men and women at the front desks, 'and if you ask me they're doing a crap job.' He holds out his hand, 'I'm Luke Carter, Commissioner Wilks said I was to help you in any way I can.'

Kate takes the proffered handshake and tries not to look surprised, but Luke has seen her reaction.

'I guess I'm a bit younger than you expected.'

'They say that once the policemen start to look young then you're getting old.'

Luke laughs and releases her hand,

'Oh I'm not a bobby on the beat. I'm an advisor for the Met, pretty much like you,' Kate finds herself warming to this young man before her as he continues, 'though maybe not in your pay-grade but still, we all have to start somewhere, right?'

She thinks of her own monthly pay-packet and answers,

'I wouldn't be so sure of the pay-grade issue, I'm still only a lowly D band.'

'In that case,' Luke says with a twinkle in his eye, 'I'm buying the coffees today.'

He walks back to the door, beckoning her to follow him.

'I've been given a little information on what you need, but we can talk about it in the dungeon more securely.'

'The dungeon?' she asks.

'The IT security team are based in the deep dark recesses of the buildings lower levels. No light, locked doors and...' he makes sure that the non-police security officers can hear him, 'prison guards that need a personality transplant.'

His words get him a glare from what looks like a solid mass of muscle that has been forced into the black uniform of the private security firm. The face is deep-set and looks as if it used to a violent and bloody end to conversations.

'See what I mean, no sense of humour.'

Kate takes a deep breath and follows Luke through the corridors and stairwells until they come to his department.

'Welcome to my world,' he says, swiping his ID card through the slot in the wall and unlocking the darkened glass doors. They swish open dramatically and Luke does a good impression of the noise from Star Trek as the doors open on the Enterprise. He notices the look on Kate's face and raises his eyebrows,

'Sorry about that, force of habit.'

They enter a brightly lit hallway with glass panels on either side. The corridor bends slightly and Kate realises the offices within must be encircled by the glass corridor. Entering another sliding security door, this time without the sound effects, they are confronted by a group of security guards who all seem to share the same bored demeanour.

'Morning guys, permission to come aboard?' Luke asks cheerily as he hands over his ID card and motions for Kate to do the same.

'Place all electrical items in the box provided and step through the security screen,' is the response.

Luke places a mobile phone in the box and Kate follows suit. Luke gestures for Kate to go first,

'Please, after you.'

'So this is like, what, airport security?'

'Sort of, no recording or electronic devices are allowed through to the dungeon. Even some watches have to be left out here in case of misuse.'

'Oh.'

'Do you have any memory sticks, flash drives or recording devices about your person?' a female security guard asks before she can step through. Kate blushes and her hand pats her trouser pocket absent-mindedly. She reaches in and pulls out a black and red coloured USB flash drive.

'Sorry,' she mumbles as she receives a stern look, 'I always carry this around in case I need to transfer any data or files.' She places the small device into the plastic tray alongside her phone.

'Don't worry about it,' Luke says, 'everyone has one nowadays. It's just not every day you have the memory stick police come down on you like a ton of bricks.'

The female guard nods at the both of them and gestures for them to walk through the gate, one at a time. To Kate's relief there are no alarm sounds or lights flashing and she waits at the other side as Luke follows her through. She stands and waits, just as if she is at an airport departure gate, for her phone and USB stick to be returned. She is met by blank stares from the security personnel and Kate looks at Luke with questioning expression on her face. His face reflects her own look of puzzlement until he understands the situation,

'Ah, your phone. I should have explained better, everything has to stay out here until you leave. Nothing is allowed in or out without written authority.'

Kate's blushes deepen as she recalls Luke's words from a just a few moments ago. The security systems have thrown her a little off balance.

'Of course,' she says, 'no problem.'

Her embarrassment quickly turns to anger as she sees a smirk appear on the female guards face. She is just about to say something when she remembers that she is here to do a job, not get into a fight. She ignores the woman and follows Luke through what she hopes is the final door and into a dimly lit room where much of the light appears to be cast from the rows of computer monitors that fill the room.

Luke's demeanour changes, becoming more businesslike as he walks along the rear most row of monitors. Kate sees that virtually every one of the brightly lit screens has at least one person sitting behind it intently peering at rows of code, images or video. There is a noticeable lack of verbal communication throughout the room which Kate finds a little disturbing.

'This is not like any police department I have been in before,' she says in a whisper, as if to speak out loud would break the spell that the men and women in the room appear to be under.

'This is no ordinary department,' Luke replies in the same tone.

He stops and peers over the shoulder of a young man who looks barely old enough to be out of school and is scratching at his forehead thoughtfully. Scanning the screen and the lines of what looks like a foreign language to Kate, he leans in and places a finger near to the monitor,

'Ben, try changing this integer to 10. That may speed up the process a little.'

The forehead scratching stops and the young man releases a long sigh,

'Shit, how did I miss that?'

Luke rests a reassuring hand on his shoulder,

'You're too close mate. Take a break and open your mind to other things for ten minutes. Go on, go and grab a cuppa,' Luke pauses and glances at Kate with a twinkle in his eye, 'actually, while you're there how do you fancy grabbing a brew for me and Miss Jeffery here? How do you take your coffee, Kate?'

'White with one sugar, please.'

'Excellent, you got that, Ben? A Julie Andrews Sound of Music and a Julie Andrews Chitty Chitty Bang Bang.'

Ben shakes his head,

'I get the white nun for you, but what the hell is the Chitty Chitty Bang Bang?'

Luke winks at Kate,

'A spoonful full of sugar, mate. Can you bring them into the pod? We'll be in there for a while.'

Ben is still shaking his head as Luke and Kate walk away. He mumbles under his breath as he rises from his console,

'Why can't he just ask for coffee like everybody else? I'm getting fed up of his Julie Andrews this and Whoopie Goldberg that. He might as well ask for an elephant and whistle, I'd have no idea what that was either.'

Kate is a few steps behind Luke and hears Ben's mutterings. It brings a smile to her face as she realises the dynamic of the men and women around her. Luke leads her to the edge of the room and yet one more door. He steps forward and punches a set of numbers on a keypad before stooping slightly so his eyes are level with a small screen. The Eye Recognition Identification System (EyeRIS) correlates the code with Luke's iris scan and the small red LED on the door handle turns to green. Luke presses down on the lever and pushes open the door. The bright light from within spills out and Kate has to narrow her eyes at the sudden glare.

'Welcome to the pod, the inner sanctum within the inner sanctum, and a place, if they knew about, the bad guys would dread.'

Kate crosses the threshold and feels as if she has just fallen down the rabbit hole so different is the transformation. The door sucks shut behind her with a small hiss of compressed air and the journey is complete.

'Now the work begins,' Luke says, 'welcome to my kingdom.'

34

After talking to Carter with the sad news of JD's death, Graham does the only thing he knows will make him feel better. He goes back to work.

Filling out paperwork is a routine that allows his mind to switch off and forget the unfolding events that are surrounding him. The time passes quickly and a few hours pass as he types up reports and follows up enquiries that make up the Chief Medical Officer's normal day to day routine. The knock on his door breaks him from the respite of the mundane work.

'DCI Dawkins body is here, Graham.'

Graham looks up and nods silently towards Chris Harris.

'I'll be there in a moment, Chris,' he says, 'Can you prep the area for me please.'

There is a look of deep compassion on Chris's face,

'Sure thing boss.'

Graham waits for his colleague to leave before standing up. He eases the stiffness from his body and as he leaves the room he grabs his lab coat from the coat rack by the door. It is only a short walk across the corridor to his gruesome place of business.

The stark white light makes the room appear colder than the 15 degrees centigrade readout that is showing on the climate control display panel. The light is bright enough to highlight the polished scratches on the metal tables and the subtle discolourations on the tiled surfaces of the walls and floor. Just one of the tables in the room is occupied, and while the person on it has been in this room many times before, this is the first and only time he will be the subject of interest.

'I can do this if you want,' says Chris, with consideration, 'I mean, I know how difficult it might be for you.'

Graham shakes his head towards his assistant as he pulls on a pair of thin rubber gloves and stretches them over the white sleeves of his medical gown.

'Thanks Chris but I owe it to JD to do this myself,' he pauses slightly before quickly looking across and adding, 'That's no reflection on your abilities. I just feel the need to do this for him. My final act as a friend, I hope you understand.'

Graham looks back down to the pale, cold face that so far is the only uncovered piece of JD before him. He won't stay covered, protected even, for long. Graham knows that over the course of the next few hours, JD will be laid bare to reveal all of his secrets as only a post-mortem can do to a person. He minutely adjusts the wireless microphone that is attached to the lapel on the gown and presses the record button at the head of the table with a rubber clad finger. As he starts talking, his mind detaches and the professional within takes over. The minutes drift by seamlessly as he cuts and dissects the flesh and organs of what he now regards as the puzzle before him on the table. A puzzle that must be solved in order to reveal the cause and reasons of why and how a person in the prime of their life has been reduced to a piece of dead meat lying open on a stainless steel autopsy table. As cuts are made, bodily fluids slowly ooze into drainage channels cut into the metal surface like warm jam. The fluids are collected for possible analysis and later disposal in polished receptacles hidden beneath the table.

Graham pauses and checks the wall clock for the time and sees that almost four hours have passed. He takes a step back from the table, removes his stained gloves and presses the stop button on the digital audio recorder. He picks up the small silver device and thrusts it through the gap in the gown into his trouser pocket.

'Chris, I'm not expecting too much from the bloods and I'd like to get this preliminary report to Commissioner Wilks as soon as I can. Would you,' he pauses as he looks down at his old friend's body as if seeing it for the first time. Chris steps between his boss and JD's body and nods his head.

'No problem. If you type up the report I'll look after JD.'

A tear rolls slowly down Graham's cheek as he reaches out his un-gloved hand and lightly touches an untouched area of JD's forehead.

'Goodbye old friend.'

As he turns away and walks across the cold, sterile room he unplugs the lapel microphone, strips off the medical gown and along with the gloves and plastic over boots, places them in a hazardous waste bag. The microphone goes into a small plastic box for cleaning and later reuse. It is only a short walk across the corridor to his office but it is just enough time to allow Graham to compose himself and wipe away the tears that had threatened to flow freely. Sitting down at his desk he reaches out a slightly trembling hand and clicks a mouse button to remove the screensaver from the monitor. Another click and the icon his mouse was hovering over opens up a preliminary autopsy report form. This is used to quickly disseminate the important information before the full report has been completed and is for police use only. Graham starts to type;

Subject is a white male submitted for post mortem medical examination with wound to right hand side of upper torso. Wound found to be a single penetrating gunshot trauma with no obvious exit route. Site of wound has been exposed by medical staff during attempted treatment and resuscitation of the subject.

Examination of the subject also found contusion and tearing of the upper lip that corresponds to blunt force trauma to the lower jaw which has also damaged two teeth. Subject's teeth found to be the cause of the damage to the internal lip surface.

External signs of struggle are indicated by bruising to right hand side of neck consistent with electrical stimuli, possibly by some kind of charged weapon, e.g. Tazer.
Gum residue and contusions found around subjects wrists are indicative of restraints being used whilst subject still mobile.
Incision to right earlobe and blunt force contusions also found around this area.
No other discernable marks or abnormal features found.

Exploration of gunshot area and subject's clothing found no traces of powder residue; therefore it is probable that the shooting took place at a distance greater than one metre.
No perforation, i.e. no exit point found from the projectile and internal examination commenced.

Entry point is consistent with small calibre and discovery of fragments within body cavity suggest non jacketed 9mm parabellum round as used in handguns and machine pistols. Tissue damage due to cavitation effect found along route of entry through subject.
Fragmentation of the round was caused by the tumbling track of projectile through soft tissue which then struck upper edge of right rib cage.
Multiple tracks discovered through tissue and organs from fragments of 9mm round and bone injury with exploration channels made by emergency medical staff in attempts to stem blood loss.

Internal blood loss discovered pooled in body cavity. Major trauma to lingula (middle lobe of left lung) and heart caused by bone and metal fragments discovered to be the main cause for blood loss in subject.

It is my medical opinion that the injuries sustained to these organs were the main contributing factors to the death of subject. It is improbable that even on the spot surgery by a full medical team would have allowed any chance of survival due to the extent of rupturing and blood loss sustained by the subject.

Awaiting results from labs for bloods and toxicology reports, but preliminary testing shows no abnormalities in this area.

Full report to follow.

G. Young – Chief Medical Examiner

Graham reads through his report twice before sending a copy through the secure e-mail system to Wilks. As good measure he also prints off two copies, one he keeps for his own records, the other he places in a cheap brown envelope and after scrawling Wilks name on the front he places it in his out tray. It will be collected later and sent up to the commissioner.

Graham is staring into space when a small knock comes from the open doorway.

'It's all done, just thought you would like to know.' Chris's voice is quiet from the doorway. Graham turns to face him and beckons his colleague in. At the same time he reaches into his desk drawer and retrieves a bottle from within along with two white cups with no handles. As Chris sits down, Graham pulls the cork with a smooth pop from the top of the bottle and pours out two generous measures of the Laphroaig whisky.

They both raise their cups and clink them chunkily together,

'To JD.'

35

It's the blood I notice first, spreading, blossoming out in a widening pool. Paul's mouth is moving soundlessly as he gasps short convulsive breaths, and as his eyes lock on to mine I know he's not going to make it.

Replaying the events of the last few moments in my mind I still cannot comprehend the enormity of the situation. My phone is still grasped in my hand and the tinny voice is questioning, shouting to find out what is happening.

'Peter? Are you OK? What's going on?'

I kneel down, my own breath coming in short bursts from the exertion of the run from the café and also due to shock. I feel warm liquid leaking into my trousers at the knee and feel the sticky heat cooling against my skin. I grasp Paul's hand and his eyes desperately seek out mine. For an instant we are as one and I feel as if I am looking into my own soul, and then he is gone. All I am left with is the vision of his lifeless eyes as they turn glassy. Feeling like a robot I place the phone next to my ear,

'You're too late. The hit has taken place but they got the wrong man. They've killed my brother.'

I look up as one of the waiters appears cautiously in the doorway with his own mobile phone secured to his ear in much the same way as mine.

'The police and an ambulance are coming, is he...?'

I slowly nod my head and his mouth drops open in a silent O.

'What about the lady?' he asks, not moving from the doorway and ready to duck back inside to safety if more shots start flying through the air.

My confused mind takes a moment to consider his words. A woman? Shit,

'Ann!' I cry as I lay Paul's hand back across his chest and stand up in an awkward, uncoordinated movement. Congealing blood drips from my trouser legs with gentle splashes.

'Ann,' I cry again, moving towards the overturned table which hides her body from view. The first thing I notice is how her white blouse is now a sodden red rag and a hole the size of my fist is oozing blood from its ragged cavity. I can tell by the way the blood is hardly flowing that she has gone already and to my sense of guilt and revulsion at the sight before me, I feel a wave of relief wash over me.

'What's going on? What's happened? Talk to me Peter.' Masterson's voice on the telephone drags me back into the real world with all the grace of a man being pulled out of sucking quicksand.

'They're dead, both dead,' I manage to say, 'they've been shot.'

'Take a breath Peter, look around you. Is the shooter still there?'

I turn away from Ann's body, thankful of the command that rip my eyes from the bloody scene. A gathering crowd of curious onlookers and gore seekers has formed at the front of the restaurant blocking my view of the harbour. Some people are already taking photos and videos with their mobile phones to record the scene for their own grisly posterity or for posting to social media. 'Look what we saw on holiday,' I can almost hear them saying, 'Much better than some stuffy old museum pieces.'

'Show some fucking respect,' I can't help myself as I shout out to these grisly bystanders, 'this is a crime scene and people have died here.'

The camera's pan towards me as if in unison and I recall a snippet of information from my media training – don't make yourself the target of their attention. On this occasion the meaning has more than one connotation as I attempt to look beyond the gawkers and search for a glimpse of the shooter.

Masterson's voice crackles out from my mobile again,

'Peter, you have to get out of there now. I'm sorry about what's happened but you will have to mourn later. It was meant to be you on the floor and you could still be a target if you stay in the area.'

I understand he is making sense but I am in a foreign country and have no idea where is safe. As if he can read my mind, Masterson continues,

'Get to a cheap hotel, pay cash and use an alias. Find somewhere off the main routes and if they ask for ID or a passport tell them your wallet was stolen and you are waiting for a replacement. Once you find somewhere, contact me and I should be able to get to you within 24 hours.'

'Shouldn't I wait for the police and…' I try to reply but he cuts me off.

'No police. As soon as your name gets in the system they will find you. You know if they find you…' his voice trails off as the unspoken words sink in and I have no trouble in filling in the blank spaces.

'Go Peter. Just do as I say and I will come and get you.'

Paranoia kicks in about taking orders from this man I hardly know over the phone, but it doesn't stop me pushing my way through the crowd which parts almost comically before I get to touch anyone. I mentally put the thought to one side that in order to get through a human barricade you just need to be covered in blood and looking desperate. With those colours on your shirt no one will stop you.

'How did you know?' I ask Masterson as I half walk, half stumble away.

'Because they came for me too. It's my fault this has happened, I thought I was protecting you but I have only made matters worse and now three people have died.'

'Three?'

'They killed Angie when they came for me.'

I recall the stunning blonde woman from an interview I had during a recent murder investigation and I can't imagine her dead as Masterson says. Then my mind flashes up images of Paul and Ann just a few metres behind me and I realise that anything is possible. The sound of a siren, police or ambulance I don't know, echoes off the tightly packed buildings around me. With people still pointing their cameras at me and the waiter's protestations saying I should not leave, I dart into a narrow passageway and am immediately engulfed by the cold shade away from the sunshine's glare. I quicken my pace to put distance between myself and the bodies behind me. 'Who is behind this?' I say a little breathlessly into the phone.

'I'll tell you in person. Just get to a hotel, lay low and call me back when you have the details.'

'Whoever it is, I want them to pay for what they've done.'

'I promise you they will, now go.'

The phone line falls silent as Masterson disconnects. I scroll through the settings to save his contact details as I wander aimlessly through the narrow back streets of Chania. I manage to keep walking on a heading that makes the volume of the sirens recede in the distance until I can barely hear them. It is more by luck than judgement that I find myself standing before a large set of dirty glass double doors. They may once have been regal and imposing but the neighbourhood looks like it has seen a bit of an economic meltdown over the past few years and the hotel has followed its decline in sympathy.

I push on the glass leaving behind a smear of dust and grime on the glass and enter the dimly lit lobby. A faint smell of citrus furniture polish is fighting to counter the odour of stale sweat and cigarette smoke, and failing miserably. A stereotypical Greek man is sitting behind the scratched and water stained counter. His thick dark hair and beard are ragged and unkempt and he has a cigarette dangling from the corner of his mouth. He doesn't even raise an eyebrow as I walk towards him, as if he is used to seeing blood soaked foreigners in his hotel. As I look at the surroundings I do in fact wonder if it is a regular occurrence.

'A room please, whatever you have available.' I ask him.

'It's a minimum two night stay and cash upfront,' he answers, tapping his ash onto the floor behind the counter. I notice his English is tinted with an American-Greek accent.

'No problem, I need it for three nights anyway,' I blurt out without thinking, 'how much will that be?'

He looks me up and down as if assessing my worth and perhaps my desperation,

'Three-hundred Euros.'

It is my turn to look him up and down and I also turn to the gloomy lobby about me. I take in the faded and shabby furniture, the plastic flowers and the overflowing ash-trays which are probably the reason he is now using the floor to deposit his cigarette ash.

'I'll give you one hundred and fifty, take it or leave it.'

His eyes narrow as he gestures towards my stained trousers,

'Two-hundred and I'll have those dry-cleaned. No questions.'

I pull out my wallet and place four crisp fifty Euro notes fresh from the ATM on the counter. They disappear quickly and a key replaces their position in front of me.

'Room 316, third floor. It has a nice view of the city and you can see everyone coming and going in the street if you want to.' He winks conspiratorially.

I nod my head in thanks as I pick up the key.

'The fire escape is next to your room also,' he continues, 'you know, in case of any sudden emergencies.' He lets out a little laugh which turns into a coughing fit as I walk away and towards the elevator. 'I'll give you a few minutes to get settled in then send up my niece to pick up your dry cleaning.'

As I go to press the UP button with my thumb, his voice booms out across the lobby,

'Out of order, you have to use the stairs.'

I barely miss a stride as I turn towards the stairs, flakes of dried blood dropping from my trousers and falling heavily to the floor as I walk towards the dark stairwell. I am surprised to find a light come on automatically as I climb. I had expected to have to make the three story journey in darkness.

On the third and top floor of the hotel I walk into the hallway to look for my room. As promised it is next to the fire escape at the far end. I peer through the safety glass of the fire door and wonder if the rusting and aged metal staircase that has been attached to the building would hold my weight if I had to use it. Shaking my head I take a step back and unlock the door to my room. I am pleasantly pleased with the spacious area that opens up for me. There is a small seating area off to one side of the king-size bed where I can sit and look out over the city and the road leading to the hotel. A large and clean bathroom sits behind a door to my left and I can imagine that this hotel may once been a much grander place than it is now.

I walk over to the window and gaze out across the buildings before me. I can make out the Venetian lighthouse at the harbour and I can see blue lights reflecting off the yellow stone of the thick walls. My mind is numb as I stare out, looking yet seeing nothing as I try to come to terms with the events of the last few hours. As I stand there I attempt to place my hands in my trouser pockets and my left hand bumps into my mobile phone. It breaks me from my spell and I know I must call Masterson to let him know where I am.

*

Masterson is in deep conversation with an aircraft mechanic who is checking the undercarriage of a sleek private jet which is sitting alone in a brightly hangar. Masterson knows that as much as some celebrities and politicians like to brag about their own aircraft to colleagues and chat-show hosts, the reality is that many aircraft are actually run by a discreet leasing firm that has a bank of pilots and engineers which are ready at a moment's notice. It is often the case that these aircraft are flown in and out of cities all around the world with no one but the crew onboard if they are required to do a pick up for a person with more money than sense. This is what Masterson is counting on and the conversation with the chief engineer proves his point. He hands over a few hundred dollar bills and is told to come back at 4pm for a flight to Dallas, Texas. He is also advised to bring nothing more than hand luggage if he wants to avoid customs and immigration. He smiles at the advice. For a man used to travelling with no more than the clothes on his back, hand luggage can sometimes seem like a luxury.

As he walks away, heading towards the small yet busy bar that is conveniently placed on the roadside opposite the hangar's entrance, his phone vibrates in his pocket. He scans the caller ID before answering with a grim smile,

'Where are you?'

Masterson's voice on the phone brings the harsh reality of current events back to me, but I manage to hold myself together and give him the details of the hotel and my location.

'OK, stay off the grid and don't talk to anyone.'

I think of Julia and Wilks and how I am going to explain the situation to both of them.

'In fact,' Masterson continues, 'turn off your phone when we're done, remove the sim and battery and only replace them at...' he does some quick mental calculations of flying times and time differences, '7am your time. I'll contact you before 0730 and if you don't answer I will have to assume you have been compromised, or worse.'

'Why can't I ring you?' I ask, more for something to say than for any real answer.

'I'm going to change this phone now, I would suggest you do the same after my call in the morning.'

'Isn't this being a bit over dramatic and paranoid?'

His harsh reply makes me realise just how naïve I can be and how much trouble I am in,

'Ask that question to your brother,' there is a pause as he lets his words sink in, 'Look, I'm sorry. That was uncalled for.'

I stay silent.

'I'll ring between 0700 and 0730 tomorrow. Make sure you answer.' He disconnects.

After his curt response I stare out of the window to the street below in an attempt to gather my thoughts. They drift to Julia and I know I have to contact her and explain the situation. I have already put her through so much that to leave at this point without talking is a sure fire way to destroy what little chance I have of making our relationship work. With my thumb resting on the call button I think about Masterson's warnings, and decide to ignore them. I press lightly on the green symbol and take a deep breath.

'Hi Peter, how's the day out with your brother?'

Her voice is happy and light but I feel my heart sink at her question.

'Julia, please just listen to me. Something terrible is going on. Paul has been shot and I have to return to the UK for a while.'

There is only silence as a response and I can almost see her beautiful face in shock.

'I have to leave Crete and try and find out what has happened. Somebody tried to kill me but they made a mistake and Paul,' I have to take another deep, shuddering breath, 'Paul was killed instead of me.'

'What...?'

'Please no, Julia. I can't speak for long and I just had to let you know what was happening. I didn't want you to feel I was abandoning you.'

'Abandoning me?' Julia's tone is angry, not what I expected, 'Your break the news that someone is trying to kill you, murdered your brother and you have to run away and I'm supposed to just accept this like it's an everyday occurrence. Maybe to you this is a routine thing, and I am beginning to see that it is, but this is just so like you.'

'Julia, please…'

'No Peter, I can't do this anymore.'

'Julia, I love you.'

'You say that like it's true, but it's the job you love. The job and whichever old flame you happen to fall into bed with. It's all about the thrill of the chase and you don't seem to care if you are doing the chasing or the one being chased. I'm truly sorry about your brother, really I am, but can't you see that this all of your own doing?' She pauses and I stay silent as her words cut through me, 'Did you actually come here to see me, Peter? Or was it just a happy coincidence that I was here in Crete, and you are actually on a job and Paul was sucked up into it somehow?'

'I came here to be with you, to try and save what we have.'

'What we had, Peter, not what we have. I don't think we have anything anymore.'

'Look, once this is all over we can talk about us and get back to normal. We can…'

'There is no normal with you. Your life revolves around death and mayhem and 2 a.m. calls to drag you away to another murder. I don't want to live like that anymore. I want someone I know will be there in the morning, someone to share a conversation with that doesn't involve broken promises about being there for me.'

I close my eyes as she speaks, wanting, no, wishing that she could see things from my perspective.

'Julia, I can change. I can be the man you want me to be.'

'The only way you will change is if you leave your job. Are you willing to do that? Would you leave your job if it meant saving our relationship?'

'Are you giving me an ultimatum? It's the job or you?'

'Exactly that, Peter.' Her voice softens, 'If we have any chance of being together you must leave the force. Will you do that, will you leave for me?'

I pause as I consider the enormity of the question. My whole life has revolved around the Met. Could I give it up for a woman I love? Does she know the enormity of what she is asking me to do? The silence over the phone is deafening for a few moments until Julia breaks it.

'I guess that's my answer. If you loved me then you would have answered straight away. The fact you have to think about it says more than anything you can say.' She lets out a long sigh over the phone, 'Goodbye Peter. I hope you get this... whatever this is you are involved in sorted out and I'm sorry about Paul, but please don't contact me again.'

'Julia, I can...' but I realise I am already talking to a dead line.

36

It takes a few seconds for Kate's eyes to adjust to the change in the lighting and she looks up instinctively to see where the glow is coming from. There are no lights that she can make out and it is as if the walls themselves are producing their own glow.

'Artificial light and ionised air panels,' Luke explains, 'they have been designed to produce 30% more natural light than natural light, although how you can manage that is beyond me. I looked up the scientific methods and calculations behind it once and I was just baffled.'

After the first second or two of squinting, Kate finds her eyes are actually feeling soothed by the glow.

'Wow, that actually feels good,' she exclaims.

'Amazing isn't it? The light frequency has been set to give the eyes a chance to relax. It's like a massage for the optic nerves.'

'Surely the Met hasn't invested money in something like this? It must cost a fortune.'

Luke shakes his head, 'Private investments. This area has been financed by a security consultancy on the proviso they can use it to filter information on an ad-hoc basis. Of course, they have to ask for access, but they can use it whenever they like so long as it doesn't interfere with police business.'

'And what exactly goes on in here?'

Luke smiles, 'This is the Facial Acquisition and Capture Identification Assessment Laboratory. FACIAL for short.'

Kate's eyes narrow, 'And how is this meant to help us catch my suspect?'

'Using this system we can assess in real time any CCTV images from all over the UK. We are tapped in to all points of entry and exit around the country as well as many ports and airports around the world. If your suspect shows up, we'll find him.'

'Her,' Kate corrects him, 'find her. But that must take time, obviously. By the time you go through the feeds she will be long gone.'

'That's what we like to people to think, when in fact the POD can search for an individual from the feeds and correlate it within a few seconds to the millions of pictures within our databases in seconds. The world's most wanted are constantly being searched for and in some cases are in known locations, yet they are left alone because we get to disrupt their operations further down the line. The best thing is they don't have a clue how we do it.'

'Surely it would be in the greater interests to stop them at source. Stop the rot before it sets in.'

'If the powers that be did as you say then someone else would simply step up and take over. Someone who may be under the radar when it comes to us and then we really would be in trouble. I mean, you remember Bin-Laden getting captured and killed? I heard he was under surveillance for years without his knowledge and it was only when he had served his useful purpose that he was zapped. Apparently by keeping him alive all those years the Yanks had managed to intercept at least three 9/11 sized operations, including one here in the UK.'

'It doesn't bear thinking about,' Kate mutters, 'but knowing they could be caught anytime and we just stand by, well the public would be up in arms.'

'The rumours that come out about this just sound like crazy conspiracy theories, and besides, we have all signed the official secrets act or we wouldn't be here.'

Kate thinks back to the huge number of forms that were

presented to her for her signature before she was allowed to officially start work for the Metropolitan Police. She also recalls the Deep Vetting, or DV, interviews by two unsmiling detectives who seemed to know more about her background than she could remember herself. As her mind is wandering, Luke rolls out a pair of comfortable looking black office chairs from under a workstation and sits himself down in one with a contented sigh.

'Let's get to work,' he says as he gestures to the empty chair for Kate to sit in. As she eases herself down, Luke types in his username and password combination to access the FACIAL system.

'Right, what's your suspects name and we'll do a quick scan to see if she is already in our system. If she isn't then I can spread the net wider, which normally means resorting to Facebook to get a decent photo.'

'Her name is Ewelina Jankowska,' Kate can't stop a grin appearing as Luke's fingers pause over the keyboard.

'Perhaps you had better type that in,' he says leaning back and relinquishing control to Kate.

After she has typed in the name, Luke moves back into position and with a few taps and keyword entries, a list of names, dates and locations appear on the screen. Each is accompanied by a thumbnail of a picture or paused video footage of Ewelina at that moment in time.

'Hmmm, it seems that she has been a very busy girl.' Luke taps a key and one of the thumbnails zooms out to show a larger picture of Ewelina.

'That's her,' Kate says with excitement, 'but she's much older now. She looks barely in her twenties in this picture.'

Luke goes to work on the keyboard and a paragraph appears next to the picture.

'Her charge sheet,' he explains. 'She was arrested for smuggling and selling illicit tobacco. It was, and still is, a major way for East European gangs to raise capital quickly.'

'What, selling the odd packet of fags to get around the system. That can't be that much of a problem can it?' Kate asks him.

'That's part of the problem in trying to stop this because that is just what most people think, yet tobacco smuggling accounts for around 130 million pounds in London alone. Not a bad little earner if you control the supply.'

'I know I'm surrounded by the police here and they're all about fighting crime, but isn't that money just in lost taxes and a matter for Customs and Excise to deal with.'

'It used to be but it's taken over as the number one smuggling product in the UK. It's also integrated with people trafficking, the sex trade and harder drugs. We've seen countless people killed because of it, not just turf wars, but the innocent punters who are smoking counterfeit cigarettes laced with things like rat poison and other kinds of crap that's used as a cheap filler.'

Luke types rapidly and brings up different pages of information.

'Her first charge was eight years ago in Sheffield, then two more in the following six months in the same court,' he taps the screen, 'she moved on to Cardiff here. Larger quantities were involved there and a bigger fine for her, then it goes quiet until she is questioned in a kidnap and murder enquiry a few months ago.'

'That's when I first heard about her. Why didn't I see the charge sheets when I asked for her information?'

'Unless you specifically ask for them, or they are related in terms of crime, then they remain locked down to avoid discrimination in any cases brought against the accused.'

Kate shakes her head, 'So what can we do with this information?'

'I was waiting for you to ask that.'

Luke's fingers start dancing across the keyboard with a skill set that would rival a master piano player, caressing and cajoling the keys to get the desired results. On the screen, Kate watches as Ewelina's pictures are merged and manipulated to form an accurate 3d rendition.

'Now all I need to do is input this data into the FACIAL system and...' he strikes the ENTER key and turns to Kate, 'where would you like to start the search? I mean, do you have a date and location for me to start looking?'

Kate reels off the date, time and location of the shooting at

Helen's apartment. As she does so, Luke is inputting the figures into the FACIAL search box.

Kate is amazed when a small map appears on the monitor showing the locations of the CCTV cameras that have been linked in to FACIAL. Luke clicks on the camera nearest to Helen's apartment and a video window pops up. Within 3 seconds of it playing, Ewelina appears in view, walking with urgency towards the camera.

'Gotcha,' Luke exclaims, 'now I just have to...' his voice trails off as he concentrates on the task before him.

For ten minutes, Kate watches the young man at work as he manipulates video and still images on the screen. She is afraid to say anything in case she breaks his concentration, but when he turns towards her she risks asking a simple question.

'Well?'

'I can give you a run through of her movements from when she left the scene, here she hailed a black cab and I even have footage of her in the taxi before she was dropped off at,' he checks the details on the screen, 'at Victoria Station. From there it gets a bit hit and miss as some of the systems were under maintenance, but we have her leaving Liverpool Street where she gets into a white Transit van.'

He clicks the mouse and a still image flashes up of Ewelina just about to enter the open passenger door of a white van.

'From here I can trace her route through London using the number plate recognition cameras and this,' one more mouse click and a line of text appears over the image, 'is her last known address.'

Luke's enthusiasm is infectious and Kate shuffles forward in her seat,

'How long ago?' she asks breathlessly.

'The last images were taken just over an hour ago.'

Kate is staring at the screen intently,

'I need a phone,' she says, not taking her eyes from the image or the address as if that would stop Ewelina from leaving.

Luke reaches behind the monitor and pulls out the handset of a landline phone from its bracket. He hands it to Kate who quickly taps in the numbers on the keypad before stabbing the 'dial' button with her thumb.

It is picked up on the first ring and Kate does not wait to hear the answer before talking,

'Ma'am, we've found her.'

Luke watches as her head rapidly nods to the voice of Wilks on the line.

'I have it in front of me now. Yes that's correct,' she turns her gaze away from the screen with an effort and looks at Luke, 'Can you get this information sent over to the Commissioner?'

Luke gives a thumbs up and his fingers fly once again over the keyboard,

'Done,' he says simply.

'Ma'am you should... ah good. Can I ask,' there is a pause, 'yes I understand. I'll continue working here and wait for your instructions.' She nods once more, 'Thank you ma'am.'

She hands the phone back to Luke.

'Now why don't you show me what else we can find out with this sparkly little machine of yours?'

'With pleasure, Kate. What would you say about trying to find more about our Polish friend from less conventional means? Perhaps we should look at the European enforcement agencies and see what they hold on her.'

'I didn't realise we had such a good relationship with other agencies.'

Luke chews on his bottom lip and his eyes flick from the keyboard, to the screen, to Kate.

'Well, ummm, we may not have that good a friendship, but...'

'I don't want to know, but if we can find out more information and it won't get thrown out of a job, let's do it.'

They both lean forward in their seats as Luke starts inputting commands to bypass security protocols and search for more information.

'I love my job,' Luke says with a smile.

37

Masterson hangs up on Carter and immediately starts dialling another number from memory. He grins when a cheery voice answers on the third ring,

'Welsh war office, who wants a fight?'

'Taff, you rabid sheep shagger, how are those funny shaped balls of yours?'

'Bloody hell mate,' the lilting accent says in surprise, 'how's tricks with you then, butt? You still chasing those five dollar bar girls?'

Masterson stops in the bar's car park to continue his conversation,

'Those were the days, Taff, good memories. But as for the bar girls I seem to remember them being your speciality especially if they had a little a something between their legs. Didn't you used to knock a dollar off for every inch bigger than yours?'

'You were only jealous 'cos the lady-boys were more endowed than you.'

There is laughter at both ends of the phone before the Welsh accent comes back on the line, more serious now,

'I take it this isn't a social call.'

'Sorry Taff, not really. Are you busy at the moment?'

'Like you wouldn't fucking believe mate. Actually if you've got a spare few days I've got a job that would be right up your street.'

'Maybe later, right now I'm after a favour.'

Masterson can almost feel the ground move from where he stands as the big Welshman shifts in his seat.

'Are you in trouble?'

'You could say that. I really need a lift.'

Taff looks up at the board attached to the wall in front of his desk. It shows a table of radio call-signs, aircraft tail numbers, locations and operation or exercise names. There is stark black lettering in large print stencilled above it, SECRET – UK EYES ONLY.

Taff's voice instantly turns professional,

'Where are you, where do you need to go and what are the timing requirements?'

Masterson closes his eyes and gives thanks that once again it is who you know and not what you know that matters in this world.

'I need a pick up from Dallas and I'm hoping to get to…' he pauses knowing that he is on an unsecure line, 'do you remember where Chipper had that little trouble with the APC?'

'Christ man, how could I forget, he drove that damn armoured personnel carrier over the commandant's car.'

'That's the place, well I…'

'Yeah I remember we all had to chip in to buy a new fucking car. It was lucky we had that great big fucking bonus that year or my missus would have torn me a new one. I'm sure that was the year Simmo promised his wife the new furniture which had to be cancelled because of Chipper's APC run. God, there was…'

'Taff,' Masterson has to break in. He had forgotten how much Taff liked to talk, 'TAFF,' louder this time.

'Great fucking times mate, great fucking times.'

'Taff, can we get back to more recent times?'

'Oh, sorry mate, you know what it's like when you're stuck flying this desk. Look, let me work something out here. Wait one…'

Masterson stands silently in the car park as he waits for Taff to look for a solution to his problem.

Searching through the list of names and numbers on the board, Taff starts jotting down information on the pad in front of him. The note pad has numbered pages, all of which must be accounted for at the end of each shift and the page he is scribbling on will be signed off and shredded when his replacement comes in to take over. It takes less than a minute for a plan to come together.

'Bloody hell, you always did come up smelling of roses,' Taff says eventually, 'I've got some septic clubbers leaving the big BX and stopping off at Chipper's car park tomorrow for breakfast.'

Masterson automatically translates the slang in his head,

Septic – septic tank – Yank

Clubbers – Seals – US Navy Sea Air and Land special forces

Big BX – Large shopping area on a US base, the nearest US base to his location in Dallas is Fort Worth.

So, there is a US aircraft planned to fly a group of US Navy SEALS to Souda Bay on Crete, due to arrive in the morning.

Taff relays the timings and Masterson calculates he can just about make it.

'I need one more favour, Taff,' he says quietly.

'Go on,' even Taff's voice is cautious now.

'I also need an onward trip to the UK, anywhere in the UK with a plus one. A civilian. I need this as soon as you can and it needs to be black.'

'How black?'

'Like fucking midnight. No records in, no records out.'

Taff blows out a breath between pursed lips,

'That might take some time.'

'How long?'

'Give me 48 hours to see what I can do.'

'Taff, you're a star mate and a real life saver.'

'Yeah I know. Next thing you'll be wanting my babies,' he sighs, 'This is going to have to cost you, you know that. I can't make this happen easily.'

'Just name your price.'

The now, not so jovial Welshman stands up and pulls a dark sheet away from the wall to reveal a second board hidden behind. He takes a moment to scan the list printed upon it, picks up a red marker and places a bold asterisk next to one of the names. He then writes 'TASKED' in the blank box next to it.

'I've got a job for you,' he says almost reluctantly.

38

Wilks is tapping the address from Kate into her own computer as fast as she can. The map that appears on the screen shifts automatically and centres a red circle over a street in Hackney. Her hand taps restlessly on her desk as she considers her options. The tapping stops as she comes to a decision. She stands up and walks to her open door, she does not want to shout out these instructions as she addresses her personal assistant.

'Get me tasking on the phone and tell them I need two ARU teams with at least a dozen uniforms for cordon control,' she pauses as she thinks through the enormity of the situation and the possible consequences, 'actually, make that three armed response units and thirty officers. We don't fully know what we may be dealing with here. Thanks, Steve. Patch them through when you get them.'

Back at her desk she changes the simple map to a satellite picture of the area. It looks like it was taken in summer by the state of the lush green trees and slightly yellowing grass in the small gardens that populate the area. She zooms into street-view and pans around on screen. The address she has been given is for a small shop that has a launderette attached. The window is full of advertisements for mobile SIM cards that allow you to ring overseas for pennies. She pans around again to try and take in more detail and sees that the street is bisected by a bridge that carries the overground rail line. The street is also tightly packed with terraced houses with an old school building and a warehouse at the western end forming a dead end. Zooming back out she starts to draw lines on the image where street junctions would need to be secured. This might be their only chance of stopping Ewelina and any accomplices from escaping, and she wants to be sure in the knowledge that she has all the bases covered. Her desk phone does not even manage to finish its first ring before she snaps it up.

'This is Wilks.'

'Ma'am, Sergeant Margon in tasking. I have your basic request here for a task. Could I get more information please, you know tasking number, operation name etcetera.'

'Sergeant, I hope you can understand this is a time critical situation and I'm hoping we can get this sorted ASAP.'

'OK ma'am, no problem. Give me the requirements, location and basic details over the phone and I'll get the paperwork sorted out later.'

'Thank you sergeant, I appreciate that. I have location details of the suspect in the DI Dawkins murder and…'

'Ma'am, sorry to butt in. Give me the location and I'll scramble the teams straight away as the highest priority. I'll get all available team members in on this and I can supply two canine teams as well.'

'Thank you sergeant.'

Wilks relays the details over the phone.

'Thanks ma'am. I've just sent a text to the ARU team leader and he's already replied to say he's on his way to your office now. Good luck.'

As the tasking sergeant disconnects, Wilks goes back to her map to concentrate on getting a plan organised. It is barely five minutes before a heavy knock on her door breaks her from her spell.

'You have a job for me, ma'am.'

She looks up to see a man dressed in a black police jumpsuit with various shaped pouches attached to harness points on his vest, standing in the doorway.

'Inspector Grieves, come in. When did you take control of the armed response unit?' she asks her old colleague from her time as a detective sergeant.

They had come through training together, and while her rise through the ranks had been meteoric, his had stuttered due to cuts and office realignments.

'It's been about three months now. It's a good team to be on.'

'I'm glad to see someone I know. Look, we have a situation here that could lead us to the killer of one of our own.'

'Dawkins?'

'Yes. We have an address for the suspect that is very recent and she has accomplices at the address.'

'Weapons, numbers, intent?'

'Unknown on all counts but we must assume they are armed due to the nature of the crime.'

'What do you have I can use?'

Wilks turns the monitor round and shows him the location and possible pinch points she has found. For the next ten minute they thrash out a basic plan for Grieves to take back to his men and plan a more detailed raid on the address.

'I'll send some plain clothes in to stake the place out until the operation is mounted. If she moves, or if anyone leaves that building I want somebody on them.'

Grieves looks at his old friend as he gets up to leave,

'Do we need to involve our friends across the river?'

Wilks shakes her head,

'I think we can leave MI6 out of this at the moment and concentrate on it as a Met operation.'

'It's your call but I would suggest giving them a heads up. We may need their expertise later on and it would be good to have them on our side from the get-go.'

'I see where you're coming from. I'll get hold of someone over there before I join you.'

'Join me?'

'It's my operation. I want to be on the ground when it happens.'

Grieves shakes his head,

'Patricia,' he gestures to the office around them, '*this* is your realm. It might be better if you wait this one out and let us guys and girls on the ground deal with this.'

'Are you pushing me out of my own operation?' Wilks can feel her voice rising in anger.

'Not pushing you out, protecting you. You're the Commissioner of the Metropolitan Police Force for crying out loud. Your place is not on a raiding team with the very real danger of firearms being used. Didn't the loss of Derek Temple teach you anything?'

Wilks is bristling in anger and frustration, but the mention of her predecessor's name, killed in a similar operation, calms her down instantly. She knows what must be done and who is best suited to deal with it. She clasps her hands in front of her and looks up to Grieves who is standing half turned towards the exit.

'I'll get on to the suits at MI6. Please, keep me informed of the operation.'

Her old friend and colleague nods his head, turns on his heels and walks out of her office. As he makes his way through the hallways she can hear him barking orders and updates into his team's communication link.

She picks up her phone to call the liaison officer in the MI6 building and wonders why she wanted this job at all when the excitement of the chase is out there on the street.

'I must be bloody mad,' she says aloud to her empty office as she waits for her call to be answered.

39

After the owner's niece has left the room with my blood stained trousers for dry-cleaning I have a restless night as I try and get my mind around the day's events and Julia's ultimatum. I don't even remove my dressing gown or get under the covers in case I have to move quickly. The sounds from the streets outside do nothing to put me at ease and every time I hear a car drive past the hotel I am up to the window to see if it is the police, or someone looking to kill me. My thoughts drift from Paul's wife and family and how they must be feeling, to Ann and then on my own predicament and brush with death. But the main focus of my attention is Julia. My sweet, precious Julia and how I have managed to ruin everything we had between us.

Countless times I pick up my phone and toy with calling her, but I know that I have nothing to say that would help the situation. A few times during the long night I was on the verge of calling JD, just to hear a friendly voice but Masterson's warning kept repeating in my head and even though I see I have voicemail waiting I heed his advice and do not make any more calls, not even to the voicemail service. Instead I lie on the sheets and doze in fits and starts until the phone's ringtone breaks through my confused and scattered thoughts and I realise that somehow it is just after 7am.

I push myself up wearily from the bed and make my way to the bathroom where I splash some cold water on my face and run my wet hands through my unkempt hair. I glance at myself in the mirror, God I look like shit. Unwrapping the small square of soap from its thin plastic wrapper I make a paltry attempt to clean myself up. But a little soap and water cannot clear away the way I feel, or the guilt that has a grip on my heart. I stare intently into my own eyes in the reflection of the mirror's surface, trying to seek answers to questions that are running through my head. My thoughts are broken by the mobile phone's shrill ringing and I stumble out of the bathroom to answer it.

'Carter,' I answer.

'Peter, get yourself to Souda Bay war cemetery for 11am this morning. I'll be there to pick you up so just wait by the entrance. We'll talk when we meet up. OK?'

Masterson's voice is tired sounding, just like I feel.

'What's going to happen?' I ask. I'm feeling numb and to be ordered around is what I need, in fact, it is all I can manage at the moment to follow instructions.

'We're going to London to discuss our predicament with some old acquaintances. I'm going to get to the bottom of this once and for all, and you're going to help me.' There is a pause, 'Look, we'll talk on the way. Get to Souda Bay for 11am and wait for your pickup.' Masterson's tone turns serious, 'Now remove the SIM from your phone and flush it away. Then dispose of the battery and the phone's body in two separate locations so it can't be found together and traced back to you and I'll see you soon.'

The phone beeps twice as he disconnects and I blindly follow his orders. I not only flush the SIM away, but I break it in two just to make sure.

The gentle knocking on the door makes my head snap around

and I move quickly to the window to check the street outside. Empty.

The soft knock is repeated and a girl's voice follows,

'Mr. Carter, are you awake?' she asks timidly.

I relax as I recognise the voice of the hotel owner's niece. When I open the door she is standing outside with my trousers draped neatly over her arm. The clear, thin plastic cover that covers them does not hide the fresh linen smell that exudes from the material inside. She hands the trousers over to me and I can still feel the warmth of the laundry through the bag. I open my mouth to thank her but she has already turned away and is walking urgently along the corridor.

'Thank you,' I say to her back and she turns and gives me a smile.

'Parakalo,' she answers without breaking stride.

Closing the door I look at my watch on the bedside table and see that I have plenty of time before the scheduled meet. After a long shower where I let the warm water beat down upon my head until it turns cold, I dress and make my way downstairs to the lobby. The same guy is sitting behind the desk as if he has not moved. He even looks to be wearing the same clothes, but who am I to talk.

'Can you get me a cab to, umm,' I have to think to get the unfamiliar name right, 'is it Souda cemetery?'

He nods his head,

'The war graves, yes?'

It is my turn to nod my head.

'No problem,' he replies, 'in fact I am going that way to my home soon. I can drive you myself for twenty euros.'

I can't be bothered to argue even though I can assume a taxi would be at least half the price.

'Sounds good, when can we leave?'

He pulls a cigarette from the packet in front of him and taps it on the desk twice. He holds it up for me to see,

'After I have my breakfast, yes?' he says with a smile.

I smile and nod my head in return. I point at the shabby two seater couch near the front door where the air looks a little clearer from the haze of cigarette smoke that surrounds the front desk.

'I'll just wait over there,' I say.

In response he flicks a match expertly with his thumbnail and lights up his 'breakfast'.

'I'll come and get you,' he says between a racking cough and phlegmy clearing of his throat.

The sofa is lumpy and uncomfortable as I sit there in silence. I gaze through the dusty window, not seeing anything, just staring into space, lost in my jumbled thoughts. The hand on my shoulder startles me and I am snapped out of my spell.

'Hey, you not hear me when I say we go?'

I stand up and shake my head as if to clear out the cobwebs.

'Sorry, I was miles away.'

'Let's go my friend. My car is just around the corner.'

I follow him out of the hotel as he strides away, cigarette in one hand and a newspaper slapping against his leg at irregular intervals as if keeping time with a musical beat only he can hear. I don't look back, I don't even think about where I may be spending the next night. I am completely numb and I realise I am entering the stages of delayed shock. Realising this fact and doing something about it are two separate things and I follow silently, listening as my informal taxi service gives me a running commentary.

'This used to be a beautiful area. Kids playing, clean and tidy you know? Everybody happy and helping one another.' He waves an arm around the litter strewn street, 'Now it is not so good. The tourists don't come anymore because they want everything free from the all-inclusive holidays. Tavernas have to close, families have no money, kids have no future. We used to have a full hotel and a tour operator who would pay us to keep rooms for them. One day they say, Dimitri, for us to work with you, you must give your guests food and drink all day and we will you pay 10 Euros for each person. 10 Euro for everything.' He spits a large globule out in disgust, 'Malakas, 10 Euros won't even get you a souvlaki in this city anymore. I say no and they leave me to fend for myself,' he pauses as he reaches a surprisingly clean black

BMW. He pulls open the unlocked car door and nods his head for me to get in the passenger side, 'no loyalty, that is the problem,' he continues where he left off, 'before we had loyalty. Now it is every man for himself.'

As I pull my seatbelt around me I notice the keys have been left in the ignition. Dimitri sees my look.

'Nobody messes with me in this area. I am the boss here, I know everything, I see everything.' He taps his nose, 'You know my friend, respect we still have,' he throws his newspaper into my lap, 'and a man like you I respect.' He points down at the picture on the front page, 'After all, who would not respect a man who is dead.'

I look down and see the photo from my passport next to the scene of carnage at the restaurant. Mercifully the bodies of my brother and Ann have been covered by a tablecloth, but the dark stains that have soaked through the white material show their violent end.

ENGLISH POLICEMAN AND LOVER KILLED the headline reads in English above my picture. I look up slowly to see Dimitri looking at me with a very serious expression on his face.

'So mister dead man, what do we do now?'

40

'OK sir. What information do we have on the interior? Any news on occupants, layout, weapons etcetera?'

Inspector Grieves smiles grimly at the police officer asking the question and shakes his head almost apologetically.

'Nothing,' he states simply, 'but we do know that the chief suspect in the murder of DI Dawkins has been linked to the location and to me this is the perfect excuse to ignore the softly softly approach and enter with our trademark speed and aggression.'

The nods from the three detective sergeants of the armed response units is all the confirmation he needs to understand their state of mind.

'We've got four teams for the assault so will be making a standard two pronged entry with teams one and two, whilst teams three and four will offer reserve options whilst also controlling and cordoning this area here.' On the ruggedized tablet on the table in front of him he uses his finger to draw a ring around the area on the map. He then swipes the screen to the right and is greeted by a series of beeps from the room as the information is shared to the tactical tablets each officer has attached to his body armour.

'Now you all have as much information as I have. It's not the best but we have been in situations where the tactical awareness has been even less revealing and got the job done. Teams one and two will be led by myself and Banks. Three and four are Evans and Wallace respectively.

Team one, we are going through the front door, team two will take the back and I want your guys, Evans, supporting from the East and yours, Wallace, to the West. Expect to be involved as I am sure there will be runners.'

Grieves waits for the nods of assent and any questions, but there are none forthcoming.

'We do this fast with maximum aggression, but we also do it by the numbers. We can't afford any mistakes. We all know the scrutiny the force is under at the moment so I want everyone operating with the rules of engagement.' Grieves pauses, 'This could get noisy so ensure your teams are prepared for that,' he checks his watch, 'I want you back here in thirty minutes after meeting with your teams and discussing your objectives. I want to know if there are any questions or ideas before we start the operation. By that time we should have received Home Office approval via the commissioner.'

As his team leaders disperse, Grieves pulls his mobile phone from the pouch on the front of his black nomex suit and dials the number for Wilks.

'Ma'am, Inspector Grieves. Do we have the green light for our project?' he asks.

Wilks releases a deep sigh down the phone,

'I have expressed the urgency of the situation on the right honourable lady and she is discussing the options with the PM as we speak. I have to let you know that her first comment was, "Is it terrorism related?", which makes me think she finds the situation beneath her.'

Grieves lets out a snort of disgust as Wilks continues.

'Don't worry, I have re-educated the minister of our, and her, priorities.'

'What about MI6? Are they on board and can they offer any more awareness of the situation?'

'I have been informed they are aware of the address and have had it under surveillance for the last twelve months for something they are calling, Operation Hawkwind. They are collating the information and I am waiting for it to arrive. As soon as it does I will send it straight on to you.'

'Thank you, anything at this stage would be helpful. I hate going in blind. Can I ask whatever information you get be sent across the ARU network so each team member receives it. It saves a lot of time and allows everyone to work on the problem at once whilst avoiding communication errors and silly mistakes.'

Wilks recalls past operations of the Met's ARU's where unarmed civilians have been involved in shootings, and can see Grieves logic behind his request.

'I want no mistakes on this operation and I want to see Jankowska in custody by close of play. She must be made to face justice for her actions.'

A soft tone from her laptop grabs her attention.

'One moment, Grieves. I have something coming in on secure mail,' she says as she opens the message.

'What the...?' she exclaims, 'Grieves, I'll have to get back to you. You have to hold the operation until I do. I repeat, hold the operation. I don't believe what's just come through!'

Knowing his place in the pecking order, Grieves responds in the only way he can.

'Yes ma'am.'

Wilks has already disconnected and is rapidly punching numbers into her phone from memory. The call is answered immediately, almost as if the recipient was expecting the call.

'Patricia, before you start shouting this decision has been taken out of my hands. Another department has blocked any activity in and around the location. I've been informed they have high quality targets providing information that is deemed a higher priority than any domestic issues we may have.'

The anger in Wilks' voice is plainly evident,

'Since when does the murder of a decorated police officer become as simple a factor as a domestic issue, John? Which department is responsible for this shambles? I want to speak to them directly.'

'That's something I am not at liberty to say and I have to inform you that there is no way you will be able to speak to anyone involved. As I say, this is out of my hands and I need you to get your teams to stand down and return to base.'

'I'm not telling anyone to RTB until I get to the bottom of this and I will require ministerial acknowledgment before I abort this operation.'

'Ok Patricia, if that's how you want to play this out. Please let me hand you over to the Home Secretary.'

Wilks is stunned as she hears the instantly recognisable voice.

'Commissioner Wilks? This is the Home Secretary and I reiterate what your colleague has told you. This operation is a no-go. Stand down your officers.'

'Ma'am, this is an on-going operation to apprehend the killer of one of my officers. I have to I ask the reasons for this?'

There is a tired inflection to the cultured voice of the Home Secretary,

'You may ask but in the interests of national security I cannot answer. I am truly sorry.'

Wilks knows when she is beaten,

'Of course ma'am, I may not understand your response but I do recognise the chain of command.'

'Thank you Commissioner Wilks, and thank you for your understanding.'

The call is disconnected and Wilks has to take a moment to keep her anger in check before relaying the information to Grieves.

'Inspector, I hate to say this but recall your team and stand down,' to his stunned silence she continues, 'I can't give you a reason just yet, but I aim to find out why.'

As she hangs up she is already striding out of her office to make the short journey across London to the MI6 building to look for answers.

41

Luke is leaning forward over the keyboard and typing commands quicker than Kate can think when suddenly, the screen goes blank.

'What the hell just happened?' she asks.

His fingers are paused over the keys as he looks at the black screen with a simple flashing cursor in the top left hand corner, that a moment before had been a wealth of information about Ewelina and her past.

'I don't understand it,' he mumbles, 'it's like the whole database has been wiped of any trace of her.'

'Is it something we've done?' Kate asks, thinking of the consequences to her career of dabbling on the edge of legality.

'No. We were just accessing found on servers from all over the country, all over Europe in fact. It's like she has just been erased.'

'How can that be?'

Luke suddenly sits bolt upright.

'Shit!'

His hands are now flying and typing in commands at an even more frenetic pace.

'What is it Luke? You're making me a little nervous.' Kate shuffles back in her seat as if to try and distance herself from whatever is happening in front of her.

Without pausing his typing, Luke answers softly, almost whispering,

'I'm deleting all traces of our search history parameters and evidence that we were ever here. The only people who could do this,' he pauses and looks at her, 'who would do this can just as easily remove us from the files...and once that happens you can be deleted in real life. These guys can make you cease to exist in more ways than one.'

He returns to his work with a desperation that is shared by Kate.

'But they can't, I mean, they wouldn't...'

Kate, listen to me. We've stumbled on something here that we weren't meant to see.' He gestures to the small stack of printouts between them, 'Take these and get out of here. I've still got a bit of work to do here but these have to get to Commissioner Wilks. She might know who to contact if things go bad for us.'

'Go bad for us?'

He grabs her by the wrists and stares intently into her eyes, he notices a small fleck of grey set in the hazel of her right eye like a chip in moss covered rock,

'Kate, if you don't hear from me within the next 24 hours you have to get these papers to her and tell what we have found here.' He nods his head to the screen now filled with commands she doesn't understand, 'I've managed to erase all details of your visit to the pod, but I need to erase any traces from the whole building. That includes any video and not just our id swipes at entry points. I won't be able to do anything about my log-in details, but I can at least muddy the waters for you so that if, when, they come looking they might just miss you ever being here.'

He releases her wrists and gets back to work.

'Can't you just erase your log-in?'

He shakes his head, 'All log-ins within the pod are fireproof, but I can move some details around and make it look like I was here for a different reason.'

How the hell can you do that?'

Luke gives a wry smile,

'I designed it.'

He picks up the papers and places them in her hands. Kate notices goosebumps on his arms and understands it's not from the air-conditioning within the pod. He also gives her the ID tag from around his neck.

'Use this to get out. I can bypass the system when someone comes in.'

'But Luke, what should I do now?'

'Go back to work, act normally and,' with eyes wide he stares into hers, 'get these papers to Wilks if you don't hear from me and pray I've done enough to shield you from whoever is behind this, and also that Wilks can do something with this information. Now go!'

Standing up she tucks the sheaf of papers into the waistband of her trousers and pulls her blouse over to cover them. Walking towards the door she glances back to see Luke fully focussed on the screen in front of him. She swipes his card and waits for the red LED to blink green and the door to pop open with a soft beep. As she steps through she takes one last look back,

'Good luck,' she whispers.

Stepping from the bright light of the pod into the semi-darkness causes her to take a moment to adjust her eyes. She is glad of the shadowy gloom of the computer room as it shields her from prying eyes.

No-one pays her any attention as she moves between the aisles of desks, so intent are they on their own tasks of keeping the people of London and the UK safe. Stepping out into the circular corridor she pulls the papers out from their hiding place beneath her blouse knowing that concealing things in plain sight is often the best deception. She holds them high to her chest, like a high-school girl clutching text books on her way to a lecture. It's only when she reaches the known sanctuary of corridors and halls she recognises that she lets out a long sigh of relief, and is brought rudely back to her senses as two large men in dark suits barge into her. Knocked to the ground and with papers scattered all around her she notices one man turn quickly towards her with a look of anger on his face before they both continue their determined journey through the building. As she gathers up the papers in a panic she is startled by a friendly voice,

'What a couple of arrogant pricks.'

Kate looks up to see a slim uniformed police woman, her face framed by blonde hair tied back in a tight bun. The police woman holds a few sheets of paper in her left hand and with the right she helps Kate to her feet.

'Bloody MI6 think they own the place. Are you OK?'

Kate nods, her face a bright red of guilt.

'I think these belong to you,' the police-woman holds out the papers, 'they certainly did a job on you.'

'Thank you,' Kate manages to mumble before the stress of the situation comes bursting out of her in full, racking sobs. A gentle hand is placed on her shoulder.

'C'mon love. Let's get you a cup of tea, I'm on my break anyway.'

Kate, grateful for the reassuring hand and voice allows herself to be led away from the scene, yet she is still acutely aware of the situation she finds herself in. Two minutes later she is sat at a cheap formica topped table with a steaming mug of tea in front of her.

'So what do you do here Kate?'

She looks up sharply,

'I didn't tell you my name.'

'And I didn't tell you mine, but yours is written on your ID tag that is helpfully displayed around your neck,' the officer smiles as she blows the whispy steam from her own mug. 'My name's Leanne by the way.'

Kate looks dumbly down at her tag and realises she has to get a grip on her rising paranoia and panic.

'I'm sorry Leanne. It's just been a tough day.'

'Tell me about it. Anything to do with these?' she asks, motioning towards the papers on the table that are covered, protected almost, by Kate's hand.

Kate just stares at her, frozen and unable to speak.

'It's OK Kate. I'm as pissed off as anyone. I couldn't believe it when they made me call the teams back to base, I mean, she,' Leanne plucks the top piece of paper from underneath Kate's left hand before she has time to react and holds it up. The image on the sheet shows a picture of a younger Ewelina. 'She deserves to be locked up for sure.' She sighs and looks at the picture whilst sipping her tea, 'But ours is not reason why and all that rubbish. I just hope they have some good surveillance on the bitch.'

Kate reaches out and takes the paper from Leanne's fingers.

'Who ordered the recall?'

Leanne takes another sip from her tea before answering,

'It came from the very top. From the ivory tower itself.'

'Commissioner Wilks?' Kate's voice trembles as she voices the question, afraid of the answer.

Leanne shakes her head and blows out a soft hiss between clenched teeth,

'No, much higher than that. I was told it came direct from the Home Secretary herself. I mean, what does she know about policing, right? Has she ever been on the streets on a Saturday night? I tell you, this latest round of cuts is a kick in the teeth to all of us.' She shakes her head in disgust, 'A bloody kick in the teeth.'

Kate stands up suddenly, rocking the table and causing hot brown liquid to spill from her mug onto the table. It spreads slowly outwards, like a virus.

'I'm sorry, I have to go.'

Leanne narrows her eyes at the sudden change of Kate's demeanour.

'Oh, now I get it. You're one of her lackeys aren't you? You're probably here doing case studies of working hours and,' she swirls her tea around in front of Kate, 'how many tea breaks we bloody have. Is that it? Was it your advice that pulled the operation?'

Kate shakes her head, confusion filling the tumbled thoughts on her head,

'I'm so sorry,' she says as she hurries away leaving her spilt tea on the table with Leanne as the only evidence of her being there.

Glancing angrily at her watch, Leanne switches her gaze to the spare mug and her expression softens.

'Waste not, want not,' she says as she softly blows ripples across the top of the light coloured liquid.

42

Masterson's flight over from the States proved uneventful. The best thing about the dark circles he moved in was the anonymity and the no questions asked mentality. Sure you could get curious, but you never asked any operative for details. Curiosity could get you killed, or worse.

As he walks off the C-17 transport aircraft the December sun provided a welcome surprise. The military side of Chania airport was far enough away from the civilian terminal so as to avoid prying and inquisitive eyes and the Navy SEALs he was travelling with were all in low-profile civilian clothing so as not to attract attention. He blends in quite well as he walks across the tarmac with them. The only difference between him and his companions was that he was the only one not carrying a large black holdall. All he had to carry was his daysack.

He said his farewells and bid the US SEAL team happy hunting as they boarded a battered blue bus that was waiting for them. He watches in silence as it drives slowly off the aircraft pan to reveal a light green Daewoo that was almost as run-down as the bus. The driver rolls down his window and in a thick Yorkshire accent asks, 'Masterson?'

He nods and makes his way over to climb in the passenger seat.

'Taff sends his regards and asked me to help you with owt you need. He also said to stay away from the APC's, whatever the fuck that means. Sometimes I just don't understand that bloke.'

As Masterson closes the door he slams the small car into gear and heads at a speed that seems incredible for a small track through the rough scrub undergrowth.

'Did Taff give you my shopping list?' Masterson asks as the car swings drunkenly on the winding dusty route.

'Yeah, but it was a bit vague so I've got you a couple of longs to keep you happy and a short if you need it. Also a range of accessories to that always come in useful.'

'Cheers mate, where are they?'

The big man in the driver's seat jerks his head to the right, 'Right there on the back seat.'

Masterson swivels around to see a bright orange Mountain Equipment duffle bag bouncing in the back.

'Thanks, that's great. What specifically have you got for me?'

'Well I didn't know if you were going for distance or firepower, so you've got both. There's an MP5 with four 30 round mags and ten boxes of nine mil, a G3 also with 10 boxes and a couple of magazines. Thought you might appreciate them what with you being old school. The short is a CZ75 Shadow, don't know if you know it but it's a damn fine pistol that knocks socks off the old Browning you probably grew up with. That was confiscated last week after an altercation in a bar. No serial numbers on any of them.'

'All sounds good to this old man. What about the accessories you mentioned?'

'The usual mostly. Again I went for the stuff you may have use for. A few pounds of C4, det cord, NVG's a few flash bangs and I managed to toss in a couple of HE for good measure. To save you getting your clothes dirty there's also a couple of Nomex suits in there...you never know right?'

Masterson can't help but grin, 'You're an absolute star mate, what's the total? How much do I owe you?'

The driver shakes his head, 'Naff all mate. I owed Taff a huge favour and now that debt has passed on to you. Let me tell you, since he was put on that fucking desk I hate owing that Welsh bastard anything. He can really make your life hell, but then I'm sure you know that.'

Masterson nods his head, 'Yeah, but when you need pulling out of the shit, he knows when and where to find the perfect tow truck.

Both men look out of the window in silence. They don't see the glistening snow on the White Mountains or the buzzards lazily drifting on the air currents. Each is lost in their own thoughts for a few moments.

The road straightens and the car approaches a large metal gate that is guarded by two Greek soldiers. Both are kitted out in full battle order; helmets, webbing and a loaded M16. The driver lets the car roll to a gentle stop between the two men and Masterson notices one of them stifling a yawn with a hand that also holds a mobile phone.

'Evening chaps, lovely fuckin' day to stag on eh?' the driver says with a smile.

'Dave, it's shit,' says the guard on the left, also grinning. 'One day we will get a job like you and you do ours. You can stand here and we go drinking with whores.'

'Trust me Lambi, my life is a whole more dangerous than you think, after all, never turn your back on an angry hooker especially when you know she has a big boyfriend in the next room.'

Dave holds his hand out of his window and the two men shake hands briefly. Masterson sees a note palmed across and the guard barks out rapid words of Greek to his bored compatriot with the mobile phone who quickly moves to open the gate.

Glancing down at the note in his hand, Lambi's smile grows wider, 'Come back anytime my friend,' he says as he waves the two men through.

Leaving the airfield behind them, Dave adjusts the rear view mirror and asks, 'Right then, where do you need to go?'

Masterson looks at his watch before replying.

'Souda Bay cemetery, but I need to check out the lay of the land first as it's been a while. Can you park in the area in front of the naval accommodation?'

'Not a problem, I know the guys there. Do you need another pair of eyes on the ground? I told Taff I would help in any way I can.'

Masterson mulls this over for a second before shaking his head.

'Thanks, but it might spook my guy. If you see any water activity that is getting too close I would appreciate a heads up. Just give three blasts on the horn. I think we should be OK from what I remember of the place.'

'What about the high ground?'

Masterson shrugs his shoulders, 'From what I recall there's good cover from the olive groves, plus,' he pauses and looks out over the sparkling blue waters of Souda Bay as they drop down on the steep hillside road, 'If they've had time to prep the high ground then we're fucked the moment I get out of the car. Sorry about that.'

Dave turns to Masterson, still grinning, 'I thought Taff was letting me off lightly.'

Then under his breath, 'What the fuck have I gotten myself into?'

Masterson laughs, 'Mate, never trust a Welshman, especially one that says he is doing you a favour.'

43

'Commissioner Wilks, what a pleasant surprise.'

Connor Harman stands and smiles as he stretches out his hand from behind his expansive, oak desk. He deliberately ignores the look on Wilks' face, just as she ignores his proffered hand.

'Let's cut the crap Connor. What the hell is going on and why was my operation scrubbed?'

'Please Patricia, at least have a seat while we discuss this, yes?'

Wilks slumps, almost wearily into the soft, plump chair. Only her eyes betray her emotion and she is doing all she can to stop from exploding angrily at the man before her.

'As you know, Patricia, I am unable to comment on any ongoing operation and...'

Wilks lets out a bark that almost resembles a laugh, 'And there I was, thinking we were all on the same side.' She closes her eyes and bows her head, trying desperately to compose herself. Her next words are spoken softly, 'I lost a good officer yesterday and we should have apprehended the person responsible. The problem is our hands were tied by your operation,' she looks back up to him, 'Please Connor, help me out here.'

Wilks pauses, hoping the fact that losing a police officer in the line of duty will strike a chord. She glances around the large, windowless office. It has more the look of a rich playboy's study with leather bound books lining the walls in old fashioned bookcases, than that of the office of the head of counter intelligence for the United Kingdom. The office itself is set deep within the heart of the modern building that sits awkwardly on the Thames. The warren like maze to find this room and the metal lined walls are to try and make sure that any conversations held within are kept secure from prying ears. She wonders if the room has any internal surveillance, and decides that is probably the case. It is MI6 after all.

'Look, Connor, is there anything you can give me that will assist me and my officers in the investigation, or at least give them hope that we are taking measures to apprehend DI Dawkins killer.'

Harman clasps his hands together on the leather writing pad, almost as if in prayer.

'All I can say, Patricia, is that the order to cancel your operation did not come from my department. Personally I want the same outcome as you, but my superiors have other plans in place.'

'Anti-terrorism?'

He shakes his head.

'National security concerns?'

Again a negative shake and Wilks notices Harman's lips are pressed tightly together.

'Deniable ops?'

There is no response, and that is enough of a response to Wilks. She points a finger upward and tilts her head sideways in a querying manner. Her indication is towards the upper floors where the government sanctioned programs are planned and operated from.

She gets another negative shake of the head. Wilks reverses the direction of her finger, now pointing down to the shadowy underworld of government sponsored but deniable projects. This is an area that has almost no rules and receives no official recognition for its work. Its budget is siphoned from other departments or is produced from its own clandestine, risky and sometimes illegal work.

Wilks has heard the rumours that 'downstairs' has even raised funds through armament sales to terrorist organisations, of course this can never be proved or UK Plc would find itself in a whole world of political pain.

Her worst fears are founded when Harman points his own finger downward and nods. The silent routine also impresses on Wilks that there may be others listening in what should be the most secure building in the capital. For the benefit of any and all listeners, domestic or otherwise, she asks,

'So there is absolutely nothing you can tell me?'

Harman sighs, 'Patricia, we have been friends for a long time and if there was anything else I could tell you, you know I would. I would suggest you speak to the Home Secretary and voice your concerns. She may be able to offer more details of the parties involved and perhaps help you understand who is running this particular operation. Unless you get that approval, then I am afraid my hands are tied.'

Wilks eases herself slowly, almost painfully from her chair, knowing there is nothing to gain from pursuing this line of conversation.

'So justice is truly blind and we are just meant to try and do our jobs with both hands tied behind our backs.' She says this with resignation in her voice.

'You and I both know that we are here to uphold and protect democracy, not practice it,' Harman holds out his hand and Wilks recognises it for the conciliatory gesture he is intending, 'I really do offer my sincerest condolences to you and the Metropolitan Police service for your loss. I truly wish for a speedy and satisfactory conclusion to this terrible case.'

As she leans across the desk to grasp his hand, Wilks replies, 'Thank you Connor. I hope so too.'

She leaves in a much slower manner than her hurried and angry trip over from the new Met offices. She has much to think about before she makes any further decisions.

She's standing alone in the elevator on the way up to her office, when the mobile phone in her pocket breaks her from her dark thoughts.

'This is Wilks.'

'Commissioner, my name is David Warwick. I work in the UK consulate here in Crete, Greece. I'm afraid I have some sad news regarding one of your officers. I'm very sorry to say that according to local police there was an incident two days involving a Mr. Peter Carter in which he lost his life.'

Wilks feels her stomach drop, 'What? Oh God no. What happened?'

'Details are still coming through, but first accounts seem to suggest he may have been shot. There are no suspects in custody and the investigation is already underway to try and piece together the timeline leading up to the event, and who may be involved, including the identity of the woman who was also fatally wounded in the attack'

'Julia,' Wilks says automatically, 'Peter was in Crete to see his fiancée. Her name is Julia. She has family on the island, so does Peter. Has his brother been informed?'

'That's something I don't have any information on. I'm sorry but I can look into it and get back to you. Do you have a surname for Peter's fiancée?'

'Pardalakis, Julia Pardalakis.'

'Thank you. I'll pass that information on to the local police here. The reason I decided to contact you directly is with this being an incident involving a British national, I can ask for assistance from the UK police in the investigation. I already have the permissions from the relevant authorities and would like to offer you and your officers a role in this terrible tragedy.'

'David, thank you for the offer. I need to get back to my office and brief my international crimes team about the situation. Can I use this number to contact you?'

'24 hours a day. I will also send you details of what we have so far on the incident and a liaison for your officers to contact directly in the Chania police force.'

The elevator slows to a stop and the doors open with a soft ping. Wilks walks slowly out, trying to hold back tears of sadness and anger.

'David, I'll get back to you within the hour and I thank you again for contacting me.'

'Commissioner Wilks, I'm so sorry it had to be at such a tragic time. I wish to offer you and your fellow officers my deepest condolences on your loss.'

'I offer the full support of the Metropolitan police and we will use every resource to assist the local police in resolving the investigation as soon as possible. You have my word.'

She terminates the call before the tremor in her voice becomes noticeable.

44

I see no point in arguing with Dimitri or telling any further lies, so I decide to let him know exactly what has happened over the last few days. After all, what's the worst thing that could happen now?

His reaction is not what I expect. He nods, smiles and reaches out, turns the key and starts the engine.

'Ok dead man, let's get you to Souda Bay. You may find it difficult to believe but my brother had similar problems.'

My look of disbelief sets a huge grin on his face and he gives me a none to subtle wink.

'Just joking, my friend. I have to tell you that you, out of all the people I have known in trouble, you my friend are in a world of shit.'

As he manoeuvres the car with the finesse of a house brick to the face into the traffic, the screeching of tyres and wail of horns almost hides my reply.

'Thanks for the support.' It may sound curt but inwardly I am breathing a huge sigh of relief at his reaction. The relief is short lived as we hurtle through the narrow streets of Chania barely avoiding pedestrians in the car lined streets of this pretty, yet overcrowded little city.

As the streets open up into a long, straight road full of car dealerships and agricultural shops I actually begin to relax a little. At least we now have two lanes of traffic, but drivers seem to think there are four as all sizes of vehicles weave and overtake with apparent disdain for the rules of the road.

We skirt the harbour of Souda and the December sun glints innocently off the sea causing a kaleidoscope of colours against the dust speckled windscreen.

An ANEK Lines ferry, its engines rumbling noisily, is making its way out from the large berth against the docks and moving slowly out towards the open sea. I notice a few military vessels further along the coast, their drab grey colours standing out against the browns and greens of the landscape they are resting near. Dimitri, watching me says,

'British ships. They come here from their patrols very often. Good money for the bars and keeps the brothels busy too. You English are better behaved than the Americans and you have more money to spend than the Greeks. That is why we love them.'

We pass a couple of busy beachfront tavernas and the smell of cooking meat fills the car. My stomach rumbles involuntarily and noisily.

'We are almost here,' Dimitri points ahead to a small sign that states *Allied War Cemetery – Souda Bay*. 'You will find a small periptero, a kiosk, where you can buy some food. Nothing much but I'm sure it has sandwiches and drinks for tourists.'

We turn right at the sign and follow a narrow, tree lined road for a few hundred yards. After the larger streets of the last few moments I suddenly feel hemmed in. The overhanging branches are full of olives and the road surface is greasy from the windfalls that have been crushed by passing traffic. Without indication, Dimitri makes a right turn and I find myself staring out of the front window at the vista of Souda Bay spread out before me.

A tall, white monolith stands proudly at the centre of this view. Atop it is a large cross that towers above the pale headstones that are laid out neatly in blocks and rows. Beyond this scene is the open mouth of the bay with the steep hills rising up on either side of this strangely peaceful little parcel of land. After feeling constricted in the lane outside, this view helps me breathe a little easier.

Dimitri brings the car to a halt in the shade of a huge olive tree that has been left to grow in the centre of the parking area as a form of natural roundabout. He turns off the engine and turns to look at me.

'It is not much for me to say but I wish you good luck for what comes. I thank you for your honesty with me and I know you have much to do and much to avenge, and for a Cretan, vengeance is a thing to respect and to nurture. I know you will not be returning to my hotel, and I hope to never see you again until your journey out of this darkness is complete.'

I don't know how to reply so I reach for my wallet to pay him for my safe delivery. As I try to do so he leans over and grasps my hands in his.

'For now you will forget me as I will forget you. We never met and I have never seen you, but if you return you will be my brother for your path is a difficult one to take.' He releases his grip, 'Now go my friend and meet your destiny.'

With these words he leans over me and with an almost intimate touch, releases the door catch. He pushes the door gently and it swings open.

'But I need to pay you.'

'You have paid enough and you will need it, and more, where you are going. Kalo taxidi file mou.'

I get out and close the door behind me. I don't even have time to thank him before the car engine roars into life and he drives off with a squeal of rubber on tarmac. All I am left with as he disappears around the corner is the dirty taste of exhaust fumes in my mouth.

I have never felt more alone.

Here I am surrounded by the dead of the past and I wonder what the future holds for me. Will I end up like these poor souls; like Paul, Ann and JD?

I walk slowly into the cemetery, lost in my thoughts. Masterson is nowhere to be seen as I walk through the low, wrought iron gates. My stomach rumbles again and I look back towards the car park and only now notice a caravan with a faded sign advertising cold drinks and snacks. But it is boarded up and closed so I will get no respite for my hunger there.

I step off the flagstone path onto the well kept and strangely sponge like grass. Now I am amongst the gravestones I notice there are hundreds, if not thousands of them all lined up in an orderly, regimented fashion. Amongst the individual headstones are groups of three, four and more. I wander over to one group to see what makes these different from the others, why these men have some special status compared to the others. The names and ranks of the young soldiers, sailors and airmen stare back at me indifferently from their delicately carved inscriptions. I stop in front of five markers all closely packed together, their grey stone sides touching each other, creating a bond between them. Each is that of a member of aircrew who were all on the same bomber that was lost over Crete in 1941. None are over the age of 30 and I shake my head at this waste of young lives.

As I turn from this far corner, my eyes are drawn across the countless number of similar graves and my emotions come crushing out. I feel wetness in my eyes at the loss, not just of these poor souls, but for my family, my friends, my lover. As I stand here fighting back the tears I feel another emotion rise inside me; anger.

It is then I notice Masterson walking towards me from the far corner of the site. His slow gait matches my mood, and the blazing dark purple and deep red colours of the tall shrubs behind him that line the boundary of the cemetery also coincides with my bruised emotions.

I walk purposefully towards him knowing he is the only one who can help me.

45

'Could you come with me please?'
Luke is not surprised to hear the voice. What surprises him is
how quickly the owner of it, and the large man next to the
speaker arrived.
'I'm just in the middle of some routine maintenance,' Luke
answers as he peers with feigned intensity at the screens before
him.   'Can   you   just   give   me...'
'Stop what you're doing right now. I won't ask again. Take your
hands away from the keyboard and stand up.' The soft tone
doesn't   hide   the   menace   in   the   words.
Luke pushes his chair slowly away from the desk and as
instructed, stands up. Now, taking his first proper look at the two
men who are stood in front of him, he realises he may be in a lot
of trouble. He also sees two uniformed officers at the door to the
pod, trying to look menacing.
'May I ask why you need me?
'Matters of national security.'
'And who are you exactly?' Luke is amazed at how calm he is,
but knows that by stalling these goons he is giving Kate a better
chance to get to the Commissioner with their information.
'We're the people who are here to take you where you need to be.
Don't worry; it's just down the hall. There's a few questions that
need answering and your name came up on our list.'
'Right, OK. I'll just log out,' Luke leans forward but his hands
don't reach the keyboard. For two large men they move
deceptively quickly. Luke is pulled away by his collar, which lets
out a loud ripping sound as he is spun around, and deposited on
the floor in an untidy heap. His head knocks against the hard
plastic of the chair support and he sees stars for a second or two.
When he recovers his hands have been secured in front of him by
plasticuffs. The hard plastic edges are digging painfully into his

wrists and he can already feel the circulation being constricted as his fingertips are starting to feel tingly and slightly numb.

'You two, no one in or out of this room until you receive orders from me. Got it?'

The two uniformed officers nod their heads as Luke is manhandled to his feet and half dragged, half frog-marched out of the pod. As he is led away the gentle hiss of the door closing is the only sound in the computer room. In the dim light all heads have turned to stare as one of their own is taken away by these official intruders into their domain.

It takes a few moments after the three men leave the area that people start to get back to their work. One or two look at each other warily, but no-one wants to be the first to speak out about the events that have just unfolded in front of them.

It's one of the uniforms at the now sealed door of the pod that breaks the silence.

'Fuck me.'

*

The very same words are running through Luke's mind as he is taken to the elevator. He is running through his last few moments at the terminal and wondering if he has done enough to cover their tracks. He knows they, and he thinks, he hopes, 'they' are MI6, will be able to see his logon and the searches, but he's sure that he's erased any proof of Kate's involvement and the print-outs and the hard copies made on Ewelina's history. He knows his only hope is that Kate manages to get to Wilks before someone speaks up on the fact that two people were in the pod when the searches were being conducted.

'What would MI6 want with a data analyst like me?' he asks as the doors close shut.

'We're not MI6,' says the man that until now has stayed silent. He gets a glare from his partner that is changed to a look of disgust and a shake of the head.

Luke flicks his eyes between the two. He sees no sign of any passes; visitor or permanent. There are no badges of rank or name tags on either of his captors. They are not quite 'men in black', but they come damn close to being so. If they were wearing dark glasses they could possibly pull it off, he thinks.

He also wishes they would pull out some kind of magic wand and make him forget the last 48 hours.But that's just fiction from a movie.

And he knows it...

46

Masterson smiles as he looks at me. All I want to do is wipe that grin off his face. Does he realise the sacrifices I have made to be here? The brutal murders of my brother, and on/off lover, only a few hours ago?

I look at him and see only my own brutal past. It takes all of my strength and imagination to see that that this squat, taut figure could hold the key to my future. As he comes closer I realise his smile is not that of condescension. His eyes actually show a genuine sign of consoling me.

'Peter, I'm so sorry,' he says.

I want to punch him until my fists are bloody pulps...but I wait; my hands clenched by sides.

I want to know...I want to realise just what the fuck is going on as I stand here on this barren, forgotten soil of the sanctuary that is the Allied War Cemetery at Souda Bay.

Before I can say or do anything else, he hugs me.

'Pete, I know your pain. I know you've lost people close to you and I know you want to make those responsible pay.'

There's a pause and the embrace seems to last an eternity. I want to throw him off and expose his actions to the world. I wait as he talks softly into my ear.

'But I also know you want justice. You want to bring those responsible for what has happened to a swift and proper execution.'

With his arms wrapped around me I don't know how to react. His words make sense, but how do I know that what Masterson says can make any effect on my outcome?

I say the only thing I can under the circumstances, 'Get the fuck off me.' And I push him away.

My head is in turmoil. Here I am in a foreign country, my life is in total pieces, and this wanker wants to hug me for whatever reason he sees fit. Does he think I need reassurance? Does he need to give me help... well OK, yes I need his help, but the hug was just a step too far.

'I've lost people too.' He says without emotion.

It's his face that breaks my barriers. In his weary expression I see a reflection in my own eyes, but it's his eyes that stop my anger.

I recall a drug dealer from many years ago. We had been after this guy for so many years that we thought we would never catch him because he was always so careful. Then one day he came to us.

His wife had been abducted from their house by a rival dealer. He thought it was all an elaborate plan to get him to turn over a prime bit of turf. He thought he was the king of the area, until they sent his wife's two thumbs in the post with a warning that the next two body parts would be her breasts.

That's when he came to us, and that's the look I see in Masterson's eyes. It's a look without hope, without any form of redemption.

I take a small breath when I realise it is a look I have seen in the mirror from my own face since the shooting at the harbour.

'Peter,' he says urgently, before taking a breath and speaking more calmly, 'Pete, I've got a flight booked for the two of us that is bound for the UK. It leaves the military side of the airfield in about an hour. At the moment you're on that flight with me because I need you when we get back to London. I know you have a lot to process, but I need to know you're aware I'm on your side and want to help.'

As I look at Masterson with a numb face I realise that he is the only option I have. He knows I'm still alive and is willing to take me with him back to the UK. In my eyes that makes him almost trustworthy.

But I also know his past.

'Look Masterson, I've taken everything you've said so far on trust. I've seen my,' I catch my breath for a second, 'I've seen my brother dead on the street along with a woman who should have been having a simple meeting, I've just found out my best friend and colleague has been murdered , and my sister is hospital after being released from a murder charge for fuck's sake. Now, as far as I know, everyone is in this position because of me. What if I hand myself in and say enough's enough. I'll go to the local police station and await the outcome of whatever they want to do.'

'Jesus, are you really that naive? I thought we had an understanding. The people that came after Angie and me, they're the same people that want to see you removed. And when I say removed, I mean, never to be seen again on this planet. Do you understand?'

I take a deep breath and nod my head. I know what's going on; I just choose to ignore it.

'So what's the plan?' I ask.

*

Twenty minutes later I'm sat in the back of the largest Royal Air Force aircraft I have ever seen. Through the centre of the fuselage are rows of seats that are fully laden with young men in camouflage uniforms. I'm sat at the right rear of the immense, cavernous interior and I notice Masterson feels right at home. He's walking amongst the aisles, swapping a bottle of fruit juice for a sandwich from the white cardboard box we've all been given on entry to the aircraft. He stops next to a guy with a red arm band on his upper left arm. After a few moments of conversation I watch as they both stand up and head towards a plywood crate close to where I'm sitting. I catch the briefest of their conversation.

'...Taff said you wouldn't need a...' the engines start their high pitched whine and I try to lip-read the rest of the conversation.

'...well in that case, send the glocks back and...'

'...only four cases of ammunition...'

'...ditch the copper and...'

I'm just about to unbuckle my seatbelt at this when I see Masterson shake his head,

'I need him.'

The two then proceed to the front of the plane where they climb a short ladder to the flight deck. It's only a few short steps but the uniformed serviceman at the bottom of the ladder puts paid to any ideas I have about following them.

The rest of the flight passes in relative peace, apart from the fight between the troops on board the aircraft. It seems to be about who should find the best spot on the cargo netting that covers the multitude of boxes at the rear of the aircraft. As soon as the voices lower to a level less than that of a busy city street, I fall asleep.

47

As Wilks reaches the corridor to her office back in the relative tranquillity of the upper floors of New Scotland Yard, she notices Kate waiting for her. She lets out an angry breath.

'Kate, I really don't have the time to see you just at the moment. There is an ongoing operation that requires my full attention. Please schedule a meeting with...'

Kate interrupts her,

'Would this operation be anything to do with a certain Polish woman?'

Wilks pauses.

'I can't comment on any live operation with a civilian.'

Kate holds out the papers in her hands almost reverently, 'You may want to take a look at these and ask yourself why your live operation is now dead.'

'How do you know about...' Wilks catches herself before continuing further. It only takes a second of thought before her response. 'You'd better come into my office.'

*

Sitting at her desk, which apart from three chairs, is the only furniture left in her office in preparation for the move to the new building, Wilks has the loose bundle of papers in front of her. She has only scanned through four or five pages but she's already seen enough.

'Who else knows about this?'

'Luke and I found this information only a few hours ago. We had just started to print these when someone started to erase everything from the servers.'

'Erase? Why would anyone do that?' Wilks' eyes drift to the right as her thoughts contemplate the consequences of what she is being told. 'Where is Luke now?'

Kate shakes her head, 'He stayed in the Pod to try and remove any traces of what we were looking at. He looked scared when I left him.'

Wilks gathers the papers together and puts them in her desk drawer. She locks it and stands up.

'He has full reason to be if it's who I think is behind this. I'm also starting to wonder if this has something to do with Peter's death. Come on, we're going to find Luke and get some answers.'

Kate looks incredulously at Wilks.

'Don't you mean JD's death?'

'Oh damn, I'm sorry Kate. I can't believe how quickly the events of the last few days have been unfolding.' She draws a deep breath before continuing, 'Peter Carter has been killed in Crete. I've no further information or details, but it appears he was shot.'

'Oh my God!'

'It's a shock, but from what I've seen today it could all be related and that means that Luke may need to brought in for his own protection.'

Kate nods her head to the desk, 'Are the papers safe there?'

Wilks lets out a dry smile that seems more like a grimace, 'They're in the office of the Commissioner of the Metropolitan Police Force in one of the most secure buildings in the city. I don't think they could be any more secure, do you?'

'Of course Commissioner, I'm sorry. It's just there's so much going on I don't know what to think anymore.'

'Look, Kate. You and Luke may have stumbled onto something that goes above even my pay grade. I have some ideas about the situation and I hope to God I'm thinking correctly, but this is a very delicate matter. A matter that involves, MI6, national security and departments we aren't meant to know about who follow a very blurred set of regulations. But trust me when I say that I'm going to get to the bottom of this and ensure that justice is brought down on those who deserve it.'

'Are we in any danger?'

'Not on my watch, I promise you. But we have to get to Luke before anybody else gets to him first. I won't have anyone in my building being picked up and carted off who knows where for an illegal interrogation...or worse.'

Kate stares at the Commissioner for a few moments with an incredulous look on her face.

'But you're the head of the highest and most respected police department in the UK, surely...'

'Kate, there are other departments and secretariats far above me. I and my colleagues look after the relatively small scale area of the metropolitan city of London. What we are dealing with here are those government departments which are responsible for the security of the United Kingdom. But saying that, I'll not let one of my most trusted employees take the fall for investigations I should have condoned. I hope, Kate, you take note of the fact that this is an investigation I should have been made aware of!'

'Ma'am I came here as soon as was possible with the information that Luke...'

'I have to interrupt you again, why were you conducting this investigation and who authorised it?'

Kate says nothing as her mind races. Should she reveal the talks and discussions she has had with Graham?

She decides to say nothing.

'Right, in that case,' says Wilks, 'you're coming with me to see if we can get some answers. You can drive us to Vauxhall Cross; we're going to rattle some cages with MI6.'

48

I smell the rain and the dampness from the uncomfortable position I find myself in. This is before I am fully awake, but it's the taste and aromas of England, and I have to say it's a refreshing way to wake up. I'm still not completely aware of where I am, yet somehow that makes me feel more alert to my surroundings.

The rear door of the cargo plane is fully down and I see the airport buildings to one side from my strapped in cargo seat. The uniformed men and women from the flight are being directed into a narrow doorway, but I notice Stuart is talking to a Military Policeman with a vicious looking German Shepherd held by a thick cord leash, off to one side. They shake hands and he starts walking back to the aircraft.

'C'mon Peter, we don't have time to spare.' He says to me.

Picking up a few black holdalls, he grabs my hand and almost physically drags me from the cavernous cargo bay. The MP we are following allows us to bypass the queuing troops, who all look ecstatic to be standing in the rain on a drab airfield, and takes us into the building by a small side door.

We pause at a door next to a security booth, where more military police personnel are watching CCTV feeds, and x-ray images of bags and holdalls.

They all look bored and only one woman looks across at us with a questioning look on her face.

Our friendly MP says, 'VIP's boss. Gonna get them through to transit before the mob make it too busy and I need to get Jake here into arrivals as well.'

Behind the booth the woman leans over and presses a small button on her desk. There is a buzzing sound and our door is pushed open.

Large plate glass windows frame the large, open area beyond the door and the MP points to the wide double doors.

'That way for vehicles and transit accommodation turn left for the jump school and you'll find who you're looking for there.' He reaches across and shakes Masterson's hand, 'Good luck sir and it's great to see you again.'

'You too, and it's good to see you staying out of trouble.'

Masterson hands me a holdall as we exit the terminal, a moment before a surge of people start pouring in through the doors.

'What was all that about?' I ask him as we walk away in the light drizzle.

'We got lucky there. I met that kid a few years back on an operation in Helmand Province. He and his section were looking after a few contractors when they got in a bit of bother. Myself and a few guys helped them out.' He pauses his speech but doesn't break stride, 'Unfortunately not all of them made it.'

We continue on in silence and I take the time to take in my surroundings. The red brick buildings and open spaces remind me of my time at the police training college at Hendon. The utilitarian facade hides the thousands of people working within, and I know that it's only at lunch and the end of the working day that the empty roads will become filled with people.

We pass a training ground where around 50 men and women are being put through a series of sprints and other exercises. Normally you would expect a range of garishly coloured clothing, but of course this is the military.

Each one is wearing identical black shorts, light blue V-neck t-shirt, knee high white socks and silver coloured trainers.

It's like watching blue worker ants as they work around their nest.

I shift the heavy holdall from hand to the other.

Masterson points ahead to a triple story building that looks incredibly large.

'That's us, the parachute training school. There's a guy there who'll get us to London and set up the meet.'

'I'm still a little worried about that. You've not told me just what it is you're hoping to achieve and who it is we're meeting.'

'Well, first off, there's no we at this meeting. You're going to contact your boss and get set up with protection while I go and sort out this mess. One way or the other.'

I stop and put the holdall down on the damp pavement.

'From what you've been saying about who we're dealing with, what makes you think the Met can protect me?'

Masterson stops and faces me.

'It'll only be for a few days. That should be all the time I need to square things away.' He smiles tightly, 'I can be very persuasive when needs be.' He turns away and starts walking, 'Come on, I need a cuppa.'

*

I'm sitting at a stained formica table in an area like something from a sixties TV show about bad places to eat and drink in the UK. The surroundings are bare walls and concrete with a smell of desperation in the air.

'This is the UK's premier school for military parachuting.' Masterson explains as he sits opposite me. His hot cup of tea matches my coffee with the small air currents of white steam that dance in the air between us.

'I remember coming through here quite a few years back. Nothing changes, even the crap tea bar.'

I sip the scalding liquid slowly as I try to think. My exhaustion is hitting me hard as we sit in the warmth of the empty room. Around us I hear the murmurs and calls from the training rooms, but nothing registers.

'Why do you want me to call the Met? Do you think they can help us?'

Masterson sips from his Styrofoam cup before answering.

'Mate, nothing can help us until I sort out a few details. The only reason I want you back in the fold is to ensure your safety. Once people know the hit in Crete went south and involved your brother instead of you...well, you might have a chance. I need to speak to a few people after you're declared alive to ensure there will be no more attempts on your life.'

'For fucks sake. What have I done that's made myself, my family and others a target? Is Julia in danger?'

'She has nothing to do with this, and I hate to say that it seems your brother and the journalist, Ann was it, have nothing to do with this either. They were unfortunately in the wrong place at the wrong time. I know it's no consolation, but the only people to blame are the ones I want to bring to justice.'

'How can I help?'

'Go back to your boss, explain what's happened and wait for me to contact you. What I have to do isn't something I want the police involved in.'

I take another small sip of foul tasting coffee.

'Are you going to look for justice?' I ask, looking at him over the top of my cup.

'Only in the biblical sense. And you don't want to be involved in that.'

With everything that's occurred over the last few days I can only nod my head in agreement.

Masterson slides a mobile phone across the table.

'To save your career and to save your life, ring your boss.'

I push the foul coffee to one side and pick up the phone.

My only hope is that Commissioner Wilks will answer it.

49

'When was the information compromised?

Which agency ran the searches and what information did they find before we were aware of their intrusion into the system?'

Jim Groark is barking these questions at the young brunette woman who only moments before had brought him the news of the security breach.

'Sir,' she replies calmly, 'we have already apprehended the person responsible and ops are bringing him in for questioning now. Any sensitive material has been recovered or removed from the system and this department's involvement remains deniable.'

Christ, she thinks, why is it the men who are always so excitable? 'The information requests were not through an external source, but it appears to be from the Met. They've been conducting an investigation into our asset and this was an unauthorised response from one of their IT techs.'

'I was informed the investigation had been shut down.'

'That's correct sir, but it appears that not everyone was following orders.'

Groark leans back in his chair, 'So we have a rogue tech who has taken it upon himself to hack into our servers and access our information.' His pause is not for dramatic effect, although that is how it comes across. 'I want him destroyed.'

The brunette raises her eyebrows at such a direct request. Groark lets out a small laugh at her expression.

'I mean destroyed as in never to be able to work again, his financial records wiped, bank accounts frozen. Whatever you need to do, just do it.'

'Yes, sir'

Her response is automatic yet she knows that the request is far from routine for a UK national. Already her mind is working on which departments need to be involved, especially as the target is a member of the Met Police's team...albeit a civilian.

'Sir?' she asks, 'Can I ask for an operational clearance certificate on this request please?'

The man opposite gives her a withering look before replying curtly.

'Just get it fucking done.'

As the door is closing behind her, Groark is already picking up the phone and dialling numbers rapidly. The phone rings once before being picked up without a word being said by the recipient. Groark waits half a second, listening to the breathing of the person on the other end of the line.

'We have a problem that needs to be addressed immediately. An asset of ours has become a nuisance to Op Hawkwind and has to be let go. The Polish girl is to be given early retirement from our service with a suitable severance package.'

There is silence for a second or two before a deep voice with a Scottish accent replies,

'I'll start on the paperwork straight away. Do you require notification of redundancy?'

'That won't be necessary, just let me know when it's done.'

Groark receives no answer before the line goes dead.

He puts his own phone down on the table in front of him and rubs his temples softly, as if doing so will somehow relieve his problems.

50

Luke sits in a metal chair that's bolted to the ground. His wrists are handcuffed to the thin, yet strong arms of the chair and the only other furniture in the area is a basic metal table and two chairs that sit opposite him.

He looks across at the wide mirror that encompasses the wall opposite his seat and waits. He knows his movements are being watched and possibly recorded. He just wishes he knew by whom.

Breathing slowly and deeply he tries to relax his body, but his mind is working overtime.

Who was it that shut down the search for Ewelina and why is he being held? Also what the hell are they going to ask him?

Fuck me, he thinks, what the hell have I got myself into? His mind drifts and he wonders if Kate has managed to contact the commissioner. If she has and the goons behind the window know, what would be their next move?

As he's still pondering different scenarios in his mind, the door is flung open and a man and a woman enter the room.

'Luke, how are you doing mate? Can I take these cuffs off you as there seems to have been a huge mistake this morning.'

The woman closes the door behind them as this is being said.

'Please do. I was just at work running routine checks about operations when I was dragged out. I really have no idea what the hell is going on.'

'Yeah no problem,' the man says, dropping the keys on the table between them, 'but I need to know who authorised your routine checks and why was it based on that particular subject of your search?'

Luke looks between the man and woman in the room.

'Do I need to have a lawyer present and is this under caution?'

'Luke,' the woman says softly, 'why would you need a lawyer unless you've done something wrong? Besides, you said you were working on routine checks. All we want to know is why and who for.'

'So I'm not under arrest or detained?'

'No of course not.'

'Then let me out and allow me to leave.'

'Sorry, Luke. We can't do that. You see the information you accessed is classified way above your pay scale. You're not being detained or arrested, but you are being held for questioning under the anti-terrorism act. This means we can hold you here, in whatever way we deem acceptable for up to 28 days.'

The man slowly slides the keys back across the table towards him. There's a small screech of metal against metal that accentuates his words.

'That also means you have no recourse to contact anyone in the outside world unless we deem it fit. Do you understand the predicament you're in here, Luke?'

Luke nods his head slowly.

'Yeah I do. It means I'm not going to find out who wins the final of Love Island.'

The man lets out a small laugh.

'I fuckin' love comedians, especially when they stop telling jokes and start crying...start spilling every little secret about their sad, little lives Normally it takes a whole lot less than 28 days.'

He picks up the keys and nods his head towards the woman in the room.

'Turn off the lights, no food, no water, no comfort breaks for 24 hours, and let's see if he wants to talk after that.'

She nods sternly, opens the door and walks out. The man follows and moments later the light goes out leaving Luke in complete and utter darkness.

'Oh shit.' He mutters under his breath.

The words are clearly picked up by the microphones around the room.

52

My call is answered on the third ring by a questioning Wilks.

'Who is this and why have you got Peter Carter's phone?' She has stopped mid-stride in the cavernous hallway of the SIS Building, the home of MI6. Kate is aware of the strange looks they're getting from the always cautious security staff.

'Ma'am, it's me, Peter. I can't go into too much detail over the phone, but there's been a mistake over the reports of my death. It was my brother... and Ann, that were murdered in Crete. I need your help.'

The line is silent as Wilks takes in what she has just heard.

'Ma'am, are you still there?' I ask, more for something to say than for any other reason.

'Peter! My God, it's such a relief,' she stutters momentarily wrong footed by the news, 'I mean I am obviously so sorry to hear about your brother, but with DI Dawkins' murder and the ongoing cock-ups with the investigation...What happened, how are you?'

'To be fair boss, I'd prefer to talk it through with you during a face to face.'

'Yes, of course, I understand. Are you still in Crete? Where are you?'

'It's better if I don't tell you that as I don't know if this line has been compromised. I'll be back in London sometime over the next 24 hours and I'll call again from a different phone,' I see Masterson nodding his head in agreement, 'but I need you to understand that I think I may have been caught up in something that relates to the TSI activity and who was orchestrating those events.'

Wilks' eyes narrow as three security guards detach themselves from their post at the entrance and start walking towards her and Kate. One of them, a female, is speaking into a small microphone on her wrist. Her mind is racing as she starts to mentally fill in the pieces of the jigsaw puzzle she is faced with.

'Peter, I believe you're not the only one being manoeuvred by others. If what I'm thinking is correct, this is all linked in with something Luke found out, and also a reason for JD's death.'

'I can't believe I'm hearing this. Am I just a pawn in someone's game? JD is dead...my brother is dead...Ann is dead. Why?' As my voice rises Masterson walks towards me to find out the reason for my increasing anger.

'Peter, I'm sorry. It's only now just beginning to make sense. Look, if you're in the UK I can send someone to pick you up and bring you to me. I'm at Vauxhall House at the moment, looking for answers and I may be some time.' As she says these last words the female member of security approaches her, flanked by the two male officers.

'I'm sorry ma'am, but you'll have to end the call. We've been ordered to take you downstairs.'

Wilks firmly holds up a single finger, like a schoolteacher asking for silence in class.

'Peter, I have to go. I'm passing you over to Kate and she will pick you up, wherever you are.'

Wilks hands the phone over, 'Kate, get Carter and bring him to the Yard. Go to my office and wait for me there.'

I hear Kate come on the line, and she sounds nervous, 'Peter, where are you? Commissioner Wilks is being escorted to somewhere in the MI6 building and we believe they are also holding Luke here.'

I realise she has said this to ensure the security detail knows there are witnesses to their actions.

Masterson is next to me and has heard the last part of the conversation.

'Peter, this could work out for us. We'll take the lift back to London and you then follow everything your boss says. I'll meet you when my part is over in this.'

At this point I have no idea what's going on. Wilks seems to have a bigger picture, but I am in the dark. I realise that Masterson is right. If I get back to London I'll at least be in familiar territory.

'Kate,' I say down the phone, 'I'm at RAF Brize Norton. I'll be waiting for you.'

'I'll be with you in around two hours. I know where it is.'

Kate ends the call and pockets the phone. She watches as Wilks and the security officers wait at the metal detector area for a side door to be unlocked. Wilks looks back over her shoulder, 'Call the Deputy Commissioner and let him know I won't be making the briefing this afternoon. Tell him what's happening here and present him with the file.' A hand is placed on her shoulder and she is gently, but firmly, guided through the barrier and disappears from view.

Kate moves back the way they came and take the elevator to the underground car park. As she pulls out of the non-descript entry and exit point she hands the electronic car tag, which opened two of the four automatic security gates around the car park, to the stern faced guard. Her eyes drift to the rear view mirror and she wonders if she would notice if anyone was tailing her. Kate shakes her head as her eyes focus once more on the busy London traffic.

'Stop being so paranoid.' She tells herself.

The two vehicles that have fallen into place a few cars behind her manage to keep a discrete distance all the way to Brize Norton.

53

'Commissioner Wilks, so pleased to finally meet you.'

Jim Groark stands up from behind his desk and extends his hand. Wilks just stares at him coldly.

'You have one of my staff I believe. A young man by the name of Luke Carter, who was removed from my building a few hours ago. I want him released and I want to know why you have stopped an active investigation into Ewelina Jankowska, and by the way, why is Connor Harman not here and who the hell are you?'

Groark lets his hand drop to his side and he sits back down in his chair. He leans back as if to appraise the police woman in front of him, the chair creaking with the movement. Wilks crosses her arms in front of her, not impressed by the games being played.

'Firstly, Mr Harman, capable as his department is, is not involved in this matter.'

'So you're not MI6?'

Groark continues without registering her question, 'Luke Carter is being questioned over his involvement in actively removing classified information from UK Eyes Only archives. The accusations brought against him range from terror offences to breaching the official secrets act. As for who I am, names are not important, but I have taken over *this* department following the unfortunate demise of my predecessor.' Groark leans forward, resting his elbows on the desk, 'I'm sure you are aware of the implications this could have on Luke's career should he be charged. Also, commissioner, the problems for your own advancement, hell, possibly even being able to draw your pension could become, shall we say complicated. He was, after all, recruited directly by you.'

Wilks takes an angry step forward her hands now in front of her like a boxer and tightly balled up.

'We both know this is bullshit. How can somebody doing their job be classed as terrorism, and both you and I know the CPS will not even consider any charges once I get involved.'

A small red light flashes on the desk between them. Groark leans over and depresses the intercom switch, 'Thank you, please ask her to come in.' He says with a smile. 'You may be the commissioner of police, but I have bigger guns on my side.'

He leans back once more in the creaking chair as the door opens behind Wilks.

'Commisioner Wilks, I'm sure you know the Home Secretary.'

The woman enters the room with a nod to Groark.

'Patricia, I understand how upset you are regarding this incident and...'

'Oh my God! Are you involved in this?'

The Home Secretary sits down in the right hand of the two seats opposite Groark and gestures for Wilks to sit in the other. Wilks dumbly follows suit and sits down; her mind racing with possible scenarios.

'This, commissioner, is a matter of what our friends across the pond love to call homeland security, and your employee has stumbled across a huge area of information that should never be allowed to see the light of day, let alone be in the public domain.'

Groark watches the exchange with amusement.

'And what about the people who have died? Is that just to be swept under the carpet as well?'

Groark cuts in, 'Of course we are all deeply saddened by the deaths of two Metropolitan police officers, especially ones so decorated and...'

'Two officers?' Wilks asks.

'Yes, Carter and Dawkins.' Groarks answers.

Wilks pauses a moment before replying, 'Oh of course, you don't know that DCI Carter is still alive, do you? Plus why would you even mention his name when only DI Dawkins was involved in this investigation?'

Groark looks stunned but has enough of his wits about him to stay quiet. Instead he looks over at the Home Secretary for her support.

'Patricia, I know nothing about a DCI Carter, but I am truly saddened by the death of any Metropolitan police officer.' The home secretary turns briefly to Groark. The steel in her voice is like a physical presence to everyone in the room, 'And I want to promise you that there will be no more deaths involving our brave men and women of the Met because the threat from your suspect has been neutralised...isn't that right Mr Groark.' The last words came out as a statement rather than a question.

'Yes, I have a team working on that now.'

Wilks cannot hide her shock, 'Does that mean you're...'

The Home Secretary interrupts, 'It's perhaps better we don't go into the details of the matter. Let me just say that Miss Jankowska has been dealt with and deported for past crimes in her native Poland. She is no longer a concern for the UK's security services.'

'But I must have justice for the deaths of Zoe Walker and DI Dawkins.'

The Home Secretary nods solemnly, 'And you will be able to pursue this justice once the Polish courts have dealt with her. You may start any paperwork for international extradition which is relevant to your investigations, but your operations concerning her recent activities are to close. There can be no discussion about that, do you understand, commissioner?'

'And what about Luke? When will he be released back to us at the Met?'

The Home Secretary raises her eyebrows at Groark. He takes the not so subtle hint and leans forward to talk into the intercom.

'Get the young man out of the interrogation rooms and take him to the lobby. Commissioner Wilks will be there momentarily for the transfer from our custidy.' He says curtly.

'Yes sir,' is the tinny response, 'and should I continue with his financial...'

Groark hits the transmit switch angrily, 'Stop all processing and investigations. Just have him taken there immediately.' He looks up at Wilks's angry face, 'You may leave now commissioner.'

Wilks looks between the two of them with barely disguised contempt.

'You two deserve each other. I will not be complicit in this matter and I will be taking it further.'

The Home Secretary offers a sickly smile, 'And just who will you complain to my dear? I am the head of your organisation and what I say, goes. I'm not sure even if you took your complaints to the PM you would get very far. He is, after all, the man who held this position before me...the man who briefed me on all operations and responsibilities this position must be aware of.'

Wilks knows in her heart she's been out manoeuvred, but hopes to see some swift justice brought down on these two people in the office with her. She bites her tongue, rises from her chair and heads for the door.

Groark has to have one last dig before she leaves.

'Your man is lucky, Wilks. Whatever he was looking at, well, how can we charge him with breaking the official secrets act when there's no longer any information to be found. If there's no evidence, there' can be no crime. As for Carter, if what you say is true, tell him I'm sorry about his girlfriend.'

The Home Secretary shoots Groark a withering glare, which he just smiles benignly at. Wilks hesitates at the heavy wooden door a fraction of a second. The room is silent as she contemplates what she wants to say, and the others wait intently for her outburst. The moment passes and she pulls open the door and steps out. Wilks doesn't even give them the satisfaction of slamming the door behind her, instead she just leaves it open as she walks away to find Luke. The security detail that brought her to this office, fall in line beside her to ensure she makes no detours on her back.

54

It starts to rain softly as Masterson and I wait outside the main gates of RAF Brize Norton. After finishing our terrible coffee, it takes us just under 40 minutes to walk from the hangar to the exit through the vast grounds of this military airfield. The two guards manning the gates have moved inside a small hut, which sits between the barriers, to get out of the rain. I watch silently as Masterson shifts his black duffle bag over one shoulder.

'C'mon Peter. There's a garage just down the road where we can grab a hot drink and get out of the rain. Text your driver and tell her we'll be there. She should only be about 20 minutes out.' With that he moves off, away from the curious glances of the camp's guards.

I follow him, texting Kate the new pick-up point as I walk. It's only about 200 meters away from the entrance, and the bright lights cut through the winter's afternoon gloom. Inside there are a few tall, round tables next to an automatic hot drinks machine. I slip in the required coins and press the buttons. Cars go by in a blur of mist and hissing tyres as the rain increases. My drink is made and I look at the contents to find something that is almost something like tea...almost. I hand it to Masterson; my stomach has had enough of crap tea.

'What are you going to do when this is all over?' I ask him as he sips at the hot liquid.

'I'm not sure there is an after for me with this one.' Masterson says thoughtfully. He scratches absent mindedly at the healing wound on his arm. 'I think I may have burned my bridges one last time, and if not, what I am about to do will definitely see me watching my back for the next few decades.'

'Then why do it?' I ask, 'Why put yourself through the torment?'

He stops staring into his tea and looks me straight in the eye, 'Because they made it personal. Because they took from me the one thing I've loved in a long, long time. If they had decided to come after me alone, that's fine. That's business. But...' His voice trails off as his eyes drift out of focus to look at something, or someone only he can see.

My mobile chirrups away to tell me I have text message. I glance down at it,' She's five minutes away.' I say.

Masterson tosses the two-thirds full cup into the waste bin.

'That tea was shit, let's go.'

Once again I find myself following this dangerous man; a man I know virtually nothing about except his capacity for vengeance and violence. We stand and wait under the forecourt in silence as Kate arrives. She drives up to the pumps and gets out of the car. She smiles grimly at me, not even noticing Masterson, 'Can you fill her up, I really need to use the bathroom. I'll only be a second.'

I walk over and grab the petrol pump, push the petrol cover on the car to release it, and unscrew the filler cap. I push the nozzle in and depress the cold lever in my hand. The fumes of petrol get stronger as the fuel rushes into the tank.

'Thanks Peter, I'll pay on the way out.' She pauses awkwardly, 'I'm so sorry about your brother and JD.'

She looks as if she wants to say something else, but I wave her away, 'Go on and use the toilet. The quicker we're back in the London, the quicker I'll feel normal again.'

I see compassion in her eyes, along with something more troubling on her face. It looks to me like guilt, but I don't want to get into whatever she may have on her mind at the moment. I need to find answers to what the hell is going on.

As I fill the tank, Masterson opens the boot, deposits his bag of weapons and slams it closed. He then opens the backdoor, lays down on the seat and closes his eyes. Within seconds it seems as if he's asleep.

A black Porsche Cayenne pulls up at the pump opposite me and I feel the gaze of the two occupants, one male and one female, linger on me for a second too long. I get an uneasy feeling in the pit of my stomach. For an instant I think about tapping on the window to wake Masterson. The woman gets out and smiles at me before heading inside. My stomach unclenches and my butterflies recede as the man gets out and starts putting petrol in his car. He doesn't look at me or even register I'm there. Paranoia is only a problem if there's nobody out to get you, I think to myself.

The pump clicks as the tank is filled and I place the nozzle back in its holder. Looking over to the cashier's window I see Kate standing there with a cup from the drink machine in one hand. She points to the station I'm at and has a quick discussion with the assistant, before handing over her credit card. I get into the passenger seat and wait for her.

She comes out of the shop area and walks slowly to the car, just behind her I see the woman from the Porsche walking back to her car carrying two plastic cartons of sandwiches. I watch Kate's face screw up as she takes a sip from the cup before throwing it into the waste bin next to the petrol pumps. Her hand is on the door handle when she catches sight of Masterson on the back seat. She freezes.

'Who's that?' she asks me through the closed door.

'A friend, I think. Without him I'd still be stuck in the middle of nowhere and wondering what to do.'

Kate looks at me and decides that whatever is going on she's already involved, 'Another person won't make any difference I suppose,' she opens the door and eases herself into the driver's seat, 'Their tea is shit,' she says, starting the car and turning the fans to the screen to clear them of condensation.

I smile as we move slowly out of the petrol station, heading back to London. Heading home.

55

Patricia Wilks, Commissioner of the London Metropolitan police force, is not used to being ordered around. Nor is she used to being kept waiting for over 30 minutes. Her patience is growing extremely thin as she stands next to the metal detecting archways which span the main hall of the MI6 building. Even the three guards that have been with her take a hesitant few steps away from her. They sense her anger and want it to be someone else's problem to deal with. She looks directly at the female security guard, asking softly but firmly 'Where is he and why is this taking so long?'

Her focus of interest stares back impassively, saying nothing. Wilks notices a slight turning of her head and realises she is receiving a radio message from her discrete earpiece. The female guards nods to her two accomplices and they all walk off behind the barriers with a relief that their job here is done.

Wilks scans the lobby and the area beyond the security entrance. A door opens and Luke walks out. He notices Wilks and gives out a huge smile of relief. The man next to him, tall, broad shouldered and in an ill-fitting, single breasted black suit leans inward and says something that stops Luke's smile immediately. Luke glances between his thuggish looking escort and Wilks, and nods his head.

'Let him through,' the man in black says.

Luke steps forward mechanically as the scuffed metal security barrier is opened. Nothing is said between the two of them until they are on the wide white steps of the building. The Thames is moving slowly and murkily in the cold December afternoon and it matches Wilks' mood as they walk along the Albert Embankment towards Lambeth Bridge and Millbank.

'Are you OK Luke? What did they do to you in there?'

'Nothing at all. That's what I can't understand, they put me in a room and left me there until about five minutes ago when they brought me up to you.'

'And what was said when you were let go? I saw that brute say something.'

Luke stops walking and looks out over the muddy Thames river towards the Westminster city buildings. He doesn't face Wilks as he speaks, 'He said they're watching us, he asked if I understood and then said, we'll always be watching you.'

Wilks looks around the riverside pathway. It's not busy but she can sense that some of the people chatting, walking or just sitting on the scattered benches are not as innocent as they look. A taxi cab's horn blares as traffic lights turn from red to green and the car in front of it takes a second longer than necessary to move forward. A few people turn to look at the noise, but a man and woman walking slowly arm in arm look in the opposite direction, towards Luke and Wilks. She feels a shiver go down her spine.

'Come on Luke, let's get back to my office and I'll take a proper look at those printouts of yours.'

'Is that wise?' he asks, turning now to face her.

Wilks bites her bottom lip in deep thought, 'I really don't see what choice we have. I'm not letting this go and if that means upsetting the bastards in MI6, and the incompetents in that building,' she points towards the Houses of Parliament, 'then I'm prepared to do anything it takes.' She pauses and looks back to the man and woman, still arm in arm but now apparently looking at something extremely interesting the dark, muddy waters of the river. 'Even it means losing my job.'

'Well in that case boss, how about a drink first? I don't care if you're on duty, this could be the last time to relax in a while and I for one could do with a stiff drink after the last few hours.'

He gestures to the brightly coloured, 1930's era Dutch barge floating on the Thames. It has a fine view of the Houses of Parliament and best of all, the outside spaces are quiet on this drab afternoon. Wilks considers Luke's proposal for a moment before smiling grimly.

'You're on and you're buying. I'll have a gin and tonic and then we go.' She glances at her watch, 'By the time we finish up and get to the Yard I imagine Kate and Peter will be there too.'

Luke looks shocked, 'But I thought Peter was...'

'So did I until this morning,' she glances back at the couple and wonder if they will follow them in to the bar of Tamesis Dock, 'Come on, I've got a lot to tell you.'

Luke lets her enter the bar area first, this time it's his turn to glance at his watch as he recalls the last words said by his interrogator before releasing him to Wilks.

'Keep her occupied for at least an hour, do that and we'll forget everything.'

*

Forty-five minutes and two gin and tonics later, Wilks has told Luke everything she thinks might be going on. She has also kept a close watch on the entrance and the couple from the embankment have not come in. An old gent with a copy of The Times and an umbrella is the only other customer, but their conversation has been kept low, all the same.

Luke is trying to come to terms with everything as well as keeping an eye on the clock.

'I need another to allow all this to sink in. You?' He asks.

'No, I think two G and T's is enough for any afternoon. We have to go.'

Luke mentally checks off the distance from the Tamesis Dock to New Scotland Yard in his head and estimates it's at least a twenty minute walk.

'Yeah, sure.'

He waves over at the young Eastern European barmaid in thank, as they exit the warm bar, back out into the chilly air. As they walk in silence, side by side, Luke is trying to piece together the theories behind Wilks' words in the bar.

'Boss, if the Home Secretary is involved, does that mean she's taking a cut from the activity?'

'If we can prove that to be true, we can hang her out to dry. If we can also trace the funds back to a government department we are really going to be worrying some high profile people.' She pulls her jacket a little bit tighter around her to stave off the cold, 'We also have to look into the human slavery aspect as well as the international gun running operations. Your and Kate's printouts will give us a good start point, I just don't know who to trust with the investigation. This could go deep into the heart of not just the government and MI6, but MI5 and many different police departments too. I'm not sure I can even trust the deputy Commissioner. I've seen him sucking up to the Home Secretary on many occasions.'

'What about DCI Carter? With the threat on his life, surely he can be trusted?'

'I thought that too, but he could be too close to the situation, with his sister still in hospital and Jankowska now the pin that seems to hold everything together. If we can find her we can bring all this crashing down and get some form of justice for JD.'

Dusk falls quickly in London in December and its dark when they reach the entrance to New Scotland Yard. They make their way up to Wilks' office to find two men in grey overalls struggling to remove her desk through the door to her secretary's area.

'What the hell do you think you're doing?' Wilks thunders.

Standing half in and half out of the room, with the desk on its side in the doorway, the man in the hallway looks slightly shocked to see her.

'We were told to get this down to Southeby's by the morning, Commissioner Wilks. The other team are tasked with bringing the rest of your office materials down tomorrow to your new place on Victoria Embankment. We've been told your move is coming through early because this room is needed.'

Wilks shakes her head angrily and pushes past the removal man to open the drawer which luckily is on the side of the desk outside her office. One glance and she whips her head round, 'Where are my documents that were in here?'

The man points through into her office, 'Everything is in those boxes. Your secretary was placing everything away when we arrived. He said it was alright to take the desk away today.'

'He?' Wilks asks.

'Yeah, big bloke in a black suit. He was already boxing everything up in preparation for the transfer. I think he took a box with him when he left.'

Wilks moves surprisingly fast and Luke smiles involuntarily as she vaults over the desk and into the rooms beyond.

'My secretary is a female sergeant officer,' she says on her way through the doorway.

It's only a few seconds later that they hear her voice shout out.

'Motherfuckers!'

56

The gentle hiss of the tyres on the wet road surface, the warm air from the heater, along with the gentle rocking motion of the car have the not undesired effect of sending me to sleep. So it comes as a shock to hear the irritating ring of a mobile phone penetrating my groggy state.

Kate presses a button on the steering wheel to make the Bluetooth connection through her car stereo. She has already seen the caller ID, but I'm still struggling to ease my aching neck away from its uncomfortable position against the foggy window to see the display.

'I'm almost with you Commissioner. Only about another ten minutes.'

I hear Wilks' voice from the speakers.

'Please tell me you have the printouts from my desk, Kate. Tell me you came here before going off to pick up Carter.'

Both Masterson and I are shocked fully awake on hearing the panic in Wilks' voice.

'Um, uh, no, I uh, I left straight away for Brize Norton.'

'Shit!'

'Boss, what's the matter?' I ask.

'It's all gone. Everything has gone.'

'What has all gone?' I'm mentally kicking myself for not staying awake and questioning Kate over recent events, that plus I am too wrapped up in my own problems to have cared, I realise.

'The printouts. The evidence linking Ewelina to covert and deniable departments within MI6 and their dealings in everything from tobacco smuggling and people trafficking, to much, much more. They've raided my office and taken it all.'

Kate talks rapidly, 'But Luke can get back in the system and find the information, he can...'

'No he can't. It's all been erased. Those were the only copies.'

'I'll testify,' Kate says again, 'We'll testify, me and Luke. We saw the records; you can do something with that, surely?'

'There's no hard evidence to back up your claims...unless we can get Ewelina to talk, and I think that's extremely unlikely as we're not allowed to touch her.'

'So let me get Ewelina, bring her in and get her to tell her side of events.' I say.

We all hear Wilks long sigh over the speaker, 'Peter, you just don't understand what's been happening since you were away. Ewelina is off limits, I've been ordered by the Home Secretary, no less, to leave her well enough alone. The Metropolitan police force cannot touch her.'

I think to what Julie said to me in Crete and my mind is made up.

'Then I quit. Consider this my resignation and I'll get an official letter to you as soon as possible. I am no longer an officer of the Met.'

As I say this I feel a weight lifted from my shoulders, and then my world screeches to a halt as a black Porsche Cayenne pulls dangerously close in front of us and hits its brakes. I have a vague sense of satisfaction that it's the same one from the petrol station before Masterson is thrown through the gap between the front seats, where he had been listening in on the conversation, as Kate slams both feet down on the brake pedal. I feel my body forced into the strapping of the seatbelt and I wait for the crunch of metal on metal that comes with a high speed crash. I notice from the corner of my eye, Kate wrenching the wheel to one side in a vain bid to avoid the looming bulk of the 4x4 vehicle in front of us. Because of the wet roads she only succeeds in turning the car sideways as we aquaplane.

I watch almost as in slow motion the rear of the Porsche burst through my side window, spraying me with safety glass. Masterson gets thrown partly across Kate due to the impact, and then it's over. Silence descends for a brief moment, and only then am I aware of the shouting from outside.

I shake my head to clear the glass away and find I am surprisingly intact. There is a distorted v shaped point on my door that is pressing into my arm, but apart from that, and the shattered window, the car and I, are both relatively undamaged.

I look across to Kate and see her sitting there in shock with Masterson pulling himself rearwards into the back seat. He opens the door and I know he's looking to get his weapons from the boot, but before he can step out of the car, the shouting increases.

'Stop right there! Let me see your hands.'

The authority in the voice gives him no choice. It's an authority that comes from the owner of it having an extremely nasty looking pistol in his hands. Masterson dejectedly raises his hands above the rim of the open door. The rain is slowly staining the sleeves of his jacket a darker colour as it soaks into the exposed material.

'You in the back, exit the vehicle slowly, keeping your arms clear of your body at all times. Take three steps away from the vehicle and lie face down. I am authorised to use force and will have no hesitation in doing so. Do you understand?'

Masterson nods his head as he swings his feet out onto the tarmac and stands up, with his hands still raised above his head.

'Driver,' this time it's a female voice giving the instructions, 'turn off the engine and exit the vehicle. Keep your hands visible at all times.'

I hear another voice and struggle to make out the words.

'...going on? Kate, Peter? Are you OK? What's going on?'

It's Wilks through the Bluetooth connection.

'Boss,' I hiss as quietly as I can, 'we've been stopped by two armed personnel, one male, one female, they're getting us out of the vehicle and I'm not sure what's going to happen next. Can you...'

I stop speaking abruptly as the cold metal of a gun barrel is placed against my left temple.

'Please get out of the car, Mr Carter.'

'Peter, what's your location. I'll get an ARU to you immediately.'

With his free hand, the man with gun to my head leans in and hits the power button on the phone which is sitting in its cradle on the dashboard.

'Now, Mr Carter, please join your friends on the floor.'

Kate is sobbing quietly as I lay down next to her.

'Look,' I say, 'whatever this is about concerning me, let these two go. They've got nothing to do with it.'

The sound of a pistol being cocked freezes my blood in my veins. I find my mind drifts away, all fear has gone as I come to the conclusion I am about to do in the rain by the roadside.

Masterson pushes himself up from the ground and launches himself at our attacker, he receives a swift and brutal bash to the head with the butt of the pistol. He falls against him and collapses to the ground in a heap .

'Sorry guys, it's just business. I'll make it quick.'

I close my eyes and wait for oblivion. All I can think of is Julia and how much I want to tell her.

Nothing happens. I hear a phone ring, then urgent whispers that are barely audible over the sound of the blood pounding in my ears. I dare to open my eyes and see a knee pressed into the soft earth next to my head.

'You are one lucky bastard, you know that. Ten more seconds, that's how close you were. Ten fucking seconds.'

I let out a breath I didn't realise I was holding in. The knee shifts slightly as the moisture from the ground seeps into the material.

'Stay here for ten minutes. Don't try to follow us and don't bother to call this in. You've been given a reprieve and my boss is happy to let this be a warning as long as you all forget all about this little accident.' The knee swivels again and I follow the movement to see the pistol is placed against the back of Kate's head. 'You won't get a second chance. Nod if you agree my terms.'

Kate and I both nod in unison, but Masterson is out cold and doesn't move a muscle.

With a squelch, the knee is removed from my vision and I reach out to grab Kate's hand. She is still sobbing, but whether it's from fear or relief I can't tell. We both lie there in the mud and the rain until we hear the Porsche car doors slam shut, the engine rev and it drives off. Masterson groans and slowly pushes himself off the floor. I follow suit and then move to help Kate. She shrugs me off angrily, her tears still flowing, mixing with the rain drops and mud splatter on her face.

The whole incident has probably taken only two or three minutes, yet I feel I've aged ten years.

'Well,' says Masterson, 'it looks like you've just been taken off the shit list.' He rubs his head and checks his fingers for blood, 'Thank fuck they didn't recognise me or things might have ended differently.'

Kate stares malevolently over to him, 'Differently, fucking differently. We could have died here!' Her voice has risen to a shout.

'Yeah love,' he replies, 'That's what would have happened if they'd recognised me.'

He stands up a little unsteady on his feet and shakes his head 'Woah, that was a cheap shot.' He walks to the back of the car and pulls out his duffel bag. 'I think I'd better make my own way to London from here. It'll probably be safer for all of us.'

He walks over to me and holds out his hand, I grab it and he helps me to my feet. He offers a hand to Kate but she ignores it, getting to her feet on her own.

'Yes I think that is for the best,' she spits out before getting in to the car through the open drivers door. It slams shut behind her.

'Did you mean what you said about retirement?' he asks me.

'I think so,' I mutter, running my fingers through my wet hair. 'I just don't know what else to do to end this.'

'You'll know when you know,' Masterson says cryptically, 'I'll be in touch when you do.'

He walks away into the rain and I get back into the passenger seat. The door groans as I pull it shut and I feel glass crunching under me, but I don't care anymore.

'Come on Kate, let's get to Wilks. This isn't over yet.'

57

Jim Groark hangs up the phone and looks over his desk at the Home Secretary.

'It's done. My people are no longer actively engaged with Carter.' His eyes drift along the back wall of the office, taking in the wood panelling and random pictures that came with the office when he moved in a few short weeks ago. He has yet to put his mark on the place. 'Although I think it's a mistake to have called it off. He could become a problem.'

'Leave that to me. I can keep Wilks under control, which means I can keep Carter under control. We'll have no more issues from either of those two.'

'Which brings us back to our major problem. The Polish girl has dropped off the grid.'

'Do you think someone tipped her off?'

'I don't know who could. As far as I'm aware there were only a few people involved in the discussions about her retirement.'

The Home Secretary stands up and walks over to the window. It looks out from its first floor position into a small yard for storing waste bins. She pulls a small gold plated cigarette case from her pocket, opens it and takes one out.

'I'd prefer if you didn't smoke in here.' Groark says.

Her thumb depresses the small silver button and a jet of small blue flame erupts from the top with a subtle whoosh. She lights her cigarette and takes a deep drag before exhaling the smoke against the window pane. It swirls and spreads in a mesmerising pattern

'And I would prefer if you'd managed to have kept your fucking house in order.' She takes another deep drag on the cigarette, causing the tip to glow fiercely in the dim light, 'But neither of us is going to be satisfied today are we?'

Groark bristles at the accusation, 'My predecessor was in charge of this operation and I am just trying to pick up the pieces.'

The Home Secretary turns sharply away from the window, 'Your predecessor was an idiot who got himself killed because he did not understand the implications of his actions. I pray you do not do the same.'

Groark recalls the video of Leahy, the department head before him, being assassinated coldly by Stuart Masterson.

'I've taken care of that problem, on your orders if you remember.'
'Someone has to take responsibility for these things, and you were dithering about what to do next. We needed to make a statement. Just like we need to do with the Polish girl.' She stubs her cigarette out on Groark's desk and leaves the smouldering stub in the ashes. 'Now find her and get rid of her, or do I have to find another candidate for this department's head?'
Groark just stares at the woman as she turns and leaves his office. Only when the door closes behind her does he say anything.
'Bitch.'

58

I'm standing in Wilks' office with Kate and Luke. Kate hasn't said a word since our incident apart from to phone and relay the information to Wilks that we are OK, and were on our way to New Scotland Yard. Wilks is looking around her empty office with an indecipherable look on her face.
'I won't accept your resignation.' She says, finally looking at me.
'It's the only option we have.' I reply, 'I can do this and not bring about any consequences to you or the Met.'
'And what happens when you find her? What will you do then? Make a citizen's arrest? Do you think she'll come quietly...for God's sake, Peter, this woman is armed and especially dangerous. She has already killed JD, probably Zoe Walker as well, and I don't want any more people hurt.'
'Neither do I. This is why I have to do this.'
'There's more to this situation than just finding this woman. There's more than just involves you.' She waves her hand at Luke and Kate. 'If we get this wrong there are consequences...deadly consequences for all of us.'
'Then I won't get it wrong. I'll bring her in and we blow this heap wide open. I want to see everyone involved in this to be exposed and prosecuted to the full extent of the law.'

Luke speaks up, 'We all do Peter, but this is bigger than anything we thought. This goes right to the very top and I can't see what we can do against people like that.'

'Nobody is above the law,' I explode angrily at Luke, 'Nobody.'

'We're not saying they are, Peter,' Wilks says calmly, 'but we must make sure everything is by the book. Any discrepancies and the case falls apart before it's even begun.'

'That's right,' I confirm, 'Which is why you must let me do this without any knowledge to you. You can deny everything until you have a watertight case. You'll be bulletproof,' I look at each in turn, 'all of you.'

'I'm not sure I can go along with this.' Kate looks at me as she speaks. Her face is still smudged with mud and I can see she is at the end of her mental tether. 'I don't think I can be involved after...after,' she is sucking in huge breaths as she fights to hold back tears.

Luke puts his arm around her to comfort her, 'It's OK, it's OK,' he repeats.

Wilks nods her head as she makes a decision.

'Luke, Kate, it's time for you to leave.'

Kate nods her own head and pulls out of Luke's arm. She starts walking towards the door. She pauses to look back at the young man who is standing motionless.

'Are you coming, Luke?' she asks him.

He shakes his head, 'I'm not going anywhere. They need a computer guy to help with this. Maybe the information has been deleted, maybe not. Without me you won't know where to look, what to look for, and more importantly, how to cover your tracks.' He stands up straight and thrusts out his chin in defiance. 'I'm in this to the end.'

Kate's fingers grasp the doorhandle. She looks at us and says simply, 'I'm sorry.' She pulls open the door, exits, and closes it softly behind her.

There is a moment of silence after she leaves which is only broken by Luke as he gazes intently around the empty space, 'Has this room been swept for bugs?'

59

Three days later I'm sitting in a car at six in the morning, around the corner of a small cafe in East London. Luckily the Commissioner's old office hadn't been bugged, but where Luke managed to get his equipment from so quickly kind of disturbed me. He had also swept her new office on Victoria Embankment and found nothing out of the ordinary. I have been in contact with Luke every day since and he has been feeding me information on any sightings of Ewelina. During that fateful meeting it had been decided I wouldn't contact Wilks until I had a positive sighting. As far as the rest of the Met was concerned, I had resigned with immediate effect due to personal reasons. In police speak, this means everyone assumed I had suffered a mental breakdown. An assumption I am happy to keep up if it means I can find Ewelina Jankowska.

So far I hadn't seen anything of her, and this tip off came from an intercepted text message that mentioned her name. Luke couldn't tell me how it was intercepted, or whose phones were involved. All he could say was that she was meant to be in this cafe at seven-thirty this morning. So here I am. Waiting.

The car's demister is working overtime on the back window and I have the blower on low to keep the front and side windows clear. I don't care if the battery runs low, it's not my car. I check my watch for the sixth time in as many minutes; 06:06. I've always hated stakeouts.

There's a knock on the window and I look around expecting to see a traffic warden or curious police constable asking me to either move on, or find out why I'm sitting in a car at this hour of the morning. Instead I'm shocked to see Masterson grinning at me through the passenger window.

'Open the door, it's freezing out here.'

I lean over and flip the handle. He climbs in and starts rubbing his hands together to warm them up.

'How the hell did you know I was here?'

He smiles again at me, 'Who do you think sent that message about Ewelina? She's not here you know.'

'For Christ's sake, why are you sending me on a wild goose chase?'

'Look, Peter, I didn't know for certain you would be on the case after what happened. When I heard you were off the force,'

I interrupt him, 'Who told you that?'

'Well you did resign the other day over the phone, but I had to make sure. I also had to find out who was monitoring the phone systems. There are a lot of dodgy characters about, as we found out last week. Look, do you want to take Ewelina in or not?'

'Of course I do. Without her we have nothing.'

'Good, because I've been tasked with finding her as well. Only the person who wants me to find her, doesn't want her going to the police.'

'Who is this person?'

'It's better you don't know just yet. But don't worry, when the time is right they will be brought to justice for their actions.'

'This is all too cloak and dagger for me. Why can't anyone give clear answers anymore?'

Masterson puts his hand on my shoulder, 'Because there are no clear questions, and right from wrong is not on the agenda for these people. Please just trust me.'

Once again I think, what other options do I have. I nod, 'OK, I'll take your word for it. So, where is she?'

'Dover.'

'Dover?'

'Is there an echo in here? Yes, Dover. But I don't know how long for because she's trying to get to the European mainland, so we had better get a move on. While we drive I'll tell you a little about my last few days.'

I start the car, luckily the battery is good and the engine catches first time. I pull out of my parking space and we head off on the two hour drive to Dover.

'After I left you,' Masterson starts talking as soon as we clear the city, 'I managed to hitch a lift to London.

I wanted to confront the people who had ordered the hit on you, on me and had killed Angie.' He sees I want to ask questions and shakes his head, 'just listen please, Peter.'

He stretches in the passenger seat as far as the seatbelt will allow him, and continues.

'I've done things in my past I'm not happy about. I've been places and seen sights that have hardened me, but the sight of my girl, bleeding out in front of me, made me want answers. And when I say answers, I mean blood.

I thought I'd gotten out of the job I was doing, but the job had other ideas. They sent someone I knew to kill me. That confirmed to me what I already knew, they'd never let me lead a normal life. So I went to the top dog to insist on being left alone, to be able to live a normal life. If that's even possible in this crazy world.

It was easy to get in the building, I had a pass.' He sees my quizzical look, 'Remember when we were stopped and I threw myself at that goon? Well I palmed his pass and pretended to be knocked out. I hope he gets into some serious shit for that.

Anyway, I get inside the building using his pass, it's a place I knew well, after all I worked there didn't I? Bold as brass I enter this bloke's office and sit down at his desk.

Oh Peter, you should have seen his face, he looked like he was caught between shitting his pants and seeing a ghost. I just sat there and waited for him to make the first move. I was hoping he would do something stupid, perhaps try to reach for a weapon at the very least. Instead he surprised me; he sat back down in his chair and just looked at me. We stayed that way for a few long minutes, neither of us saying a word. Just silently studying each other.

He finally broke the silence, 'I thought you were dead, I saw a picture.'

I nodded, 'Yeah, I sent that with Rowlinson's phone.'

His hands moved from the top of his desk and I brought out my silenced pistol, placing it on the desktop between us. He could probably see it was pointing at his heart. His hands slowed in their movement, but didn't stop.

He brought them up to his chin and placed his elbows on the desk, leaning forward.

He had dead eyes, black and featureless, like a sharks. He went silent again, as if considering something. He didn't look scared at this point, I guess he had gotten over the shock. Now he just looked, I don't know, curious.

'Do you want your old job back?' he asked me.

'No,' I replied succinctly.

'You're here to kill me then?'

'Yes.'

'Killing the previous head of this department didn't stop people coming after you, did it?'

'I don't care about that.'

'What if I could stop that from happening? What if you could leave all this behind and disappear to a normal life?'

'Are you bargaining for your life? I thought that was beneath men like you?'

'It is. But I don't recall a non violent end for many people in this job.

Car accidents, train wrecks, light plane crashes, it's all par for the course. What I'm doing is offering you one last project and then you're free from this life. You'll never have to look over your shoulder again.'

'And you get to live?'

'Well, Mr. Masterson, if I'm not around, who is there to oversee that orders don't get misconstrued and a retirement order goes out? I would much rather prefer to be alive to see that doesn't happen to you.'

I tapped my fingers on the pistol and am pleased to see his eyes flicker down to it.

'What's the job?' I asked him.

'I need you to retire someone.'

'I don't do that anymore.'

He smiled, can you believe that, he fucking smiled at me before smoothly saying, 'I think you'll like this one. She's the start of all these problems for everyone.'

I knew then who he was talking about.'

Masterson then turned in the car seat to face me and I already know what he's going to say.

'He wanted me to kill Ewelina Jankowska.'

My hands grip the steering wheel tightly, 'And are you going to do that?'

Masterson lets out a small laugh, 'Bloody hell no. She's too precious to you and the law, that and getting you off the hook for good. Plus you'll be able to finally get some closure.'

'Did you kill him? This man in the ivory tower?' I ask, not sure I want to know the answer.

'No. I accepted the job and got my reprieve in writing.' He holds up a mobile phone, 'He wants a picture from this phone when it's done.'

'But you said you're not going to Kill Ewelina.'

'And I'm not. I've got a written order saying my life can be normal, just like yours. I'm going to use that.'

'But if you don't carry out the job, won't he just countermand that order?'

'He won't get the chance.'

Masterson has a smile which sends a chill down my spine and I'm glad that, for the moment at least, he's on my side.

'OK, uh, where do we find Ewelina and how do you want to play this out?'

'Head for Dover...'

'Yeah, I got that.'

Masterson turns his grim smile to me and I shut up.

'As I was saying, head for Dover and look for the signs for Pencester Gardens. She's staying in a house near there. Now, I'm going to get my head down for an hour. Wake me when we're close.'

With that he adjusts the seat back as far as it will go and within seconds is snoring softly.

I consider calling Wilks to appraise her of the situation, but realise this is something I have to do without her help.

I can't be sure her phone isn't being monitored and anything I say could lead to Ewelina being picked up by the wrong people. I stifle a yawn and turn the heater down from thermonuclear hot to mild frost in an attempt to stay fresh and awake.

The traffic is fairly light to Dover this morning. Mainly goods wagons and the odd small van, probably doing cigarette and booze runs for Christmas. The cooler air in the car does its job and I manage to stay awake for the next two hours until we top the rise to come down into the busy little town.

I reach over and nudge Masterson.

'We're here.' I say as he comes slowly to life and peers outside at the grey mid-morning view. He stretches his head side to side and I hear his bones crack.

'I needed that. Now, park up on the eastern end of Pencester Square and I'll go and get our little problem child.'

'I'm coming with you.' I say a little too loudly.

'Yeah, sure. That's just what she needs, to see a copper coming to take her in. No, I think it's best if I handle this. I can be very persuasive.'

I turn left at the junction and have the square on our right hand side. 'You said you weren't going to harm her.'

'I said, Peter, that I wasn't going to kill her.' His face is turned to mine to gauge my reaction.

'Just get her to the car so I can take her into custody.' I ignore his look and pull in to a parking spot. Masterson nimbly gets out as I pull on the handbrake and walks over to a grey and yellow parking meter. He places a few coins in the slot and retrieves a ticket. He walks around to the drivers side of the vehicle and taps on the window. Dutifully, I wind it down. He hands me the small slip of paper.

'I thought an hour would do. I don't want to be too long and I don't want you getting a ticket do I?' He winks at me, smiles, and walks towards a row of terraced houses. He disappears from view around the corner.

60

Masterson's grin drops abruptly as he enters the car lined street. He scans the area and spots the number of the house he's looking for on the opposite side of the road. He thrusts his hands deeply in his jacket pockets, as if to stave off the cold, when he is actually getting a firm grip on the silenced Sig Sauer within.

He proffers a quick look left and right, an observer would think he was checking for traffic, when in fact he's looking for surveillance, anyone out of the ordinary or CCTV cameras. In his brief scan he notices nothing and so, taking a firmer hold of the rubber chequered grips of the pistol, he crosses the road and stands at the door.

It's an unassuming door on an unassuming street, but Masterson knows what goes on behind it. The intelligence for the address states it's a holding and processing area for young women, girls really, who have been smuggled into the UK. They are promised jobs and the opportunity to send money back to family in whatever shithole of a village they may have come from in Eastern Europe, the Middle East or even China. Of course the jobs are false, unless you count enforced prostitution as a viable occupation. The girls are held, photographed and auctioned off to gangs from all over the country. Some don't even get to move on from this address and are locked in small rooms in the basement, waiting for clients to come and use them. They are normally the ones that no gang wants and the men who come to this address pay extra for special services. There is normally a swift turnaround of women in this place as the special services can mean bruises, broken bones and worse. An old smuggling tunnel leads form the basement into the nearby church grounds, and from there it's a swift, undetected trip with bodies to a waiting small boat for disposal.

All of this is running through Masterson's mind as he stands at the plain black door. His experienced eye can see the reinforcement around the doorframe and he instinctively knows that the wooden door is a facade for a heavy steel interior. He can feel he's being watched and as he pulls his hand out of his pocket to knock on the door, he notices the small unblinking eye of a camera where the door peephole normally sits. He knocks twice and takes one step backward onto the wide pavement.

The door opens to reveal a shaven headed young man, wearing a cheap knock off DKNY tracksuit and heavy gold chain around his tattooed neck. Masterson cannot help himself, he starts to laugh at the typical stereotype of a Russian gangster.

'What's so fucking funny?' The voice is heavily accented.

Masterson stops laughing, 'Life.' He says.

Masterson's right hand twists in his pocket and he fires two shots into the young man's chest, He crumples to the floor without a sound, his eyes registering shock as he dies. Masterson quickly steps over the body, pushes it to one side with his foot, and closes the door. He removes the pistol from its tattered hiding place in his pocket, there's no need for secrecy now.

The hallway has been painted black and has dim red wall lamps as the only form of lighting along its length. From the layout given to him, Masterson knows on his right is the security room where the thug at the door would have come from. He also knows there will be another man in there.

Entering smoothly and quickly, he sees the bulk of the second man rising from a chair in front of a bank of computer screens. There is a dull thud as Masterson fires a round from the Sig into the back of the man's head, splattering gore over the monitors. The screens flicker and change view every few seconds and Masterson sees women in rooms, only just big enough for a sparse bed, in most of them. A screen flickers again and shows the person he's here to find. This room appears larger than some of the others and has a dressing table next to the bed with a few belongings strewn across it. Masterson makes out a hairbrush, small purse, a mobile phone and a semi-automatic pistol. The number 24 is displayed in the top right hand corner of the screen. Number 24 means second floor, room four. Masterson looks up at the ceiling and listens for any sound. As he does so he notices a safe door standing open towards the rear of the room. Bundles of cash have been neatly wrapped up from the week's takings. He pauses a moment, staring at the thousands of pounds in front of him before he heads out into the hallway and makes his way up the stairs.

Room 24 faces the front of the house and on his way there, Masterson thinks about the pistol on the dressing table and how best to enter the room. He stops outside the door and is still thinking of the best way of making an entrance when it opens in front of him. Ewelina is standing in front of him holding a purse in her hand, and, Masterson notices immediately, no gun. He places his hand on her mouth before she can react and pushes her back into the room. Ewelina reacts quickly and makes a lunge for her gun on the dresser. Masterson is quicker and brings the butt of his pistol down on her temple, momentarily stunning her. She stumbles and as her legs hit the bed frame, she sprawls across it. Masterson takes the brief respite to pick up the pistol place it in his waistband. He waits for Ewelina to gather her senses. She turns to look at him with hate and venom flashing in her eyes.

'Nice place you've got here,'Masterson says, waving his Sig Sauer around the room in a nonchalant fashion.

'Fuck you, just do what you came here to do and tell them all to roast in hell.' She spits back. 'What are you waiting for? Kill me and get it over with.' Ewelina stares at him defiantly.

'What if I'm not here to kill you?' Masterson asks softly.

It takes a second for the question to register in her mind.

'Why else would you be here?'

'I want to bring the whole thing down on their heads. And I need you to help me with that.'

'Hah,' she rubs her head where a small golf ball size lump is growing under a bright red mark, 'like that could happen.'

'You have information the police want. Information that can be used against the people who brought you here. The ones who pushed you into doing things you and these other women should ever have to do.'

'The police are as corrupt as anyone else.'

'Not all of them Ewelina. I have a good man waiting outside who can offer protection and a chance to survive this, if you go with him and testify.'

'Protection?' Ewelina laughs, 'Protection is not 30 years in prison and a plane ticket back to Poland.'

'We all have to pay for our actions. There are consequences to everything we do. Your only other option is death, and knowing what I know about your former employers, they will want to know what you know and who you've told before you die. And I'm damn sure they won't ask as politely as the police.'

'What if I tell you everything and you let me go?'

'That won't work. I need hard evidence.'

'I can give you that.'

Masterson lowers his pistol.

'What have you got?'

Ewlelina picks up her purse from her side. Masterson raises the gun to point at her face. Slowly Ewelina opens the purse and upends it, spilling the contents on the bed. She rummages amongst the items before holding a small object up for Masterson to see. It's a USB flash drive.

'This holds details of all transactions, dealings and the names of people I have used over the last six months. It includes pick up points across Europe, addresses in the UK and bank account details of everyone involved in this operation. Including your ministers of parliament. It can all be verified and checked.'

'Why should I believe you? That could just as easily hold the last few episodes of Eastenders for all I know.'

'There is a computer downstairs. Let me show you, but, if you have this, you can let me go, yes?'

Masterson shifts his gaze around the dingy room. He thinks about the women in the rooms below him and how Ewelina could have been forced into this line of work through no other option.

'If what you say is true, I'll give you 24 hours before I let my friends know where you were.'

Ewelina stands up, 'That will have to do.'

A few minutes later they are standing in the security room.

Ewelina doesn't look fazed by the blood, or the dead man on the floor. She wheels a chair over and, ignoring the sticky blood on the lid, opens a laptop that was sitting next to the bank of monitors.

It only takes two minutes of scrolling through a swathe of excel files, documents and photographs to know that Ewelina has been telling him the truth.

'This is incriminating stuff.' Masterson mutters as he leans over and pulls the USB drive from the laptop.

'So you will let me go?' Ewelina asks, looking between Masterson's face and the pistol in his hand.

Masterson looks at his watch to see just twenty minutes have passed since he left Carter in the car.

'Leave here, don't head towards the square. My man is waiting there. Head towards the Coastgurad buildings, you know where they are?' Ewelina nods her head, 'Good. I'm not going to lie to you. I give you 24 hours and then I'm coming after you with the police...and I pray that no-one else from our former employer comes looking for you.'

Ewelina nods again, stands up from the chair and pauses, 'You said *our* employer.'

'Yeah, from what I'm about to do, he's going to be a little upset.'

Masterson brushes past her and heads towards the door in the hallway that leads to the basement. He looks towards Ewelina as she stands watching him. He glances at his watch, '23 hours 55 minutes.'

Ewelina turns away quickly, steps over the prone body on the hall and exits by the front door. She doesn't close it behind her in the rush to get away.

Masterson grasps the handle of the heavy door when he hears two distinct sounds. The first is the sharp report of three gun shots from outside, the second is the mobile phone given to him by Groark starts ringing.

He ignores the phone and runs outside, pistol in his hand, only to see a black car turn right at the end of the street. He catches sight of a figure laying on the pavement about fifteen feet away. The bright red blood from Ewelina's head wounds is steaming slightly in the cold air.

Footsteps pounding behind him instinctively force him to turn and point his pistol.

*

I hear the shots and push my door open. I am at the entrance to the street where I saw Masterson walk down only twenty or so minutes before. I see him standing with his pistol raised and also the prone figure of a woman in front of him. I am still running when he turns to face me, pistol pointed at my head.

'You said you wouldn't kill her.' I almost scream the words at him.

He lowers his pistol and I see he's also holding a ringing mobile phone in his other hand. He presses the screen to answer it, then presses it again for speaker phone and holds it up between us.

A voice I don't recognise is talking coldly, 'You had one job to do, and you blew it. You're on the shit list now son. Wherever you go, whatever you do, you'll be doing it with one eye looking behind you, you fucking moron. But you know what, I'm going to let you go for now. I want you to suffer the torment of knowing your worthless life is in my hands and at any moment I can snuff it out.'

Masterson brings the phone horizontally towards his face, 'I'm shutting you down. I'm shutting your operation down now, and there's nothing you can do it about it.'

'Do you think I care about that place? It's a by-line for the real operation, a place to move money through. Besides, do you know how long it will be before we open again...? Fucking minutes. Do what you have to do and know that you're not doing anything ut create ripples on a pond.'

Masterson drops the phone and cruches it beneath the heel of his boot.

'I didn't kill her, Peter. Someone from the firm must have tailed us here and waited for me to do this.'

My heart sinks. Not because of the fact we have lost the case, but because another person has died on my watch. Even knowing

ONE STEP AT A TIME

Ewelina's crimes, I cannot feel she deserved to be gunned down in cold blood.

'Where do we go from here?' I ask Masterson.

He looks around as doors start to open up and down the street, the occupants drawn to the drama unfolding like moths to a flame. Some are talking into mobile phones, others are filming the scene ready for their next post on Twitter or Facebook. Masterson grabs my arm and turns me back in the direction of the car.

'He thought I was shutting this place down. I meant I was shutting everything down, everything.'

He places a small object in my hand as we walk.

'Take this and do with it what you need to do. This holds vital information to your case. Get back to London and show it to your boss. Between you I'm sure you'll know what to do with it.'

I look down at the small black USB stick in my hand. He pushes me into the car.

'Drive carefully Peter. I'll catch up with you soon.'

With those words he slams my door shut and jogs away into the greenery of Pencester Park. I pocket the flash drive and start the engine. As I drive off I can already hear in the background the wail of sirens racing to the scene which is overlaid by the ringing of my mobile phone.

61

'They've done a bloody good job,' Luke says as he struggles to find information relating to Ewelina. 'Her social media has been deleted; no that's wrong, it's been stripped clean. No references to her name anywhere on Google, Facebook, Twitter or Instagram. Her police files have disappeared, including her interviews over the Zoe Walker investigation. It's like she's ceased to exist.'

'You have to find something, Luke. What about the text message relating to her appearance in Dover?' Wilks asks the question as she stands over him, staring at the same computer screens.

'It was sent and received from two burner phones. The thing is they were both in the range of the same cell towers.'

'That's not so strange Luke. Mobile phone masts serve fairly large areas.'

'No boss, what I mean is both the transmitting phone and the receiving phone can be triangulated using these four masts to the same ten metre box in London.' He's pointing at a list of numbers on the screen.

'And you didn't think of mentioning that before?' Wilks sounds angry.

Luke shrugs in way of apology, 'I was a little busy with other things when it came through and I've only just managed to access the information from the servers.'

'Right, so where in London did these messages originate?'

Luke brings up a map on the right hand screen and types in the numbers. A string of red lines run out from different points and intersect over a point on the map.

Wilks looks at the satellite image of the large white building flanking the Thames. She closes her eyes and drops her head, 'Vauxhall House. The bastards have been playing us.'

'It could just be coincidence...' Luke's voice trails off as Wilks glares at him.

'Can you track these phone numbers and find out where they are now?' she asks.

'I've been trying that since the message came through. They're either switched off or have been dumped in the river.'

Wilks taps her fingers on the desk, 'When did you last try?'

'Last night, but nothing was there.'

'Can you locate Peter by his cell phone?'

'I don't need to; the car has a tracker fitted.'

Wilks' fingers stop their drumming, 'Where is he and try again on the burner phones.'

Luke types more commands across the keyboard and the map drifts across the screen. A red flashing circle is stationary in the middle of Dover.

'I thought Ewelina's location was meant to be in East London?' says Wilks. 'Have you got a hit on the phones?'

More clicks come from the keyboard and map moves imperceptibly. A second red circle is flashing and moving towards the car's location. It is just metres away.

Wilks grabs her phone and punches in Peter's number. She watches the screen as the circles converge and then move slowly apart. She listens to the ringing tone and is thinking the worst.

'Do you think he's OK?' Luke asks urgently.

Wilks shakes her head as the phone rings for the fourth time. She is just about to hang up and call Dover police when a voice comes through the speaker.

'Boss, Ewelina Jankowska is dead. She's been shot, but I've got something we need to look at.'

Wilks is stunned, relieved and angry at the same time, 'Who the hell was with you just now?'

I'm a little confused by the question, 'What? How do you...It was Masterson. He was trying to bring Jankowska in but someone else had other ideas.'

'Peter,' Wilks is trying to control the tremor in her voice, 'it was Masterson who sent the messages about her location.'

'I know, he told me on the way down here.'

Her voice has raised an octave when she next speaks, 'You drove to Dover and you took him with you?'

'Boss, listen to me. I think I've got something that will blow all this wide open. Where are you?'

'My office. My new office in Curtis Green.'

'I'll be with you in two hours. Make sure you've got Luke there if you can. We're going to need his help with this I think.'

'He's sat next to me. I'll arrange for you to be brought up. We'll be waiting for you.'

Luke taps her arm and mimes a snapping motion. Wilks nods in understanding, 'Now break the sim card in half, bin the phone and if you need me I'll be on phone number two as well.'

I hang up and with one hand on the steering wheel manage to remove the back from the phone and slide out the sim. I place it between my teeth and bend it in two. It gets thrown out of the window into the damp road as I climb out of Dover. The phone follows it out of the window a few miles further down the road.

I reach over and open the glove box. I rummage around and grab the phone with the number two written in Tippex on the back. I turn it on and place it on the passenger seat next to me.

Back in London, Luke and Wilks watch the computer screen as one red circle is travelling back along the motorway towards the city, while the other one blinks twice then disappears from view.

'Looks like Masterson has got rid of his burner phone too.' Luke says drily.

62

An uneventful drive and two hours later, I'm standing in the glass foyer at the entrance of the Curtis Green building. The iconic New Scotland Yard sign has already been transferred across and it stands proudly rotating on the pavement outside. A few tourists snap a picture with the sign before walking off arm in arm and wrapped up against the chill of the evening. As promised there is a visitor's pass waiting for me at the main desk.

The desk sergeant recognises me as he hands it over and I can see a look of sympathy cross his face. 'Do you know where you're going sir?' He asks.

'Not a clue,' I say as I reach out and attach the green fringed ID to my jacket with the small silver alligator clip.

'If you take the elevator to the sixth floor the commissioner will be waiting for you there.' With that he points to the far end of the room, past the curved seating that is still wrapped in plastic, to a set of glass elevator doors. 'I'll give her a ring and let her know you're here.'

I nod my head in thanks and rub my hand across my chin. The bristles rasp under my fingers and I realise how tired I really am. It's been a long day and it doesn't look like it's going to stop anytime soon. I walk to the elevator and press the call button. The doors open immediately and I walk in to the glass cocoon. I don't even think of taking in the sights of London that fill the windows of the elevator, my thoughts are on the contents of the USB drive, and the implications it will bring. I reach into my pocket and roll it between my fingers.

Wilks appears in view in reverse order. I see her polished shoes, black trousers and white shirt before her face comes into view and the door opens. I step out into an open plan office space. The tables are a sickly green colour and there are power points at each one.

'Do you have it?' she asks.

Nodding my head as I pull the drive the drive from my pocket, I find myself stifling a yawn as I hand it over. Wilks looks between my face and the USB stick now in her hand.

'Let's go to my office and get you a coffee, eh?'

'Yeah, that would be great,' I mutter back. I just feel numb, like I'm sleep walking in somebody else's dream. She takes me through the aisle created by the desks and through the door at the far end of the room.

'Welcome to my new office.' Wilks says to me, waving her hand dismissively around the room.

It's much smaller than her previous office, but it does have a better view. The Houses of Parliament frame the window in front of me and the lights from the many windows are glowing and reflecting off the dark river Thames in the early evening gloom. Luke is sitting at one of the same green desks from outside and is peering intently at a brace of computer screens. Wilks rests her hand almost affectionately on his shoulder as she hands him the USB stick.

She nods in my direction and motions to a small two seater sofa for me to sit. As I ease myself into the surprisingly comfortable chair she walks over to the window behind her desk. She grabs a half full glass jar from a coffee percolator on a shelf in the corner and pours the strong coffee into a plain white mug. I can smell it from my seat as she walks back across the room. I take it from her gratefully as Luke plugs the USB drive into his terminal.

'OK, let's see what we've got here.' He says as the computer makes a two tone sound as it recognises the drive. Luke double clicks the mouse and relays what he sees on the screen to the room. Wilks moves from next to me to stand over his shoulder.

He reads aloud the folder's names, 'Accounts in, accounts out, bank transfers, Bitcoin, client details,' as Luke continues reading I feel my eyes start to close. The heat of the room, the hours of driving and the lack of sleep are all taking their toll. I place my coffee mug onto the floor and struggle to stay awake, but it's a losing battle and I doze off for a while.

I don't know how long I've been asleep but when I open my eyes Wilks has dragged a chair over to sit next to Luke at the computer. She looks concerned, but raises a smile to me when she sees me stirring. I get up, stretch and go to join them at the computer desk.

'So, what have we got?' I enquire as I move my head in an attempt to rollaway the stiffness in my neck.

Wilks arches her back. She's obviously been crouched over the screen for too long and has her own aches to relieve.

'Name and addresses, account details and information on transactions for a lot of people and businesses. There's files on everything from arms smuggling to people trafficking to child prostitution.'

She lets out a sigh, 'We've got enough already to make a lot of people over there,' she points out of the window towards the Parliament building, 'very worried indeed.'

I peer at the information on the screen as Luke scrolls and copies details into a separate file.

'Will you open a new investigation?'

Wilks nods her head, 'Yes, but I'm going to have to be very careful in how I start any operations.'

'Because of the names in the files?' I ask.

'Exactly. We have senior politicians, a barrister or two and even some minor members of the Royal family implicated in dealings and investments within these files. Just to start an investigation is going to stir things up when I apply for permission from the Home Secretary.'

'You seem a little reticent about this.'

'I am, Peter. You see, the Home Secretary is one of those mentioned.' Wilks swivels in her chair and taps her foot nervously, 'I need to take advice on this before I start an investigation.'

'Advice?' I'm furious and it shows in my voice, 'What advice do you need on stopping this? For god's sake Commissioner, grow a pair and get the ball rolling.'

My fury is reflected back at me as Wilks stands up and spits back at me, 'I will not be rushed into blundering into something as serious and, dare I say it, as delicate as this. If I go charging in half-cocked without evidence to back up these allegations, then they win because the entire process will be flawed from the start. We do this right and we follow all protocols. That includes me seeking advice on bringing charges against a parliamentary cabinet member.'

I shake my head in disgust, 'I can't believe I'm hearing this. It sounds to me like you're scared of doing your job.'

'I am scared, Peter, and you should be too, but I'm not scared about doing my job and you know that. We both know what these people are capable of and we have to be extremely careful of every step we take.'

'I'm tired of running. They killed my brother and Ann, and one of their people was responsible for killing JD.'

'And look what they managed to do with her. I don't want to see any more deaths and I'm going to do this one step at a time.'

I am too angry to listen to Wilks as she speaks. All I want is justice and I'm blind to any arguments Wilks is putting forward. Luke is watching our discussion, but knows not to get involved in case we both vent our anger towards him.

'If you won't bring charges or start an investigation immediately then I will. I'll go around you or through you to do this, but I'm going to do it.'

I see Wilks clench her fists, the knuckles whitening under the pressure.

'And just how are you going to do anything? You resigned if you recall? I really don't see how a civilian would be able to be a part of a police investigation, do you?' Wilks puts a cruel emphasis on the word, 'police' to make me see that I am no longer a member of her beloved Met.

'Fuck this, I'm out of here.' I'm shaking with rage.

'Peter?' Wilks calls my name as I reach out to turn the door handle. It makes me pause but I refuse to turn and face her.

'Hand your pass in on the way out won't you?'

With her words still sharp in my ears I leave her and Luke behind me.

63

It's 11 o clock in the evening and Jim Groark is standing on the terrace that flanks two sides of his penthouse apartment. The red anti-collision lights of the Thames Barrier blink in the distance and he watches as a small jet aircraft descends into City Airport just behind the river and barrier, on the opposite bank. He sips at a large glass of Remy Martin X.O. savouring the pleasing, smooth burn as he swallows.

He's troubled. So troubled in fact that sat on the glass topped table, next to the bottle of brandy is a pistol. The Eastern European CZ-75 Auto is a lethal looking weapon. It was taken from a shipment on its way to the Middle East which Groark was in charge of. Apart from being able to fire all 20 rounds from the extended magazine in a couple of seconds, there is a spare magazine attached just beneath the barrel that also acts as a front grip. This not only allows the pistol to be held securely in fully automatic mode, but also means a magazine change can be completed instantly. The extensive firepower of the CZ pistol gives Groark some comfort. He knows Masterson is out there and that is what's troubling him as he watches his breath stream out in the cold night air.

He takes another sip of his drink and reaches for the bottle to refresh the glass. He wonders if the prostitute he picked up earlier has left, or if she is going to stay over. He has used her services before and knows she's worth the extra money, she has even stayed overnight for no charge once or twice, depending on what he wanted from her of course.

Groark smiles as he hears the patio window slide open and imagines she will be staying the night after all.

'Grab a glass from the bar and join me,' he says holding the elegant bottle up for her to see. He turns as he pours the Remy Martin into his half empty tumbler hoping she has kept her lingerie on...or at least some of it.

He freezes as he sees Masterson standing in the doorframe, a pistol in his hand. Groark's eyes shift to his own gun on the table.

'Do it. That would make me so happy.' Masterson says to the still form in front of him.

In a microsecond, Groark has calculated there is no way he can reach the CZ on the table, turn and fire, in the time it would take Masterson to pull the trigger.

'Would you like a drink?' He feigns indifference to the deadly character in front of him, knowing his only chance of survival is to use his wits.

'Hell,' says Masterson, 'Why not?'

He skirts around the table, gun barrel pointing at Groark the whole time. He manages to pull the machine pistol from the table and nods appreciatively, 'Nice, I haven't seen many of these.'

'I'm so glad you like. It's yours if you want it, I can always get another.'

Masterson pockets the pistol and reaches for a glass from the small outside bar. The inlaid LED lights from the bar cast a subtle glow across the terrace. He pushes the empty tumbler across the table towards Groark. The glass on the glass topped table makes a small screeching sound as it scrapes along the surface.

As Groark pours the brandy, Masterson says, 'I let your friend out. She was very appreciative of the extra cash I gave her from your wallet. She said she'd call round tomorrow.'

'Oh good, I look forward to seeing her again.' Groark holds up the glass towards Masterson, 'Here you go.'

Masterson leans across the table, reaching for the drink and is surprised to have the contents thrown is his face. The alcohol stings his eyes as he squeezes off a shot at Groark. It smashes into the double glazed window, creating a neat hole in the glass before embedding itself in the wall of the apartment. Groark makes it to the open patio door when he hears Masterson's controlled voice behind him.

'I won't miss with the next one.'

Groark is still holding the bottle of brandy in his left hand, which he considers throwing at Masterson in a vain attempt to escape. He realises the futility of such an action and raises both hands above his head.

'Inside.'

Groark does as he's ordered and takes a few steady steps into the apartment, stopping at a heavy dining table in front of the picture window looking over the Thames. He turns around slowly to face Masterson.

'Put the bottle down.'

Again he follows orders, placing the heavy glass bottle onto the wooden surface.

'Grab a chair and sit down.'

Groark, playing for time, walks around the table and sits in a light framed, wooden chair against the glass.

Masterson throws him a plasticuff tie-wrap, 'Attach your right leg to the chair.' As Groark does this in silence, Masterson walks over, just out of reach of any flailing limbs. He hands over two more tie-wraps, 'Now the other leg, then your right arm.'

Groark does so without complaint.

'Place your left arm on the chair, and don't move.'

This time Groark speaks as he follows commands, 'Is there any way I'm getting out of this alive?' He sounds almost resigned to his fate.

Masterson secures the left arm and harshly tightens the other tie-wraps, making Groark grunt slightly.

'That all depends on your answers to my questions.'

'You realise killing me won't stop a thing? Don't you see that from your actions with Leahy?'

'Killing you has nothing to do with stopping anything. Killing you is personal.'

'You said I had a chance to live.'

'Depending on your answers to my questions, yes.'

Masterson turns away from his prisoner and starts removing objects from his pockets. He places them on the table and sits down. He begins to assemble different pieces.

'Tell me, who's in charge of your operation?'

Groark can't see what is being put together on the table as he answers, knowing his life could depend on his truthfulness 'Ultimately, me, but the Secretary of State is heavily involved.'

'What decisions does she make? Is she responsible for any decision making with retirements and specific targets?'

'If the target is high value or is on the intermediate list, yes. Otherwise I have control.'

'Was she involved in the hit on Peter Carter and me?' Masterson's objects make soft clicks as parts are put together.

'On you, no. On Carter, because he was an active police officer, yes.'

Masterson pauses and looks up, 'So she sanctioned the killing of Peter Carter?'

'Yes. She has control over active operations against police officers and armed forces of the United Kingdom.'

'Can this be found in writing?'

'There's a UK Eyes Only- Cabinet Office file with all the legal requirements of ops in the UK and abroad which the Home Secretary keeps.'

'Thank you for candidness.' Masterson says as he presses a small button on the device in front of him. The last few questions and answers are replayed from the small digital recording device.

Masterson stops the recording and places it back in his pocket. He picks up the object, now assembled, from the table places it in Groark's lap.

Groark looks down in horror at the small block of C4 explosive and detonator. A mobile phone is attached to the top of the package and held in place with another tie-wrap.

'You said I would live if I answered your questions. I've answered them truthfully and you now have evidence at the Home Secretary to use.' Groark's voice finally relays his rising panic at the situation.

'That's right, but I have one last question to ask.'

'What. What is it?'

'It' simple. If you can do this last thing for me, you get to live.'

'I'll do it.'

Masterson picks up the brandy bottle and takes a swig from the neck. He examines the label and looks at Groark, 'I think you should finish this.' He pours the remaining liquid over Groark, watching as it soaks into the material of his clothes.

'OK, one last question for you. Can you bring my Angie back? Can you bring back the woman you ordered killed when you came after me?'

Groark stares in horror at Masterson as he walks away.

'I'll give you a call in a few minutes to get your answer.' Masterson exits the apartment and waits for the elevator. He's humming the theme tune to The Good Life as he descends to the ground floor, where he pulls the fire alarm to evacuate the building.

In Groark's apartment he is frantically trying to dislodge the explosive. His movements force the chair to topple over, but the restraints and the wooden frame all hold firmly. With his feet he manages to turn himself away from the package until his shoulder is pressing against the plate glass of the window. He hears the fire alarm reverberating around the apartment block and for a second thinks help is on the way.

Outside, Masterson is waiting at the brightly lit train platform. He hums the last few bars of his tune and pulls out his phone. He dials the number and it rings twice. At the same time as the third ring should start there is a huge explosion of fire, smoke and glass that blows out across the Thames from the building opposite the platform. He steps into the waiting Tube carriage and puts his phone away.

He has one more stop to make, but he thinks it can wait until morning..

64

Twelve hours have passed since the explosion and Masterson is waiting for his 11.30 appointment. He is sitting in a sturdy, high backed chair in a wooden panelled hallway. A door opens and an older gentleman, instantly recognisable in the UK's political arena, bundles past him. He is flanked by aides and they are all discussing the explosion and possible terror involvement, especially with the only victim identified is a member of the security forces. They don't even register Masterson sitting in the hall.

'...hanging on for life...' is a fragment of conversation that catches Masterson's attention.

Another door opens and an immaculately dressed, middle aged woman beckons him in.

Entering the expansive office Masterson shows an amused look at seeing a plain-clothed security officer standing at the side of the Home Secretary's desk. Masterson notices the bulge in the jacket to indicate an armed officer and nods in his direction in a friendly manner.

'Ma'am, the information I have is extremely confidential. Perhaps we could have this meeting in private?' He asks as she sits down behind her desk.

'Everything that occurs in this office can be presented in the knowledge that Bill here, will not transfer any intelligence or personal information to others. You can trust him as you trust me, and,' she narrows her eyes, 'as I hope I can trust you Mr. Masterson. You see, I know who you are and I am aware of your reputation. That is why we are having this meeting.'

Masterson nods his head with a smile on his lips, 'OK, have it your way.'

His hand reaches into his coat pocket and he's pleased to see the security detail react to the movement by rapidly reaching for his concealed weapon.

'Easy tiger,' Masterson reproaches, as his movements slow, 'I've got something your boss needs to hear.'

He places the digital recorder on the desk and hits the play button. His own voice and that of Jim Groark ring clear in the room. At the question regarding her involvement in a sanctioned killing of a police officer, the Home Secretary reaches over and stops the recording abruptly. She stares at Masterson.

Masterson feels he's being scrutinised like a bug under a magnifying glass.

'Bill,' the woman is talking in a steady voice, 'could you pop out for a moment and perhaps get some tea for Mr. Masterson and myself?'

Bill looks uncomfortably between his superior and Masterson, before nodding and leaving the room. The Home Secretary waits for the door to quietly close before speaking.

'With the unfortunate demise of Mr. Groark, I have a vacancy that needs filling. Even if he were to recover from his devastating injuries, it's quite clear that he will no longer be able to perform his departmental duties. I want you to take over his department and start running it your way. I've read your file and you've been around the block a bit haven't you? This whole sorry mess was dropped in my lap by the previous incumbent and I've been trying to work out a way to sort it out ever since.'

Masterson's eyes widen as he realises who she is talking about; the very same recognisable character that was in the hallway a few moments ago.

'That's right,' she continues, 'my immediate boss was involved in this from the start. Now if we could work something out between us it would benefit us both, don't you agree? My political future would look a lot brighter, while your immediate future would look, well, at least you would have an immediate future.' The Home Secretary pauses for a brief moment to let the implied threat sink in. 'It's about time we had a clean up around here and I believe you're the man for the job. Of course, we both know the consequences should you not take up the offer.'

'Do I get any time to think this over?'

'Certainly Mr. Masterson. You have until the moment you leave this office. Now, what is your answer?'

*

Thirty minutes later Masterson is sitting at a small table in the bar of Brunswick House. The chandeliers hanging from the ceiling catch the soft sunlight streaming in through the windows and scatter it in a thousand different patterns across the bar. He has a bottle of red wine and two glasses in front of him on the table. Only one glass has been poured and he's nursing it gently, savouring the aroma and texture of the fine wine. A woman enters the small bar and crosses to his table. She sits down without saying a word and leans across to pick up the bottle.

'Jesus Christ,' she exclaims as she sees the label, 'a 96 Domain Jean-Louis Chave, that's a £500 bottle of wine.' She pours herself a generous measure and takes an appreciative pull on the liquid, 'Now that is a nice little afternoon pick me up. Have you just won the lottery or something?'

Masterson smiles at this mousy haired woman across from him, 'How are things Evelyn? The rat race still dragging you down at The Guardian?'

Evelyn van der Vossen, sub-editor of the aforementioned newspaper sits back in the bare wooden chair.

'Let's cut the crap. I know I said I owe you one for pulling me and my team out of that carjacking in Baghdad, but I never thought I'd hear from you, calling the favour in.' As she says this her finger runs unconsciously down a small ridge of scar tissue on her right cheek. It's a memento of that day and was caused by flying glass as her car was raked with gunfire. If Masterson and his team hadn't been there to thwart the attack, Evelyn and her photographer would have been held hostage, waiting in terror for the inevitable beheading to be performed on video.

'I think that this is something that could benefit you as much as it will help me. How do you fancy the story of a lifetime?'

Evelyn's eyes narrow as she takes a longer pull on the exquisite red wine, 'What have you got for me?' she asks him.

EPILOGUE

I walk away from the graveside to gather my thoughts. JD's service was well attended by fellow officers and friends alike. As funerals go, it went as smoothly as possible, but for some reason during the memorial and eulogies I couldn't picture what JD looked like. Out in the cold morning air with the smell of damp earth filling my senses, his face comes flooding back to my mind and I feel the tears beginning to come. I walk away because I need to be alone for a while. But others have their own agenda. I wipe my eyes as three people detach themselves from the group.

Commissioner Wilks, Graham and Kate all head over towards me. Wilks is solemn faced and we all have red eyes. She holds out her hand and I reach out to shake it.

'I can't believe he's gone. He was a good man and a good officer.'

'And a good friend.' I reply to Wilks.

They all nod their heads in agreement.

'Peter?' she asks, not letting go of my hand, 'I've had a lot to consider over the last few days and I apologise for my anger at our last meeting. I have to ask if you would consider coming back to the Met?'

I look around the graveyard as I pull my hand away. I thrust both deep into my heavy woollen coat's pockets.

'I'm not doing this here, not now. At the moment I don't think I can look anyone in the eye knowing what we know.'

It's Wilks turn to look around now. Is she looking for someone in particular or is that a frightened look I see on her face for the briefest of moments?

'We have to be careful with this information, Peter. You must understand that. There are ways we can use this but it must be organised and investigated properly.'

I shake my head at her words, 'And they say justice is blind. I guess it's only blind if you can't afford to pay for the cover up.'

'That is not what I'm saying,' she takes a deep breath as she catches sight of someone over my shoulder, 'We have someone we can trust now who is higher up the chain of command. We're going to work together to clean up this rat's nest, and I assure you, Peter, everyone involved will face the justice system.'

I shrug my shoulders like a petulant schoolboy, 'I wish I could believe that.' I respond abjectedly.

'Look, I'll give you three months away from duties, with pay,' she stresses, ' so that you can decide what you want to do. You're too good a police officer to throw it all away.'

I feel a flash of anger and know I'm only feeling this way because she is right. But I have to work out what I want in life. I understand after JD's death and Helen's injuries that life is too short, especially when work is all you live for.

'Please think about it, Peter. That's all I ask.'

I nod my head silently and am a little startled when a gloved hand clasps me on the shoulder. I turn quickly to face the person.

'Hello Peter, I'm so sorry for your loss.' Masterson looks unfamiliar in his crisp suit, tie and long overcoat. He nods at Wilks, 'Do you mind if I have him a moment for a quiet chat?'

Wilks smiles thinly as I turn back to her in a daze.

'Friends in high places, Peter.' She nods her head to Masterson and walks away to a waiting car with Graham and Kate flanking her.

Masterson waits until the three have got into the car before talking.

'I truly am sorry for your colleague's and brother' death, Peter. I only hope that this can make up for it in some little way.'

He pulls a photograph from his pocket and hands it over. It shows a picture of someone lying in a hospital bed. Beneath the bandages I can see raw, red flesh, edged with dark streaks. The right arm is missing from the shoulder while the left ends at the elbow. Masterson hands me another photograph.

'This was taken when he was found.'

This time I see the skin has peeled back from his one remaining arm in a sheet that looks like discoloured cling film. The forearm is hanging at a grotesque angle and I notice his legs are missing from the knees down. But what haunts me most about the image is the white glazed eyes in the raw meat that used to be his face. The nose is gone and the lips look like they have been cut away in whatever explosion or accident this poor soul has been in.

I hand the pictures back to Masterson, 'Why are you showing me these? Who is this person?'

'This is the man who masterminded everything; you will have seen his details on the files I gave you. He had an unfortunate accident a few days ago and I can't think of a finer way for this parasite to spend the rest of his days. For some unfathomable reason he's still alive, but he will spend whatever life he has left in agony, deaf and blind.'

I shake my head angrily, 'I can't condone this action, I believe in the justice system. I believe in the guilty being punished.'

'Don't you believe this punishment fits the crime?

There is a pause as I look away from this man who delivers death as easily as hailing a taxi. My thoughts are full of memories, memories of my sister's laughter, my brother's smiling face, Julia framed against the backdrop of Crete, JD laughing away at his desk, Ann waiting for me in the rain, and I think of all of these people as the family I have lost.

'I don't think I can. This isn't what justice means. People should be held to account, pay their price to society as a whole and it should not be about personal vengeance or to make someone feel better by inflicting violence on others.'

I turn back to Masterson and see he is holding out his hand.

'That is the answer I was hoping for. Peter, I've been given a new role which requires people of integrity around me. I need men and women like you who know the difference from what is the right thing to do and what feels like the right thing to do. Because, to be honest, I sometimes get mixed up with doing what I feel to is right for personal reasons, and that has to stop. Do you understand what I'm trying to say?'

'Are you offering me a job?' I ask incredulously.

'It's a supervisory and advisory role. I need you Peter, as my voice of reason or there's every chance I could end up like this guy.' He waves the photos in the air between us.

I don't know what to say, so I do the only thing I can. I accept his handshake and wonder if I should accept the job offer. Where do I go from here and what's in store for my future? I think to myself.

'Oh, there's one more thing you should see.' He produces a newspaper from within his jacket and hands it over. 'I thought you might like to know that an investigation is forthcoming after tomorrows headlines.'

I glance at the date on the broadsheet, it's tomorrow's date.

The headline reads,

UK HOME SECRETARY FACES PARLIAMENTARY ENQUIRY OVER POLITICAL MISCONDUCT

Masterson looks at my face for any sign of my thoughts, 'It's a start, Peter. We'll be working together to clean up the quagmire this has become. I refuse to play it their way and they should all know that I'm, or we, are after them. We may not be able to make everything stick, but together we'll stop anyone else from being hurt, girls being trafficked and money being siphoned into fat offshore accounts.' He hands over a business card, blank except for a telephone number. 'Let me know OK?'

He walks away and merges with other people leaving the graveyard.

As I stand there, deep in thought and waiting for the cab to arrive, my sister comes over, a scarf covering the bandages on her head, to join me. As she does, my phone rings. My breath steams in the cold air as I pull it from my pocket to look at the caller ID.

It's Julia.

Printed in Great Britain
by Amazon

49723857R00136